The Winter of the Birds

by the same author

THE BONGLEWEED

THE BEACHCOMBERS

UP THE PIER

THE OUTLANDERS

THE NIGHT-WATCHMEN

THE PIEMAKERS

THE SIGNPOSTERS

WHERE THE WIND BLOWS

HELEN CRESSWELL

The Winter of the Birds

FABER & FABER
3 Queen Square London

First published in 1975
by Faber and Faber Limited
3 Queen Square London WC1
Printed in Great Britain
by Latimer Trend & Company Ltd Plymouth
All rights reserved

ISBN 0 571 10860 1

for the memory of my mother

I am certain of nothing but the holiness of the heart's affections, and the truth of the imagination.

John Keats: Letters

To kill fancy in childhood is to make a slave to what exists, a creature tethered to earth and therefore unable to create heaven.

Bertrand Russell

Contents

Part One

CHAPTER ONE

¶ *What Mister Rudge Said*

All the draughts in the world go past this corner. I am an old man to be living alone. Old and impossible I am and they all say it, and keep away as much as they can. I sit up late at nights and watch the moon, green as cheese over the factories and chimneys and puddlefaced in the canal and sometimes clean and sometimes dirty. I sit in the attic to be nearer the moon, and that is a little crazy because the moon is so far off that a house's height is a jot, a speck, a nothing—almost. But I sit up there for the sake of the—almost.

And because I alone in the town am awake at nights, it is only I who know of the steel birds. I see the birds who do not fly but run on wires. They sweep down in the dark straight and hard and cleanly as blades. They are terrible and purposeful. They strike. I am afraid of them.

When I say that they are steel, I only mean that they are of metal. They are not soft and warm and feathered, they do not fly as real birds do, in a kind of innocent mapping out of air. They go in straight lines and they do not sing.

If only they sang I could feel more comfortable. I tell myself that if they sang I would look at them differently, would believe they had some good in them. But on quiet nights I have heard the hiss of metal running over wires and that has become the sound of terror for me.

Here I sit in my tall house while my neighbours in this narrow street are sleeping. Mr Coombe and his weasel-faced wife go to bed at ten. I see the lights go off downstairs and then an upper window is lighted for a few minutes and then that too is darkened. How can they sleep, I ask myself, while steel birds peck at their roof? It is as if the nights creaked with frost, always . . .

And the rest of them—the Flacks, the Farrands, the Smiths and the Bakers—what do they know of these steel invaders of the night? They sleep, all of them, under their roofs, safe as houses, while all the time there is a driving hail of steel above them. The night has been taken over by these birds of the straight flight and fixed wings, while the others, the real birds, roost when the dusk comes, disappear until the dawn.

And I ask myself—what is their business, what do they mean? And you may say that a bird does not have any business, or any meaning, that it is, quite simply, a bird. For a bird to be itself is quite enough. But then a real bird is alive for joy, he is there to feed, to rear his young, to fly and sing. I have often thought that the most joyful thing to be and the most free and the most marvellous and mysterious in its comings and goings is a bird. It has a pattern (or so I believe, for I believe there is a pattern in everything) but an invisible one, and one that the bird makes up for himself as he goes along. That is to be free.

But these birds of the night are fettered. Their flight is made for them, they run on wires, there is no joy in them. That is why they must have some business. I am sure of it. And I am sure, too, that whatever their purpose is, it is an evil one. There is evil in their glitter, in their swift strike, their hissing.

And that is why I have, in a sense, appointed myself as a guard, a watchman. I alone am watching the sky at night (all night and every night, for I am an astronomer as well as a poet) and I have a kind of duty, I think.

And although the people of this town do not know me or care about me, if ever the time comes to warn them, I shall do so. It is November now, and nearly six months since I saw the first birds. There were not so many to begin with and of course it was summer then and the nights were shorter. But as the nights grow longer and the steel birds thicken, like corn, I feel a kind of doom approaching. The real birds are losing ground. They must, as the days shorten, and of course they sing less on these wet and misty days, and sometimes I even imagine that they are not so many as they used to be. Impossible to count, but it is just a feeling I have, and on some grey days I throw whole loaves in shreds out of my window to bring them to my garden and give me reassurance. I sit there and I am watching as greedily as they are eating.

I wish I did not have to be a guardian, it is a responsibility I do not want. And I can tell myself that I am an old man, a fanciful old man and even perhaps a little crazy, but it does not alter the fact that I have eyes, and can use them, and that I see those terrible birds. And so I have set a date. On New Year's Day, if those birds have not gone from here, if they are still shuttling the night and shining like an army of spears over the chimney pots and aerials, on New Year's Day I shall give my warning.

I have not decided how. It is not an easy thing to give a warning to thousands of people you do not even know. To write a poem about it would certainly not be enough. But I shall think of a way when the times comes—if the time comes. I shall warn them.

CHAPTER TWO

¶ *In Which Edward Flack Goes Into The Dark And Goes One Step Further Than He Meant*

"And talking of work," said Mrs Flack, "there'll be no harm if you get down to the shop for an hour and get the stock tidied."

"But Mum, I only did it on Sunday."

"Did, Lily," confirmed his father.

"Sunday?" she shrilled. "It's Wednesday now!"

"Yes, Mum. I'll go down now."

It was a relief, really. He went slowly down the uncarpeted stairs and tried to imagine that he was a doomed prisoner descending to the scaffold, but it was not easy. The familiar smells of scrubbing soap and disinfectant, cheese and old apples came to meet him.

"I am a prisoner," Edward thought. "As much as if I was in chains."

He went through into the stockroom behind the shop and stood detesting it.

"When I grow up," he thought, "I shall never so much as *touch* a box of soap powder. Or a tin of baked beans, or soup, or corned beef. I hate butter, I hate bacon and I hate toothpaste."

He looked slowly about, uncertain where to start. The stockroom, whenever his mother said it needed tidying, was always tidy already. And so Edward had to move things about in such a way that it would *stay* tidy, but also look different, so that he had some visible proof of his labours.

"I suppose I could always rearrange everything in alphabetical order," he thought, and for a few moments became excited by the originality of the idea, and quite ready to carry it out. But a quick survey of the shelves showed him that a gross of baked bean tins were right in the middle of the soups, and Demerara sugar was flanked on one side by currants and on the other by rice, and that the whole scheme was impracticable to the point of lunacy.

"I'll tidy up the Processed Peas," he decided.

The Processed Peas were already tidy in the sense that they stood in military rows, drawn up, tier upon tier, as if awaiting inspection

18

by some dignitary of the Processed Pea world. But their labels were untidy, and Edward could spend some time arranging the tins so that every P in Processed was directly over or under every other P, thus producing a marvellous symmetry of effect that went right beyond mere tidiness.

There was something peculiarly soothing about the process. His hands were moving and he was using his eyes, but only mechanically, in a kind of rhythm, and the result was that Edward really rather liked it because it made it easier to think. Or dream. Or both. There was an irony in this that he was aware of, too, and that pleased him. His mother did not approve of thinking— the kind that was not of the counting tins or money variety—and still less did she like dreaming. She would be very annoyed indeed if she knew that Edward was regularly using her Evaporated Milk and Processed Peas as a means to so subversive an end.

"Always mooning and dreaming around," she would say."You have to get on in this world, my lad. And that's one thing you'll never do by mooning and dreaming around."

Edward never argued, because he could not put an argument into words. But he felt very strongly that she was mistaken about this.

"I *live* inside my head," he told himself. "So does everyone, in a way. So what goes on in there, must count. It must count a lot. I shall always live inside my head, wherever I go or whatever I do for the whole of my life. So why shouldn't I be at home in there?"

Because this was what his particular kind of thinking did. It made him at home with himself. It made it perfectly clear that he, Edward John Flack, was the only reality he could be certain of. It gave him something to count on. It put things like tidying Processed Peas into their proper perspective.

"It's a windy old night out!"

He stepped back to inspect the regimental Peas. He grinned, drew himself up, and saluted.

"Atten—tion!"

The stockroom door was locked and Edward had to take the key out and then relock it from the outside, in the draughty little yard that led in turn through a tall gate into the alley that ran behind St Saviour's Street. He shut door and gate quietly for fear his mother might see him from the kitchen above, and call him back. There was bad company in St Saviour's Street, so she said, and bad company became worse at night. She meant people like

John Wardle, and the MacKay boys who were dirty and swore in every sentence and had a drunken father.

Edward was not going out either to meet this bad company or to avoid it. He was going out, as he had been doing for some time now, to test himself.

"Nearly dark!"

He started to run. If you ran in the dark it was less with you, even though it was still there, obviously, and you could not run *from* it. The worst thing you could do was stand still and get the *feeling* of darkness, growing and growing. Tonight the wind helped. The wind practically cancelled out the dark. Dark is nothing, a blackness, a void, an absence of light, but the wind is something positive and even brotherly. Edward pushed his way through the wind and heard his own breathing and told himself,

"I'm not afraid, not!"

He came out of the alley and into St James's Street, and turned back up towards St Saviour's in his usual pattern. The church was on the corner. It was empty. All the windows were boarded, the carpets had gone, the crosses, the altar. Soon it would be pulled down to make way for a supermarket. His mother dreaded the day. She had written letters to the newspapers, to councillors and M.P.s, saying how immoral it was, and what a sign of the times, that a church should make way for a supermarket.

A supermarket was a place of the devil to her because it housed banks of tins near *high* as churches, and its windows were always plastered with fluorescent, luring prices that no sensible and decent shopkeeper could keep up with. Usually she averted her eyes to avoid catching sight of them, but if ever she did, her mind would seize on them and turn them into a sermon or a refrain to last for days.

"And Tomato Sauce, I ask you, at 11p! 3p under the Recommended, that is, and you might well ask what the good is in manufacturers wasting their time in recommending prices for the likes of them to toss to the wind like so many pancakes! Lucky folks realise that what's taken off one thing's put on another, *and* more besides, and lucky some folks still put store on service and civility and *that's* something you'll never get in a supermarket. There's people glad and willing to pay Recommended for their sauce if they get it passed over with a bit of civility, and when have you ever known one of those supermarket chits on those tills stir a hand's turn to pack things proper into a customer's basket or have a proper word with them about the weather?"

Now the worst part was to come. The empty hulk of St Saviour's towered to his right, straddled the corner. Here in its shadow the darkness was darkest, so dense that it was almost palpable. Edward forced himself to walk, not run. He strode counting his paces as if counting were a kind of charm, and he knew already how many paces there were—a hundred and four to where the graveyard ended round the corner, on St Saviour's Street again. Then he was passing the high iron railings of the graveyard, grim and overgrown and never visited.

A hundred and one tonight. Edward, breathless, stopped for a moment and had his usual reward. He had a sense of enormous lightness and power as if he had taken in some kind of strength during that terrified striding.

"Not afraid—not!"

He stared down the windy street and saw in the distance figures darting, a little shoal under a lamp. The MacKay boys. Bad company. He hesitated, not sure whether or not he felt like bad company tonight. Certainly it would keep the dark at bay.

Leaves rattled and rustled nearby. He glanced over the road and saw, through the near-leafless branches of the elm, a light at the top of The House. Mad old Mister Rudge was in there alone and Edward wondered whether he were afraid of the dark, and whether he minded being right near that blind church on that black corner. They said he had taken to buying whole loaves to feed to the birds and the Street was now sure he was mad, even if not entirely a miser, as it used to say. A miser would not buy whole loaves to throw to the birds. Some of them were even calling him St Francis.

He was probably feeding the birds because he needed their company, Edward thought. The House had the only real garden in St Saviour's and to the birds it must be like paradise, sooted and overgrown though it was. Edward could see it from his window, with the high chimneys and the roofs of the warehouses by the canal beyond. Whenever he looked out his eyes went straight to it, drawn by the patch of dusty green in a brick desert.

A figure moved across the lighted window and Edward felt a sudden pang. In that moment he had a strong feeling of the solitariness of that old man, of his walking about that great empty house night and day alone. Eating in silence, winding the clock in silence, mounting the stairs to the top room in silence. He lived and moved in silence as though it were an element, or a new dimension.

Now the figure was silhouetted motionless. Perhaps Mister Rudge was looking at him, as he stood there staring upwards, locked in this sudden strange awareness of the old man's existence. Edward, prompted by some inexplicable impulse, raised his right arm then, in a kind of salute.

Then, amazed at himself, he began to run again. But not before he thought he had glimpsed the slow raising of an arm in answer. The thing was done now. Edward had put himself, by that single gesture, into a different relationship with Mister Rudge. From now on it would be impossible to jeer at him with the rest, or think of him simply as "an old madman". He had made himself an ally.

Ahead the MacKay boys still darted in their pool of light and then Edward was running to join them, to put off going home.

CHAPTER THREE

¶ *What Edward Flack Wrote In His Exercise Book, Headed "What I Would Like To Be When I Grow Up". And Which, After Reading It Through, He Carefully Tore Out And Replaced With a Harmless Piece About Wanting To Be A Footballer, An Almost Exact Replica Of All The Other Essays Sent In By The Boys In His Class*

What I would like to be when I grow up, is a hero. I read a lot of books and in all of them my favourate person is always the hero. But I do not just mean that. I mean, every book has a hero, it has to, but not necessarily what I would call a *real* hero. For instance in this book I have been reading called *Stig of the Dump* there is this boy called Barney that has all the adventures, but this does not mean that he is an actual hero. A real hero is a man who does bold and noble deeds, David in David and Goliath and Perseus and St George and so on to mention a few names.

My favourate hero is Hercules because he did not just stop at doing one or two bold deeds, but kept right on doing them the whole time (and so did Robin Hood for that matter, another of my favourates.) Practicly everything he did was a brave and noble deed and he was as strong as a lion. Even when he was only a baby he strangled a snake in his cradle, so he must have been born a hero I suppose, as the average baby would not even think of doing this. Gary Farrands who lives up our street is around the same age as Hercules was when he strangled the snake which is less than a year old, and all he does is just lie there in his pram and twang these blue plastic ducks he has. Not that I am critisising as I realise that I was proberly just the same at that age and so are most babies, but it does tend to show that heroes are born and not made and so perhaps I have not got much chance of becoming one.

You might wonder how I have got it into my head to become a hero and I think the real reason is not having a real father. I think boys like to grow up like their fathers but as I do not know who my father was or my mother I do not know what to be like. It is as if I could be *anything* if you see what I mean, and if I really can be, then I choose to be a hero. I like to think that my real father was something like an ace pilot for instance or a mountaineer who was killed performing a feat of daring. And I think my mother proberly died of a broken heart after this.

You might say why not model yourself on your foster father but this really is not the same thing at all and I know I would not really like being a bus conducter. And I expect my foster mother would like me to take over her grocery shop when I grow up but there is no chance of this though I have not told her yet.

My real trouble is that although I would like to be a hero I already know that I was not born one. And of course you cannot go and train as one, like being an engineer or a teacher for instance, and so I realise that I will have to train myself. This means for one thing doing a daily feat of daring if possible. I have already started doing this. I picked a fight with Patrick MacKay only last week and got my lip cut and blood all over my jacket and only just lost. I also climbed up Ma Briggses wall for a dare and pinched that old pair of wheels that have been in her yard for ages and which we're going to make into a go-cart. I have got hold of a book of exercises for training the RAF and am doing some each day before breakfast although in fact I do not show much prowess at press-ups etc. I have also started daring myself things, the main one of which is not to be afraid of the dark, which I am afraid I am rather. I do a kind of test or ordeal every night and am sure I am improving.

So there is a chance that I can train myself for this job in life but there is only one thing that bothers me and that is this. If for instance Hercules was alive today or St George what would they do to *be* heroes? There just do not seem to be the jobs for heroes that there used to be and of course no dragons or nine headed monsters or anything like that or at least not to my knowledge. It is obvious that David would have been no good whatever without Goliath, and I keep on wondering who or what will be my Goliath? I suppose if David had not found his he would have just been an unsung hero and no one would ever have heard of him. And the whole point of heroes is that everyone hears about them and marvels at their great and mighty deeds.

I always go through the newspaper at home to see if there is anything about a hero in them and also watch the television news, but so far there has been no sign of one. In fact all the headlines seem to be about politics and so on, and sometimes I really worry about this and wonder if nowadays we have politicians instead of heroes. If so, I think it a very bad swap. None of the politicians I ever see on television are anything like a patch on Perseus or Hercules and in fact many of them seem really silly and even my mother says they are terrible liars. Also I think you can tell a lot from people's faces and I have never yet seen a politician with a face I really like and they are usually rather fat.

There was this boy on *Blue Peter* who had got a special award for saving two other boys in a dingy which had overturned and that was certainly a very brave deed. But when you actuerly saw the boy you could not actuerly imagine him making a career out of being a hero. He was just an ordinary boy really and rather a let down when you actuerly saw him.

Mike MacKay says he is going into the army when he is old enough and I think he thinks that will be a brave and noble thing to do. But I could not disagree more. I think that all wars are wicked and stupid and when I see all those poor people in Vietnam for instance on the television I feel really sick. What point is there in killing innocent people just for a piece of land which is what most wars are about from what I can gather. And how can the soldiers bring themselves to shoot and bomb other people? Mr Brown's son is a soldier and when he comes home and walks up the Street in his uniform I often look at him and just cannot imagine him wanting to kill anyone or actually firing a gun at somebody. He is perfectly ordinary from what I can see and once even bought me an ice cream. They say it is orders that makes them do it, but what kind of orders are they to tell you to do a thing like that? No soldier is a hero in my view. In fact all soldiers are just like sheep. And there again, I *know* Mike MacKay and anything less like a hero you could not imagine. I mean he is strong all right I do not deny this, but there is more to being a hero than that.

I have rather gone off the point here but I do feel very strongly about war and so on. But to get back to my own problems. At school Mr Fowler is always saying human nature never changes and that history repeats itself and so on, and so I am quite sure that there *is* room for heroes, even nowadays, and shall not give up hope.

I do not suppose for a moment that David for instance knew about Goliath when he was my age or that Robin Hood knew that he was going to grow up to rob the rich to feed the poor. So I shall just get on with the job of training myself and trust that by the time I am old enough to be a real hero something will turn up. Heroes do not get discoraged easily and I do not mean to either.

CHAPTER FOUR

¶ *What Happened In Liverpool On The Morning Of November 4th And How A Fateful Letter Was Posted To Forty-Seven St Saviour's Street*

Alfred Graves took a last look round the little room that had been home for the past six years. It took him back those six years simply to see it again exactly as it had been when his landlady had thrown open the door and exclaimed "There!" in a voice that suggested at one and the same time that in the first place this was little less than Aladdin's Cave, and in the second that he would be a knave and a fool to grudge five pounds a week for it.

Alfred Graves, who was neither a knave nor a fool, *did* grudge five pounds a week for it, and his heart sank at its ugliness and desolation. But he was a man who had learned to be timid and to do what was expected of him and so he had made only a show of inspecting the room with its view of chimneys and a factory wall, about which even he could find nothing complimentary to say, before saying, first clearing his throat,

"Very nice. Very nice indeed. I'll take it."

His prospective landlady had shown no immediate enthusiasm.

"Supply references, I hope?" she had enquired sharply. "Recent references and a week in advance?"

She had raked him with a keen professional gaze as if for visible signs that he was either a murderer or a robber or both—or worse. But there was evidently nothing in the neat dark suit with its worn cuffs and elbows, or in Alfred's own meek expression to confirm such suspicions. As Alfred carefully took from his inside breast pocket references and money, she wiped her hands on her overall and took both.

"Right, then!" she had said. "Seems all right, I s'pose"—this handing back the reference, "but there's one or two things'll have to be made clear from the start if you and I are to get on."

She had then proceeded to make them clear. She had made it clear that there were to be no scratches found on her, Mrs Parr's, furniture and fittings nor marks on her walls. There was to be no coming and going at all hours, no using the bath more than once a week and then ten pence extra and all to be left as found, no bringing strangers into her house, no fiddling with the meters and absolutely no cooking of fish on the gas ring, if he would be so good, as the one thing she could not be doing with was a horrible evil smell of fish hanging about the place and getting into the furnishings and reminding her of her late husband who had been forever eating platefuls of finny haddock and had died of it, for all she knew.

Six years Alfred Graves had lived in this room and he knew it by heart. He knew every raised thread in the curtains, every patch on the lino and crack on the ceiling. He knew where to look for the one shaft of sunlight that ever reached it, the evening slant that lit a narrow path over the rug and across the bed and came to rest on an old brown photograph of cabhorses steaming in the rain on Liverpool Station.

Alfred Graves had lived here six years, obediently doing this and not doing that as Mrs Parr had decreed, and now he was to live here no longer. He had given in his notice a fortnight before and lived under the chill of Mrs Parr's disapproval ever since. He had hardly noticed. A chill had been setting over his whole life slowly and certainly for months now—years even, like a fog moving in from the sea. He was chilled through and through now, to the heart.

Two weeks ago he had given his notice too at the factory warehouse where he had worked six years as ledger clerk until now his very existence seemed to have narrowed to rows of figures in a neat black column. Alfred Graves had summed up these figures, cast them carefully, and made his final reckoning.

"Nothing left." Though it did not matter if there were.

He gave the room a last look and closed the door. Downstairs in the passage his two cases stood by the door, made oddly jaunty by a square of light filtered through the pane of stained glass. There were two brown paper parcels, one of which he put in either pocket of his coat before opening the door, picking up the cases, and going out for the last time.

His first visit that morning was to Liverpool Station. He had not been on a station for years and had forgotten the life and noise, the sense of endless possibility and choice of destination, of the shuttling of destinies. He almost faltered. Supposing he were to change his mind? Supposing he gave himself—and the world—

another chance? What if he were to board a train instead—any train, one picked at random—and go wherever it took him?

He stood motionless in the echoing hall while porters and passengers thronged round him, and hesitated.

"But that is what I had decided to do anyhow, in a way," he thought. "Go on a journey and not know where I am going. And a room in Crewe, say, would be the same as one in Liverpool. And ledgers are all the same the world over. No. Closing my ledger, I am."

He went to the Left Luggage Office and waited patiently in the queue. Without the suitcases he felt instantly lighter. He passed his entire worldly goods over the counter and was freed by it. He even found himself having to suppress a stir of excitement now that the thing had really begun, a strange, half-painful sensation that would even now weaken his resolve, if he let it. He groped for the parcels in his pockets and reminded himself what he had set out to do. In the Buffet he bought a cup of tea and managed to find a table to himself where he could complete his business.

The letter to Lily was already written. All he had to do was slip inside the envelope the tickets for his Left Luggage and the few remaining notes left in his pocket. He pulled out his wallet and hesitated. There were four five-pound notes and two ones.

"Not as if I'll *need* them," he thought. "More good to Lily than to me."

But some old, careful instinct refused to be quite satisfied.

"What if something were to go wrong? Need it then . . ."

Neatly he folded the notes and put them back in the wallet. He sealed the already stamped envelope and left the Buffet. There was a posting box on the station. Alfred pushed in the letter and as it fell so too his heart actually did a kind of somersaulting fall in his chest, he literally felt his heart drop.

"That's it, then. All square and tidy. No going back now."

He drew himself up as straight as his bowed ledger-clerk's spine would allow, and went out through the booking hall. There he looked irresolutely about him. How to get there? He had not thought of that.

"Should've looked up the buses," he thought. "You slipped up there, Alfred Graves. Error in calculations. Books don't balance. But . . ."

His eye fell on the waiting line of taxis. Only twice in his whole life before had Alfred Graves ever ridden in a taxi, and one of those had been to a funeral.

"Why not?"

The faintest of smiles passed over his pale face.

"Do it in style. Last fling."

He walked to the barrier and was not quite certain exactly what happened but it seemed as if a taxi shot suddenly out of nowhere right past the queue of waiting cars and stopped abruptly at—almost on—his feet. The long line of taxis behind at once set up a furious screeching of horns, like so many angry fowls, and Alfred, confused and deafened, stared at the culprit. He found himself confronted by a face so long and white and crowned by so startling a shock of red hair—*circled* by it, for there was a flaming beard too—that he actually jumped, as if faced by the devil in person.

"Yes, sir? Good morning to ye, sir! And where'll it be I can be taking you?"

He spoke loudly but pleasantly, as if the concerted hooting of twenty or so cars were a commonplace to him, a mere background music.

"Oh. Oh. The docks, please."

"Certainly, sir. Right ye are. Good as there, I promise ye! In we get and will you sit in the back or the front, sir, it being me duty to warn you there's no belts and the car a habit o' jerking like its mother was a rabbit when the fancy takes her, which is often, sir, often."

"Oh. Back. Yes. Back, thank you."

He climbed in and shut the door and sat bolt upright and next moment was shot sideways as the taxi leapt forward and he heard the driver's triumphant cry,

"Missed! Did ye see that, now? Another fraction of the least tick and he'd've had the door open, bejam, and us out—and oh, the temper of him! Will ye look at him now dancing and shaking fists and——"

Alfred had not time. The taxi took another violent swerving exit, this time out of the station yard and out into the mainstream of traffic and to the accompaniment of another chorus of horns.

"At this rate," he thought, "the fellow will do the job for me."

"Lardy!" The driver settled back comfortably. "That's better! And no good him taking me number, either, the driver of this particular vehicle being dead long since God rest his soul, and past his number being taken or anything else at all!"

"It's not—not stolen, is it?" asked Alfred faintly.

His driver lifted both hands off the wheel in a gesture of horror and Alfred cried,

"No, no! Of course not! I'm sorry—I shouldn't have—oh!"

The taxi took another violent turn and Albert lay back limply, resigned to his fate—which was, after all, what he had set out to find. Dazed as he was he was aware that neither taxi nor driver were what they should be. The back of the car was heaped with what looked like a miscellany of old clothes and camping equipment, that had surely not been absentmindedly left by the last fare? His head, which had been lolling, was jerked upright again by another sharp turn and he found himself staring into the driving mirror at a pair of light grey eyes.

"Ye're all right, sir?"

"Oh. Oh. Yes."

"Ah—sport ye are—could see it the minute I set me eyes on you, sir. Take no notice of it at all."

"Oh no. No, I don't."

"Surely to God—" both hands left the steering wheel simultaneously to bestow on their possessor a pious if hasty cross,"—a man can earn an honest wage wi'out the bats o' hell itself after him and blasting off fit to raise the souls of the damned themselves— God rest their souls—" another hasty and perilous cross, another swerve with a wake of crowing hooters.

"Am I in hell already?" wondered Alfred Graves.

"Which dock was it you was wanting then, sir?"

"Which—?" He stared stupidly into the mirrored eyes.

"The dock, sir, that ye're wanting—the number of it, perhaps, so as—whoop!"

Another swerve. Alfred found himself suddenly with his head buried in the paraphernalia beside him.

"Oh. Oh. It doesn't matter. If you just drop me off when we— when we're there."

"In the name of Jaysus, sir," said the taxi driver sweetly, "when we're *where*, I'm asking? And begging your pardon for asking, surely, but if a man's to drive a cab he must know where to he's driving it, and sweet reason that is, bejam!"

"When we get to the docks." With an attempt at firmness. "I'll get off there."

"Sea-faring man, are ye?" enquired the driver.

"No. Yes. No. I mean yes."

"Aaaah." Enigmatically. "What I was thinking—tell a sea-faring man you can—told you the minute I clapped eyes at the station. There's a first mate, I says, or I'm a Dutchman!"

Alfred said nothing.

"Which I'm not," prompted the Irishman.

"No. Oh no, you're not," said Alfred.

"Bound where?"

Alfred looked blankly and desperately into the narrowed eyes in the stripe of face in the mirror.

"Oh—er—er—"

"Foreign parts is it, p'raps?"

"Yes." Alfred was relieved. "Yes, that's it. Foreign parts."

"Was sure of it," purred the Irishman. "Sure as me own grandmother's an Indian squaw."

There was an uneasy pause. Alfred Graves, taking only the third taxi ride of his life, wished fervently that he had stuck at the second. He looked out of the window to avoid his inquisitor's gaze. The car was making a right-hand turn with the usual dramatic effects on other traffic, but shaken as he was, Alfred could see where he was now, and knew certainly that they were heading in the wrong direction. He cleared his throat.

"Er. Er—I think we have taken a wrong turn," he said.

"Short cut," said the driver succinctly, with a sagacious nod of the red mane.

Alfred said no more. He sat and wondered how going east could be a short cut to going west.

"I want to go west," he thought, and again was aware of a painful half-wakening sensation as he saw the humour of it.

"I want to go west."

"What is it ye're saying, sir?"

Alfred had not realised that he had spoken aloud.

"My name is Finn," the driver announced, stepping hard on the brake. "And the devil take that son of a fool ahead to be trying the brakes on us and us in full tilt! And if ever I do another day at driving taxis, wit' the roads awash and littered wit' mad-men and murderers my name's not Patrick Finn—and begging your pardon, sir, as there's no offence in the world meant to yeself, who's as civil and pleasant a gentleman as ever I hope to meet again, or likely to!"

Alfred felt himself reluctantly pleased to be called civil, pleasant and a gentleman, none of them terms he had ever had applied to him before, and none of them qualities he would have dreamed of claiming for himself. He strove to suppress these unaccustomed feelings because it now began to seem to him that the longer this particular taxi ride went on, the less likely he would be to go on to accomplish what he had set out to accomplish.

"Why doesn't he just drive me where I asked and keep quiet?" he thought. "If only he would keep quiet!"

"I'm not expecting to hear your name, o' course, sir," said the taxi driver. "Happy enough for you to have the advantage of knowing mine."

"Oh. Well. Of course. Graves. Alfred Graves."

"*Graves*, is it?" said the Irishman Finn thoughtfully, and Alfred found himself meeting those eyes again, and thought that it surely could not be common practice for taxi drivers to exchange introductions with their fares, and even had a sudden lunatic suspicion that he might be being kidnapped.

"Not the sort of a name to be easy to live with, Graves," went on the driver. "A superstitious man, which I am not myself—or hardly at all—" here he broke off to cross himself thoroughly, to the near-radical detriment of a passing cyclist—"but I should not want the carrying round of a name like that, bejam."

Alfred was silent.

"Change it," suggested the driver.

Alfred stared into the mirror.

"Yours," said Finn, "and no one else's. You be changing it. You change that before it's after changing *you*!"

"There is no possibility," Alfred told himself carefully, "absolutely no possibility whatever that this man knows what I am at. He is a complete stranger, a perfectly—well, almost a perfectly ordinary taxi driver, and I am his fare. And what is more, he is not taking me straight to my destination. He is taking me a long way round, so that he can charge more. He is a scoundrel, and I must deal with him."

"We are going the wrong way!"

He sank back immediately, appalled by the loudness of his own voice.

"I will tell you what, Alfred," said the driver, "and it's Alfred I shall be calling you, if you've no objection, the name of Graves being a nasty, insidious, insinuating kind of a name to be foisting itself on any man. I will tell you what. We are sure enough going the wrong way, so far as I can tell, and the reason a selfish and inconsiderate one for a man to have to own. You being the only fare, ye understand, that I have had the pleasure of a proper and enjoyable conversation with since first I ever took up taxiing."

"He is mad," Alfred thought. "Or I am mad. I think perhaps we both are."

"That being this morning," added Finn. "And give it up altogether this morning I shall, too, definite, the minute I have seen you right and properly put down where you asked. What was the time you said your ship was sailing?"

"Er—it goes at eleven," said Alfred. It sounded thin. "Half-past eleven, I mean."

"Eleven hundred hours," murmured the Irishman. " 'Tis true, then. Ah, well, if 'tis it is," with which enigmatic utterance he turned the taxi in a complete half circle and set off back at high speed in the opposite direction, with the by now familiar chorus of complainants following.

After this he said nothing. Alfred, after a few nervous minutes of waiting in vain for the exchange to reopen, sat back. They were travelling now through narrow streets with doorsteps right on the pavement. The sky was shut out from his view entirely. Alfred knew about streets such as this, and the sense of chill and oppression that had been temporarily dispersed by the Irishman, settled on him again as naturally and easily as a well-worn garment. Here and there a woman sat on a step nursing a dirty child, or a man leaned on a corner smoking. Alfred watched them and felt pity for them and he thought once more how good it would be to take that single step out of such a world. He patted his pockets for reassurance.

"Not long," he thought. "Not long now."

Past warehouses, past derelict shops with broken windows, past pubs and vacant lots. He looked to his left and saw grey water and his heart lurched.

"Here we are, then!"

The taxi came to a halt. Alfred sat stupidly for a moment collecting himself. He was there. The time had come. For an instant he felt reluctant to leave the comfort of the car, he wanted to go on and on riding forever, passenger in this vehicle with its enigmatic, loquacious driver, and he dreaded the moment of stepping out on to that cold and desolate quay.

"How much?"

"How *much* now, is it?" cried the red Irishman. "And you and me friends and have been this past half hour, and you talking of money! If ever meself I'm after asking a friend to take money for a good turn may the good Lord smite me dead!" He crossed himself hastily.

C

"I'm sorry—I thought—but this is a taxi!"

"Lardy! Taxi now, is it?" The Irishman rolled up his eyes and roared. "The man thinks because a vehicle has the word—and a word's an awful tricky thing—oh look ye, man, this here's a car wit' the word TAXI writ in red on its roof, and ye could have a man wit' the word DEVIL writ in red on his hair, and it wouldn't be making him the devil, would it?"

Alfred, in no position to follow so involved a line of reasoning, nevertheless caught its drift and shook his head helplessly.

"No," he said weakly, at length.

"There ye are, then!" cried the Irishman, and he climbed out of his cab and loped round to Alfred's side of the car. He was seen to be a lanky giant of a man a full head and shoulders higher than Alfred, whose hand he now took and wrung warmly and painfully.

"Taxi!" he cried again delightedly. "That car's no more a taxi than—was it really thinking me a proper driver ye were, or were ye mebbe wondering just a shade?"

"I was wondering," admitted Alfred.

"Ah!" The Irishman gave his hand a further pumping. "An honest man, bejab, and after me own heart! I'm telling ye truth, Alfie, I like ye. Patrick Finn likes ye, and is proud to have ye to friend!"

"Th—thank you," said Alfred, then added lamely, feeling his reaction to be lukewarm and ungracious, "and the same to you."

Though he could not help wondering if ever a friendship had been destined to be so brief.

"Aye. Well!" The Irishman Finn grinned at him then, with his white, wicked face lit within the ring of fiery beard. "And here's to the luck of our next meeting, and soon may it be. And soon it will be!"

"I don't know," Alfred mumbled. He withdrew his hand, "I must be going, I'm afraid. Ship to catch."

"Of course ye must!" The beaming Finn looked down at him with something like fondness. "A ship to catch—tide going—foreign parts. Aye—foreign parts!"

Abruptly he turned and ambled back to his cab.

"Soon!" he cried as he climbed in. He slammed the door, raised a hand in salute, and the taxi leaped forward. Alfred stepped hastily back. The taxi went out of sight behind a tall warehouse and Alfred stood alone.

Slowly he wheeled and faced the grey water. There was no one

34

else in sight, though there were ships by the dozen close at hand, their great hulks looming in the drizzle. It was going to be easy.

"He who hesitates," Alfred told himself, "is lost," and he began to walk, just as he had rehearsed it, each hand on the bulky parcels in the pockets of his jacket, and he walked and when he came to the edge of the wharf he took yet another step, the last.

"Ah!" he cried as he fell, though softly, for he wanted no help and was hardly taken unawares. But he threw up his arms instinctively as he hit the icy water and did not sink at once and only once, as he had planned. He knew only cold and dark and then light again but still cold and then,

"Ah!"

A great splash close at hand and a sudden tight grip of his collar and again, hugely and triumphantly,

"Aaaah!"

Alfred Graves spluttered and gasped and blinked and through a mist of water saw, within inches of his own, the wet white face and dark red locks of his saviour—the Irishman, Patrick Finn.

CHAPTER FIVE

¶ *In Which Edward Flack Dares Himself To The Limit And Mrs Flack Has A Telephone Call*

The Friday deliveries had been made. Edward had eaten his usual hasty Friday tea and now sat on the bed at the window staring out at a wet and darkening St Saviour's Street. It did not look at all a fit place for heroes, he thought. Heroes went with ivied pillars and marble palaces or with landscapes of caverns and towering rocks, and the sea never far away. He tried to picture David emerging from behind the corner and a Goliath striding from the opposite direction, high as the telephone kiosk and with eyes glaring like headlamps. The vision dissolved before it had even taken shape properly. David's goatskins looked merely silly and his sandalled feet on the puddled pavement ludicrous. Besides, once the slinging of stones began in earnest there would be hardly a pane of glass left unbroken in the Street, and the law would certainly step in before either David or Goliath was properly into his stride. He rejected the picture of them both being bundled into a Black Maria, and tried instead to conjure up St George.

This was, if anything, worse. By the time he had expended enormous mental effort on raising the fully armoured figure of St George against the backdrop of a Marmite advertisement, he had no heart left for the dragon.

"In any case," he thought, "first sight of a dragon and those MacKays'd have him. Always on about wanting an Alsatian to train. Have that dragon tied in their back yard, they would, doing tricks and feeding it bones. Human bones, I wouldn't wonder."

On the other hand, there was the brighter prospect that the dragon would turn on the MacKays and incinerate the whole pack of them with a single sulphureous puff, turn them into so much volcanic ash before St George had time even to poise his lance.

Edward did not really believe in either of these alternatives. The heroic life seemed very far removed from St Saviour's today and had a depressing lack of reality.

"But I mustn't get discouraged," he told himself. "The time

will come. A hero must never be faint-hearted." His eye fell on The House, and he remembered the fleeting encounter with its occupant the previous night.

"What if . . . what about going to see him . . . ?"

He felt the stirrings of excitement and fear.

"A dare . . . dare myself to go and see him."

He began to ponder on the idea while at the same time knowing at the back of his mind that the die was already cast. He had dared himself—or as good as—by the very act of having the idea in the first place, and would have to go.

Old Mister Rudge—what was he really like? Mad? Bad? There *were* memories of him in the days when he still sometimes went about the Street dressed in a long black overcoat. Edward remembered the brilliant eyes in a bony face, the wispy grey beard, the thin black umbrella, counterpointing the long jerky stride as though his powers of walking were already beginning to rust. For more than five years now he had not left The House. Mrs Cottingham, who was nearly as old herself, went in twice a week to clean for him and take his shopping.

She was a disappointment to the rest of the Street (none of whom had ever actually been inside The House), no kind of spy at all. All cross-examinations, and there had been many of them, ended with nothing more than the odd, useless hint of how the old man lived. Everyone, for instance, knew that he was fond of mulligatawny soup and rice pudding and that he had meat only on Sundays. But there is a limit to how much can be read into a shopping list. That he would not let Mrs Cottingham into the top storey of The House at all was by far the most interesting item of information so far gleaned, and even that was maddening in its being, in a sense, *non* information.

The week after this discovery the Street had been in a frenzy of conjecture. Mister Rudge was promoted to Bluebeard overnight and credited with a host of criminal activities, from unlawful holding of a person or persons against their will (which made the top floor into a jail) to forgery (which meant there was a printing press up there). Some of the crimes were nameless, to Edward at least, since if ever they were named in his presence it was in lowered tones that were just, and infuriatingly, inaudible.

Further pressure had been put on the imperturbable Mrs Cottingham to reveal more. It was put to her as a public duty that she should turn, as it were, Queen's Evidence. None of this had made any impression on the old lady as she was partially deaf, which meant that what she did not choose to hear she could cheerfully ignore—and did.

"What? What's that you say? Speak up!"

And since most of the things people were saying had bordered on the unspeakable, and were certainly unshoutable or unbawlable, in the end the scandal had died down through sheer lack of inflammatory matter with which to feed it.

Edward himself had never believed any of the theories he had heard at this time, and thought they only went to prove how silly people were. He knew, which they did not, that Mister Rudge wrote poetry. He had more than once seen it scribbled on the back of the paper Mrs Cottingham used for her shopping list.

"He burns the midnight oil . . ." thought Edward now, and recognised this as something that was, if not actually heroic, at least novel and interesting. It was something with which he could sympathise. It made Mister Rudge a little larger than life, and, this being a state Edward himself aspired to, somebody whose friendship would be worth cultivating.

Edward stared over at The House and imagined the old man going his ways in there in a kind of dim and watery silence, winding along those long stairs and corridors like a fish. Perhaps he had lived so long in silence that he could no longer speak. There was no television or radio and he did not take in a newspaper. Mister Rudge had his own world entire in that tall dark house. He was king of his own castle, mad or not.

"If I do go over there," Edward thought, "there'll be just him and me. Alone. And no one would know I was in there. I couldn't tell."

He tried to imagine knocking on that door under the boughs of the elm, hearing the shuffle of steps, the rattling of keys.

"And it's dark!"

The dare was getting out of hand. Edward tried to push it away, dismiss it. But already his training as a hero had gone too far for that. He could no longer deceive himself by giving false reasons for being a coward. In the end he tried to compromise with himself.

"Tomorrow. Tomorrow morning. Then I will."

"Because it will be light then," came this other voice inside his head, the St George voice. "Go now!"

The telephone rang in the passage outside and Edward jumped. He heard Mr Flack calling downstairs to his wife and a minute later her quick steps and sharp voice. Edward waited until he heard her replace the receiver, and then went out. This was a non-heroic act, performed in the hope that when she saw him his mother would say or do something to prevent his going out, in the near dark, to visit The House. He was not disappointed.

"Well!" she cried. "There's a thing!"

Edward and his father looked at her.

"Who was that?" she demanded of Mr Flack.

"Was what?"

"Who was that? On the phone? Large as life and so long since I'd heard his voice I all but never recognised it. Who was it?"

"Well then, Lily," said Mr Flack, doing his bit to build up the suspense. "Who was it?"

"That," she said, "was neither more nor less than Alfred Graves!"

"Your brother!" echoed Mr Flack.

"My brother," she affirmed. "And gone right off his head I do believe. You never *heard* such a muddle. You go and be clearing up in the spare room, Denis, and you give him a hand,"—this to Edward. "I shall have to get back down. There's the shop bell just gone and only Mrs Goodman down there. *She* won't go pilfering stock the minute my back's turned, but there's plenty in this street will!"

She was off, clattering swiftly down the stairs to forestall any such thing, and Edward and his father were left looking at one another.

"Better do as she says," said Mr Flack. "I suppose she'll tell us what it's all about when she's finished down there and locked up."

She did. She came back up and made herself a pot of tea and sat down to make a meal of her news and the pile of hot buttered toast together.

"I really do believe he's mad," she confided. "What *can* he mean? Posted this letter, see, this morning, so he says. Well, now he says don't open it! Not on any account to open it! So when that letter comes tomorrow morning, I'm just to pick it up, if you please, and put it on the mantel and not to open it whatever I do. Not *open* it? What kind of a letter is that to go and write, that them that it's addressed to can't open it?"

"Might not come tomorrow, Lily," said Mr Flack, sidestepping the issue.

"Well, no more it mightn't, for that matter," she agreed, "the post the way it is. But that ain't the point, Denis. What I want to know is, what's in this letter that it can't be opened in a proper straightforward way? He sounded funny, he really did, on the phone. Hardly knew him."

"So you said," agreed Mr Flack.

"And *coming* here, himself, that's the next thing! Here by tea-time tomorrow, he says, and could he stop for a few days? And what about your job, I ask him, or is this a holiday, or what? And out he comes with some rigmarole about not *going* back, ever, and about drawing lines and closing accounts and all sorts else. I could make neither head nor tail of it."

"Does sound rum," said Mr Flack.

"What's he like?" Edward asked, excited by the realisation that he had another relation, of sorts, and was actually to meet him. "And what shall I call him?"

"You'll call him Uncle Alfred, of course," said Mrs Flack. "And mind your manners while he's here, I should hope, and do me a bit of credit. He's a clever man, Alfred is, with a job in an office, and I don't want him thinking I'm bringing you up all anyhow. Very strict brought up, him and me were, and he'll expect you to be the same."

"Yes, Mum." The gilt on the new uncle began already to tarnish.

"If he took a fancy to you," went on his mother, "there's a lot he could do to help you, my lad. Get you a job like his, I shouldn't wonder, for a year or two, to get you well into the way of using figures for when you take up the shop. Ooop—what——?"

There was a thud and a roar and a crack out in the Street and Edward looked up just in time to see a shower of tiny golden sparks dwindle out into the dark. Guy Fawkes night always came early in St Saviour's Street.

"That'll be them daft MacKays!" said Mrs Flack. "Them and their bangs! Ought to be made illegitimate. Frightens the life out of you. He says he'll pay, by the way."

"Who? Pay what?" Mr Flack had lost his place in the conversation.

"Alfred, of course. For the room."

"Hmmm. But how much? And will he be under your feet all day? You want to think about it, Lily."

"Think? How do you mean think? Rung off, hasn't he? Too late now for thinking. And I don't know why *you* should object. If I cannot put up my own brother for a week or two, particular

40

for a sum that will come in handy to say the least, then the world is coming to a fine pass."

"Yes, dear," said Mr Flack, already regretting his remark. "You are right."

"*Not* that it won't mean extra work," she went on, "most of which will have to be done by You Know Who. And not that it won't mean inconvenience and fuss, neither of which things I'm fond of as you very well know, Denis."

"You're right," he agreed again. "Inconvenience and fuss."

His wife continued in a voice that implied that although Mr Flack had said she was right he had meant exactly the opposite, and she knew it.

"Not, of course, that inconvenience and fuss will worry you, you coming from a family where inconvenience and fuss is going on morning noon and night and as natural to you all as the air you breathe."

This time he did not say that she was right. Edward, who had gone behind a comic, felt bound to say something to help him out.

"He might not stay long, Mum," he said, and was at once rounded upon.

"And that's a nice thing!" she cried. "My own flesh and blood coming to stop for the first time in my whole married life, and now being wished out of the house before he's ever set foot in it!"

"I didn't mean that, Mum. I meant—you know—about the extra work, and that."

"Ah, well!" She wiped her fingers, buttered toast finished. "He's a tidy soul himself, Alfred is. Always tidy he was, even when he was a boy. Do you know," and now she sounded genuinely surprised at herself, and wondering, "do you know, blessed if I don't begin to feel half pleased he's to come! I mean, he is my brother, and flesh and blood does mean something. Oh! Oh my dear, what've I said?"

"It's all right," said Edward thinly. "I don't mind."

"Oooh, I never meant—what I meant—oh, 'tain't anything to do with flesh and blood, not really. To do with remembering, I suppose. When we were kids—you know. Tricks we'd get up to—that kind of thing."

"Her?" thought Edward incredulously. "*Tricks?*"

Another firework went off, this time much nearer home.

"Ooooh!" She jumped up and ran to the window and knocked

noisily on it and Edward heard shrieks and laughter float up from the cold and dark and exciting street and wished he were out there too. She opened the window and the marvellous firework smell came in, still smoking, on the draught.

"You get off now, all of you!" shrieked Mrs Flack. "Little devils! I shall send for the pol—ice!"—the last on a high, rising scream intended to reach every last one of the errant MacKays and their accomplices. She banged the window to and the air was at once warmer—and duller.

"Little devils!" she said again. "What that woman was at, having that number, I don't know. *Seven*, would you believe, and not one of 'em a girl!"

She evidently thought Mrs MacKay had gone in for boys deliberately, as being most trouble to other people.

"Irish," commented Mr Flack.

"And that's no excuse!" she said. "Downright untidy, a family that size, and unthinking. *Two's* right number—first a boy, then a girl. That's what I call a family—and I ain't the only one thinks so, either. Just you notice, on all those adverts on the television, and that. *Two*, that's what they always have, a boy and a girl, like I said."

The others made no comment. They were content for Mrs Flack to make a ruling on families, since it was a subject neither had the faintest interest in—or only in the merest fringe way, in so far as it affected themselves.

"Can I go out, please?" Edward asked. "Just for half an hour?"

"And get your eyes blown out?" she enquired. "No good suing those MacKays for money, either. They haven't got any."

"Oh, they wouldn't go chucking fireworks at me." He was being Hercules.

"They made your *nose* bleed last week, as I remember," she said. "But noses can be replaced, if needs be. Eyes can't."

"A blind hero . . ." thought Edward. Eyes were always being put out as a matter of course in the kind of books he read. "Wonder what it's really like, to be blind . . . ?"

He considered the possibility of daring himself to go the rest of the day with his eyes shut, but after brief thought rejected it. His mother often seemed to behave exactly as if he were not there, but as she never actually bumped into him he supposed she must know, in a way. She would be bound to notice in the end. And there was a programme he wanted to watch at half past seven.

"But I will do it!" he promised his heroic other half. "Some time when I get the chance. I'll really do it. Not just for ten minutes, but for hours and hours. It'll be a test. An ordeal. Like going into the dark, only a different kind of dark. Worse. Except that it would at least be a kind of private dark, inside yourself. The other kind is dark out *there*, and outside yourself, and full of ghosts gliding even if you can't see them, and lurking monsters, and——"

"—and you can get down to the butcher's in the morning when you've finished the orders, Edward, and get a pound or two of neck. Make a hot pot. Ever so fond of that Alfred used to be."

"*I* am," said Edward instantly. "Smashing. Stew. Can we have dumplings in it?"

CHAPTER SIX

¶ *How Alfred Graves Went To Bed Without Brushing His Teeth And How Patrick Finn Awarded Him A Birthday*

Alfred Graves awoke at just after half past eight on the morning of November 5th. He had not intended to wake at all this morning, nor on any succeeding morning, and so this in itself was, in a sense, unforeseen. But the manner of his waking and the scene of it were so bizarre, so far removed from life as he had always known it, that he was tempted, for a moment, to think that perhaps he *was* dead after all, or at least in hospital, suffering from hallucinations.

"I am in a car!" was his first thought. He raised himself on to his elbows. "I am in a *field*!"

Then, ordering his thoughts in the mathematical way he had always been used to, he added the two conclusions and deduced, "I am in a car in a field!"

The other things he noticed in those first few seconds were not framed as thoughts at all, but they struck deeper than any mere thought and stirred sensations that he had not felt for years, that he had quite mislaid. He saw a pale sun striking silvery dazzle from acres of heavily dewed turf. He saw a perfectly white sky and a milky mist bounding the horizon. Trees, hedges, gates were insubstantial and shadowy shapes, poised in space rather than rooted to earth. The whole moment seemed perfectly motionless and hushed as if time, too, were hung suspended.

Alfred swung down his legs and let out a groan. Every joint in his body was cramped and stiff. But he hardly knew this, and leaned to wind down the window and at once felt the air cold and wet on his face and heard the clear whistling of birds and again felt a wash of feeling that was almost frightening so that he hustled himself into order, and forced himself to remember the kind of awakening he was used to.

It was an effort. For six years he had woken to see a peeling wall and to the familiar stale smell of yesterday's cooking, followed by the automatic reflex of a sinking heart. He had forced himself to get up, forced himself to wash and dress, forced him-

44

self to swallow a cup of tea and a slice of toast—had forced himself to go on living.

And now it had all gone. He really could not quite remember it and was suddenly in a panic as if out of his depth in deep water, and then he *remembered* the water, and his frantic threshings and bursting lungs and let out another involuntary cry.

There came a sleepy snorting from the floor of the car and Alfred leaned over and saw below him the white face of Patrick Finn who had saved his life and brought him here, and whom Alfred had never set eyes on before until yesterday. The sun struck his red hair and beard, ringing his peaceful face with fire, and he himself was something quite extraordinary to Alfred. His whole person was as far removed from everyday life as was the scene outside. Alfred stared wonderingly down at him.

"He saved my life!"

And a stir, almost a thrill, ran through him at the thought that this marvellous, almost impossible human being had flung himself into the freezing waters of the Mersey to save himself, Alfred Graves. And not only saved him, but seemed to triumph in the act, as if it were something he had been born to do and had finally achieved, as if he Patrick Finn, had walked this earth for the sole and single purpose only of coming to that moment when he would save the life of Alfred Graves.

After pulling him out of the water, Finn had lifted Alfred bodily and strode back to his battered taxi, snorting and shaking the water from his hair and eyes. There he had grabbed a blanket from the pile in the back and roughly rolled Alfred in it and cried, "*There* ye are!"

He bundled Alfred into the back seat and went round and got in himself and started the car, while Alfred had stared blankly and uncomprehendingly at his captor's wet locks, and shivered in his sodden clothes. The first coherent thought he had, in fact, was "My feet are wet", because his feet felt wetter than the rest of him, squelching as he moved them ever so slightly. Then the brakes were on again and before Alfred had time to wonder why, Finn was out and leaning in through the other rear door, pulling out garments and muttering under his breath, "This—and this—and this!" while his teeth chattered violently and he dripped like a waterfall.

Alfred found himself being hustled over the pavement and into a white-tiled public lavatory, where Finn said briefly, "Strip!" and proceeded to do so himself, long arms and legs flailing and wet clothes tossed at random about him. Alfred himself stood dazed, fumbling with buttons, and in the end was helped by Finn as though he were a small child. One or two men had come in while all this was going on, but not a word was said.

"There, now!" Finn had stepped back to see the effect, then he reached to roll up the jeans that were folded clownlike over the enormous shoes.

"That's better!" he cried. "*There's* a proper picture of a human being, bejam!" with which surprising words he scooped up the pile of wet clothes in one hand and pulled Alfred after him by the sleeve with the other. Then they were travelling again.

"Going east," said Finn with satisfaction. "Done with going west. And where is it I'm to be taking you, man?"

Surely he was not still playing at taxi drivers?

"N—nowhere," said Alfred hollowly, at last.

"That's west," said Finn. "East we're going—somewhere. Where, now?"

"Haunton." He said it without thinking.

The hands flew off the wheel in a wild gesture.

"Haunton, he says! Two hundred miles, if you please, and'll be telling me next he's come all the way from Haunton to Merseyside to *drown* hisself!"

"Oh no! No!" Alfred was appalled by the idea of such extravagance. "But—I'd given notice at my lodgings. I wasn't going back, you see."

"Indeed you weren't," said Patrick Finn. "Not wit' a brick in either pocket, you weren't, and the look on your face as if you was a blessed ghost already!"

"Brick? But how——?"

"If you'd taken a look at the pockets on ye, man! What else but bricks? More than brown paper and string to take the weight out of a brick, bejam. And now to Haunton, is it, and why is that, if I have entitlement to ask?"

"My sister." Alfred said the words with difficulty because for years he had hardly thought or spoken of Lily and the thought that she *was* his sister was strange now, even to him. "She lives there."

A thought struck him.

"The letter!"

"And what letter'll that be?" enquired Finn, deftly turning the taxi right within yards of a 'bus, and setting up the chorus of complaining hooters that he seemed not to be quite happy with-

46

out. It was as if he needed the constant drama of the ominously close shave, and took for granted that his own life and that of others within his orbit were charmed, as if he had received a special dispensation.

"I wrote to her. Telling her. And telling her where my things were. And the money I'd saved."

"Ah, well . . ." The Irishman was thoughtful. " 'Twon't be doing, that. Nasty, untruthful, upsetting kind of a letter to be getting, that."

"But I can't stop it!" Alfred cried. "It's gone off. Posted. I posted it this morning at the station!"

"Ah, well," said Finn, "there's more ways than one of killing pussy. What ye'll do, see, is telephone."

"Telephone," repeated Alfred.

"Telephone," nodded Finn. "And you'll tell her a letter's coming, see, that's not to be opened. Absolutely not, or in peril of eternal damnation. Tell her it's not to be opened though the gates of all hell were yawning. Tell her that."

Alfred sat silent and tried to imagine giving this message over the telephone to his sister. He had not spoken to her during the six years he had lived in Liverpool—just the Christmas cards had gone between them, robins from her and holly wreaths and glitter from him. And now he was to reopen contact between them with a message about eternal damnation and yawning hell.

"You don't know her," he said. But then, neither did he.

"Tell her, too, that ye're coming to stop awhile," Finn went on, expanding his strategy. "Comfortable for ye that'll be, Alfie man, and a treat for her."

"But she's not expecting me," protested Alfred weakly.

"She wouldn't be, see," explained the Irishman patiently. "She couldn't be knowing it at all, now could she? So it'll all come in the nature of a surprise, and more of a treat, human beings being what they are and fond o' pleasant surprises. If I could be having a pleasant surprise every day of my mortal life, I t'ink I'd sell my everlasting soul, I would!"

He crossed himself automatically to indicate to the Higher Powers that he would not, of course, do anything of the sort, and went on,

"But just so as to make the surprise a bit less sudden—for a surprise *can* be too sudden, 'tis altogether true—tell her it's tomorrow you'll be coming, see?"

"Yes," said Alfred, giving up. He did not even ask where they

47

would be going tonight. He let go. Patrick Finn would work things out.

And so he did. Alfred obediently made the telephone call that afternoon. He meekly accepted the bag of fish and chips and the bottle of beer Finn fetched for supper. He did not even mention that he never drank beer. He simply drank it, and even enjoyed it and felt better for it. And when Finn had drawn up in a field in the darkness and said,

"This'll do!" Alfred had echoed, "Yes, this'll do," and helped Finn sort blankets and cushions as if he had slept in a taxi throughout his adult life and it was as natural to him as brushing his teeth.

That he had not brushed his teeth did, in fact, occur to him after they had both stretched out and settled down, Finn on the front seat, Alfred on the back, and Finn had said,

"Goodnight, Alfie man. God bless!"

"Goodnight," said Alfred. Then, timidly, "God bless!"

He lay there, his eyes wide open and seeing the branches of a tree move against the sky, and he felt a vast, incredible peacefulness as if he were, indeed, at the bottom of the sea and swaying like a weed in the tide. An owl hooted away in the distance and the sound reminded Alfred of the trains he had listened to at night in Liverpool, and thinking of going to bed in Liverpool he remembered that he had not brushed his teeth. He even began to sit up, but lay back again almost immediately.

"Nothing I can do about it."

It was something that had never happened in Alfred's life before, and was therefore as rare and strange an occurrence as any other of the extraordinary day that had just passed.

He closed his eyes then, and his last thoughts were not of the future, which had always terrified him even when he had had it tied up as neatly as humanly possible, and which now had been made at a stroke a void, a blank page. His last waking thoughts were a kind of celebratory refrain, the central theme of which was the undeniably symbolic fact that Alfred Graves had gone to bed (or to a sort of bed) without brushing his teeth, and that there was nothing he or anyone else could do about it, and that he did not care. Above all, he did not care.

And now Alfred in the early morning *remembered* that he had not brushed his teeth the night before, and was not yet sufficiently a new man to feel glad of it still, or even recognise it as a kind of victory. He opened the car door quietly and climbed out, with some vague intention of wetting a finger in the dew and rubbing it over his teeth. But the air was icy fresh, so clean and green-smelling that his head actually reeled and he drew in an enormous, snuffing breath, the biggest breath he had taken for years.

He stood uncertainly in the unexpected space and silence and stared down over the fields that lapped away into the mist. The sun came in shafts between the trunks of trees and now, as it rose, lit the last reds and golds of autumn. It seemed impossible to him that all this could have been here, coexisting, all the time he had been living out his awful life in Liverpool, and he'd not known it —or at least, not thought about it. He took a few steps forward into this suddenly remade world and found that he could hardly walk and looked down to see his feet, sized seven, encased in a pair of mocassins of such proportions that they were near skis— and laughed. It was an awkward, painful thing, near to a cough, but it was the first expression of real pleasure Alfred Graves made for years. And when he saw that he wore faded denims turned up nearly to his knees, a tee shirt sporting a large crab and a long suede waistcoat, beaded and fringed and extravagantly embroidered, he made the same strangled croak, and actually felt a pain in his side so that he had to put up his hand and press it there, hard, as with a stitch.

"I am Alfred Graves," he said out loud.

He, himself, did not believe it. It was so unlikely as to be preposterous—laughable. And so he laughed again and took a few more staggering steps into what seemed, as every moment the sun expanded and blazed on every wet leaf and twig, like Eden. He bent and pressed both palms into the grass and brought them up dripping and wiped his face. Then he dipped a finger again and rubbed at his teeth. The dew had a definite cold, sea taste and so he sucked at his fingers like a baby and squatted down so as to bring them nearer to his mouth and catch every drop. There he crouched and sucked greedily until at last his thirst was quenched. Then, gasping, he came to and was again aware of himself, and thought,

"I am mad!" And then, "Better mad than dead", and then, with a slow and joyful realisation, "I like being mad! I like it, like it!"

He straightened up and looked back and thought how per-fectly natural and at ease the old taxi looked under the elm, and already had begun to feel affection for it, take it for granted, like a real home. If anyone had suggested to Alfred at that moment that a taxi (particularly an unregistered one) did not qualify as a

D

dwelling place or fixed abode, he would have knocked him down
—or tried to.

Then Finn arose. Literally, he arose, pulling himself out and
up and stretching up his arms and straddling his legs to make a
majestic X.

"Glory!" he cried, and again, "Glory!" and he rushed down
to embrace Alfred and lifted him right off his feet and then put
him down again. Alfred shrieked and hopped as if the turf
had turned to hot coals. The giant mocassins had dropped clean
off as he dangled. Finn roared at the sight of them, and with
two great kicks freed his own feet and was scissoring in a glitter
of spray. Alfred watched for an instant, then followed suit,
doing a kind of stiff goose-step, lacking the Irishman's looseness
of limb, but with so strong an urge to caper that his disused legs
were bound to make some attempt to comply.

"Aaaah!" Finn bent down and wetted his hands in the grass
and slapped them on to his skin and Alfred, knowing the act to
be pleasurable, followed suit.

"So ye're well, then, Alfie?" enquired Finn at last, sitting back
on his heels. His long face lit mockingly. "Didn't catch your
death, then, sleeping out o' doors?"

Alfred shook his head.

"I was rather stiff," he replied, "but that's all, thank you."

"Better than *altogether* stiff, ye'd say?" Finn said innocently.

"Oh yes," said Alfred. "Definitely."

And he realised that he meant it, that he was actually, within
less than twenty-four hours of that meant-to-be-fatal plunge, glad
to be alive.

"Not that there are not the cramps and rheumatics to be
caught," Finn said, "and the way to be catching them leaving
shoes off for longer than needs be."

He put his shoes back on, and Alfred copied him.

"Like it here?" Finn waved an arm about to indicate the surrounding landscape as if he had personally made arrangements for
it, and was playing host. "D'ye like it?"

"Very much," replied Alfred. "Oh, very much."

Finn bestowed on him a rewarding beam.

"Better for me, today," he confided, "and that's truth. There
being you along with me, see."

He heaved himself up, took a final long look at the sunlit
meadow and started back towards the taxi. Alfred followed,
stepping carefully in his capacious shoes.

"Sort out—that's the ticket," Finn announced. "And then breakfast!"

He became almost housewifely then, fetching the wet clothes of the day before and shaking them thoroughly before handing them to Alfred.

"On the fence," he instructed. "Lay them on the fence for drying."

They worked companionably for half an hour or more, shaking out the bedding and refolding it, giving the taxi's jumbled and various contents a thorough going over. Then Finn fetched out a primus and boiled a kettle and soon they were sitting, each on a box, drinking hot sweet tea and listening to the birds whistle.

"I shan't part wit' her," announced Finn, waving an arm towards the taxi. "Oh no. I reckon she and me gets along, and I can tell it surely. Two days her and me've been together now and nothing but good luck for the whole of the time. I'll have a taxi, I thought, and that'll bring me good luck and a bit of company—and so it has!"

"Oh, it has," agreed Alfred.

"And runs sweet as honey," went on the Irishman. "Try her yourself when we move on, will ye, and tell me if you don't think so?"

"I can't drive, I'm afraid," said Alfred.

"Sweet Jaysus!" cried Finn, slopping his tea, "and driving as easy as dropping into a peat bog! There's nothing to it—nothing at all—I'll show ye! Just we'll get our bacon and egg and I'll put ye into the way of it!"

"But—I don't think——"

"Ah—ye'll drop straight into it, Alfie lad! There's just a couple of things I'll be needing to show ye, and ye'll be away—and take a turn or two round the field if ye like, to get you into the proper feel of it."

He leapt up, found the frying pan, and soon bacon and sausages were crackling and Alfred simply sat and watched and once again wonderingly compared the present with the past, and fingered the fringe on his gay waistcoat. At last Finn handed him a tin plate extravagantly piled and steaming deliciously, and then he made a low bow and passed over a knife and fork and said,

"And a Happy Birthday to ye, Alfie!"

"Happy—? But it isn't!" said Alfred.

"*Oh* yes!" cried the Irishman triumphantly. "For what is a

birthday but the day ye're born, bejam, and wasn't yesterday the day ye finished wit' being Alfred Graves, indeed?"

Alfred nodded slowly.

"And today ye're a new man, and *look* to be a new man, so isn't it born again ye'd say ye are?"

Again Alfred nodded.

"So if you're born again, it's surely enough another birthday ye're entitled to!" cried Finn, pressing his logic to its conclusion. "And this is it—November 5th, and Many Happy Returns of it may ye have, man!"

He raised his mug with a flourish and Alfred raised his and echoed solemnly, "Many Happy Returns", and added, "to us both!" for it seemed to him that this particular birthday was in truth less to do with himself than with the Irishman, Patrick Finn.

CHAPTER SEVEN

❡ *How Edward Flack Took A Further Lesson In Heroism And, Greatly Encouraged, Began To Record His Feats Of Daring For Posterity*

Edward opened his eyes and looked at his watch. Eight o'clock.

"Guy Fawkes," he thought. "And I've got to do it, or I'll never be a hero. It's not much, not really. All I'll do, I'll go and ring the bell. Then, when he comes, I'll say 'Good morning, Mister Rudge, I'm Edward Flack from the shop along the Street and I wondered if you'd like any errands doing?' That's all. And it'll be light."

Edward had not thought up this scheme in the few seconds between waking and beginning to rehearse it in his mind. He had lain awake a long time the night before, listening to the wind rattling the window and creaking the aerial on the chimney. He had heard the rowdies coming back from the pub (Mr MacKay's voice raised loudest among them in some rending Irish dirge) and then the Street had gone quiet. But long after that, even, Edward had knelt on his bed and looked out over towards The House to see the single light still burning at the top of the house. The old man was up there, the wind racketing about him. He had spent the day dozing, perhaps, and now, with the dark, had come alive again. He had eaten his solitary supper and wound his way up towards that upper room.

"What *does* he do?" He had wondered this a thousand times before, but never so urgently as now, because never before had it mattered to him in so real a way.

"Watch the stars?"

The solution was too simple. Why should an old man watch the stars when he could be warmly asleep and dreaming? Stars were supposed to foretell the future, but what future was there left for a man like Mister Rudge? Edward stared until his eyes began to sting. He dropped the curtain and lay back again.

"It doesn't *matter* what he does," he told himself. "It's me going that matters—performing a feat of daring."

And now the time had come—or almost. Edward spun out his

breakfast (as possibly many heroes had done before him) and asked his mother if there were any jobs he could do, in the forlorn hope that she would keep him so thoroughly occupied that there would be no time for a feat of daring. He was sent to buy a neck of lamb and a joint of pork. There was a long queue in the butcher's, and Edward walked slowly there and back, but it was still only just after eleven when he returned.

As he went out into the Street by the shop door, two of the MacKays shouted to him. They had a hastily constructed guy slumped on the go-cart that had been made with the wheels Edward himself had purloined from Mrs Briggs's yard.

"Come on! We're going up The Garden! We'll make a bomb!"

The Garden was a residential suburb within a half-hour walk where, it was known from experience, the sight of a few dirty and ragged boys pulling an improvised cart could raise untold wealth. In the Street it was more likely to promote a cuff on the ear.

"Can't!" Edward called. Going to the butcher's had been legitimate business. To go fund-raising for fireworks with the MacKays would be downright evasion. Cheating. In any case, his mother was in the shop, and would start screaming after him if she saw him go off with the MacKays, and then he would look a fool.

"You what?" yelled Mike. "Your mammy won't let you?"

"Edward Flack, Edward Flack
  Got his mammy on his back!"

This from Johnny, the sixth MacKay. They were probably going out in pairs, to swell funds even further. An older one and a little one—the little ones being proven fund-raisers.

"You watch it!" shouted Edward. "I'll black your nose!"

He had meant to say "eye".

"Yer what? Yer *what*?" The two MacKays hooted and capered with delight. "Black what? Black us *noses*?"

"Oooh—buzz off!"

He would have liked to use a stronger expression than this. To keep up with the MacKays you really did have to swear a lot. But again he was aware of his mother within possible earshot. He turned about and made towards The House, a good deal faster than he had meant to go, so that within less than a minute he was there, standing by the broken street gate. He looked back. The MacKays had gone already, doubled up the alley, fast and slippery as minnows.

He raised his eyes and looked at The House. It had always

54

been there, and he had often seen it, but never, it seemed, properly, until this morning. It loomed under the dripping boughs, a tall, melancholy house with sooted bricks. A little gust shook the elm and a spatter of water fell heavily on the sodden leaves below. It was like a gesture. Edward moved inside the gate and even this was further than he had ever been before, and a daring step. Slowly he advanced. Edward was not used to trees and felt already shut in, enclosed in a world that had suddenly gone dim and green. Was it green, or was it the air? It was green such as he had never known before. Light is white or light is yellow, but here the light was green.

He stopped. From the corner of his eye he caught the gleam of white in the long grass. Bones.

"Old man, old man, bury these bones . . ."

Who had said that? Edward actually started and looked about him, though he knew that the words had been his own, had sprung unbidden inside his own head.

"Old man, old man, bury these bones . . ."

"They are mutton bones. They are beef bones pig bones chicken bones mutton bones mutton bones . . ."

He held his ground. Murderers did not put the bones of their victims in the front garden for the birds. Edward told himself this twice, carefully, and advanced. The door before him was dark brown and peeling with panels of rich stained glass. There was a blackened knocker. Edward's hand went out and lifted it and let it fall.

The sound of it was loud and echoing and Edward nearly turned and ran because he had meant only a timid knocking that, with luck, the old man might not hear.

"I'll count twenty, then go."

He began to count, but beyond the counting his inexorable hero self was saying,

"And when you have counted twenty you must knock again. Louder."

Footsteps were advancing. Edward stiffened. His heart thudded, was in his throat, suffocating him. A bolt was drawn. The door opened. He stared at the old man, bowed and frail and greyer than he had ever imagined. The old man looked back.

"Good morning," Edward squeaked. He cleared his throat. "I'm Edward Flack." This time his voice was octaves lower, a growl. He floundered. Where was the rest of the speech—what was he to say next?

"A penny for the guy?" suggested Mister Rudge. "Please to remember the Fifth of November?"

"Oh no! No! I don't want any money! In fact—" he remembered now, "what I wondered, I thought—I wondered if there were any errands you'd like doing or something or jobs or anything?"

Mister Rudge looked at him. Then, without speaking, he stepped back and held open the door. Edward was meant to enter.

"Er—I can wait here. While you fetch the money or anything. I don't mind waiting."

Mister Rudge patiently held the door. Edward stepped inside. The door closed behind him and now the air was dimmer and greener than ever, with a curious thickness as if you could actually stir it. There was a faintly musty smell. It was cold. He shivered.

Mister Rudge went past Edward and opened another door. Again he held it open and Edward obediently went through. His first impression was of books—shelf upon shelf, pile upon pile of books and papers. The walls were lined on three sides with shelves.

"There are many books," came Mister Rudge's voice, as if he had divined Edward's thought. "Many books, but not enough time. Alas." There was a pause. He sighed. "Alas."

"I like reading," Edward told him, surprising himself. "I get told off for it at home."

How amazing, he thought, how absolutely unforeseen everything was—that he should have knocked at that formidable door, been actually admitted, and now be standing here making quite ordinary conversation with the sinister Mister Rudge. No sooner had he thought this than his feeling of triumph was checked. Mister Rudge did not reply to Edward's remark. What seemed like minutes passed and he did not reply. There *was* no conversation.

"Sometimes," Edward then said desperately, "I keep wishing it would rain. I really wish it would rain so's I can stay in and read instead of going out."

No reply.

"Sometimes I wish it would rain for ever," he said recklessly. Books seemed the one possible common bond between him and the old man, and he dared not change the subject—could not, for that matter.

"If it were to rain," said Mister Rudge thoughtfully, "if it were to rain, hard, every single day, I believe everybody would go mad."

Edward thought for a moment. There seemed the weirdest kind of truth in what the old gentleman said. There was no reason why it should rain every day, it was true, and therein lay the oddity of the remark. But if it *were* to, it was probably true that everyone *would* go mad. He certainly would.

"I think they would," he said. "I'd never thought of that."

"There is no reason why you should have thought of it," said Mister Rudge mildly. "I have only just thought of it myself. And I am a good deal older than you."

"Oh, you are," agreed Edward.

"Though not necessarily wiser," he murmured. His gaze grew keen. Then, abruptly, "Why did you say you had come?"

"To—well—you know—see if there was anything I could do. To help."

"Hmmmm."

Edward shifted uneasily under Mister Rudge's gaze and tried to look truthful—and helpful.

"That is why you say you have come," said the old man at last. "Now. Why did you come?"

"I—I—"

"Well?"

"I dared myself!" Edward burst out.

"Ah."

He went and sat down now, and waved a hand towards the other chairs in the room to indicate that Edward should follow suit.

"And so you are afraid of me?" The voice was gentle, even a little hurt. Dumbly Edward shook his head. "Were. *Were* afraid of me?"

Edward nodded.

"You thought I was mad," said Mister Rudge matter-of-factly. "Don't be ashamed, boy. There is nothing to be ashamed of. I have known for years what they say of me in the Street. And I do not care. Can you understand that? I do not care. And you, Edward Flack, are a brave boy. You say you dared yourself to come?"

"Yes. It's a sort of game. Well, not exactly a game—I *mean* it, all right. But I dare myself to do things. But I'm sorry. I'm sorry I told you. I didn't mean—I mean—well, it seems so rude!"

"If the truth is rude," said Mister Rudge, "it must still be let be. There are a thousand different faces the truth has, and some of them are ugly and some are beautiful, but they must all be let be."

"Yes, sir," said Edward respectfully. The "sir" slipped out unawares, perhaps because Mister Rudge had sounded rather like a teacher, perhaps because what he had said sounded important.

"Sometimes," said the old man, and his voice changed now, was lowered and secretive as though he were hugging something to himself. "Sometimes, boy—Edward—the truth is there to be seen, but no one sees it—or perhaps—perhaps one man alone sees it."

His eyes were intent now, he was watching Edward as though trying to read him.

"What—what kind of things, Mister Rudge?" Edward asked.

"Ah! Ah! Do you see this—?" waving his thin arms about him, to indicate the room, Edward supposed.

"Yes. Yes."

"In this house I have lived alone for more than half a century. And there are no clocks, and no mirrors. And I have taught myself to live without them, because a clock is merely an anchor for time, and a looking glass is an anchor for space. I have learned to live without them, and so I have come to move freely in my own time and my own space."

"I see," said Edward, and he did—almost.

"What I am saying, is that most men need to see themselves in a glass to be sure that they are really there. A mirror fixes a man in the world. But it also imprisons him. And he needs to cage time, or rather to parcel it out in hours and minutes, or he might find that time was slipping free like sand through his fingers, and then he would be afraid. Do you understand me, Edward Flack?"

"I—I think so."

"And you may wonder what all this has to do with the truth, and I will tell you. Before a man can recognise the truth he must first know himself, and for fifty years now I have been here alone and one by one have thrown away the crutches that men use, and now at last I think I am coming to be the one-eyed man in the blind kingdom, and I have learned to turn day into night, and night to day."

Edward sat silent because he recognised that Mister Rudge had gone off into a dream and hardly knew that he was speaking aloud. A slow flare of sunlight yawned and momentarily lit the motes of dust in its beam, then died away.

"I see them. I see the birds that do not fly but run on wires, swift and merciless in the dark. There are birds of steel that come shining and terrible out of the dark to strike . . . I hear them . . . I hear them hiss . . ."

His voice died off, and Edward, sitting perfectly still, felt a thrill of real terror, a light cold prickling about his neck and shoulders. There was no sound in the room and he was aware, actually aware of being in a near void, a clockless, mirrorless nowhere, on the very fringe of the world.

"And the real birds . . ." the soft voice began again. "It seems to me that the lovely feathered birds of the day are dying out, slowly. As the year dies and the days dwindle and the nights grow longer and those birds of steel come earlier each night to stalk upon the roofs . . . and I hear their pecking . . . their beaks are of steel . . . they glitter, and their wires glitter . . . last night, the entire sky was strung with steel . . ."

Edward, heroic, sat motionless, fixed by terror.

"*I* heard them," he thought. "Last night, on the roof . . . a kind of creaking. The aerial on the chimney in the wind I thought— but it was *them*!"

He was washed from head to foot first with cold, then hot, then cold again.

"The days are drawing in . . ."

It was Mister Rudge again but now Edward, looking up, saw that his expression had changed. It was as if he had been talking in his sleep and had now awoken.

"Oh, they are!" cried Edward, weak with relief. "That's what my mother says—and my father! They both say that!"

He knew he was talking nonsense but did not care, so long as a conversation of some kind was started, some kind of ordinary talk to stop the old man going back into that terrible dreaming again.

"Are you *sure* there aren't any jobs I could do for you? Shopping, or something? Or something in the garden? I'd like to do some gardening—we haven't got one, only a yard."

Mister Rudge smiled at him and Edward was moved almost unbearably.

"Do you *like* living alone?" he burst out. "Really? Do you have to? Couldn't you get someone to come and live with you? Keep you company?"

"Sometimes I think I would like that. But I am too old now to change my ways. I have thought of it—of there being a face across the hearth to nod to, from time to time, and exchange a word. And someone I could tell my thoughts to. But now my thoughts are so strange even to myself that I could tell them to nobody, I think. And who would come and live with me in this old house and this silence?"

Edward did not reply. The old man's voice was growing dreamy again and in another moment might be talking of those terrible birds that already he was trying to push out of his mind, forget. He stood up.

"I must be going now, I'm afraid," he said. "My mother'll be wanting me. We've got someone coming to stay."

Mister Rudge inclined his head and stood up. As he led the way out Edward was aware of the deep shadows the house had, with here and there dull gleams as of tarnished brass and silver, of faded richness. The stairs rose steeply to his right, very dark and quiet, the path to that secret upper room. Mister Rudge opened the front door and held it open for Edward to pass through.

"Thank you for your company, Edward Flack," he said.

"Oh—thank you for having me," said Edward lamely, and some heroic part of him must have been functioning quite of its own accord, because he heard himself add,

"Can I come again?"

"You *must* come again." There was just the smallest emphasis on the word "must", as if he already guessed at the workings of Edward's mind, and knew that he would go on daring himself to the limit, despite himself.

"Goodbye, then!" Edward went back under the green air and then was out in the Street again and filled with enormous lightness as he was after his nightly ordeal in the dark. He began to run.

"I did it! I did it!"

He wanted to shout aloud, proclaim his triumph to the Street, felt himself already more than halfway to being a hero. But he could not. Gradually he slowed down.

"Better not tell. Not tell anybody. Mum'd stop me going again."

Still he was left dissatisfied, as though the meeting with Mister Rudge were too momentous to treat merely as a casual visit and forget in the ordinary way.

"I'll write it down!" He stopped dead. "That's it! Keep a sort of a journal. And I could put all my exploits in it, not just Mister Rudge. I can hide it somewhere secret in my room, and keep it for ever, for posterity! All those other heroes, they had somebody to write about them and their feats of daring, but I haven't got anybody. So I'll do it myself! It could be like the Odyssey. 'The Chronicles of Edward Flack' that's what I'll call it! Yes, that'll do: 'The Chronicles of Edward Flack'! "

CHAPTER EIGHT

¶ *How There Were Fireworks In St Saviour's Street On The Night Of November 5th, And How Edward Flack Came Face To Face With A Hero*

"Not used to home cooking, of course," said Mrs Flack, "and a treat for him, however it turns out, though I do have my doubts. I shall tell that butcher. I shan't let him get away with it."

"It smells smashing, Mum. I wish he'd hurry up and come, so's we could eat it."

"He ain't *due* yet, Edward," she reminded him. "And as little likely to come early as to come late. Set your clock by Alfred, you could. I must say I *am* looking forward to seeing him."

Edward's pleasurable anticipation of the stew to come was checked. Already he had a picture of this Uncle Alfred. He saw him as small, neat, and, at best, boring. The person he would most probably resemble was Mr Fowler, who kept the little Post Office and store higher up the Street. Mr Fowler was always doing sums under his breath, lecturing while he served you, wielding rubber stamps with infuriating precision, slapping down coins in neat towers.

A car drew up outside and Edward, who had been idly watching the floating progress of a newspaper down the gutter in the wind, turned his head.

"A taxi!"

"Where?" asked his mother, who was putting out paper serviettes on a table laid with extra care, as if for a birthday (or rather Christmas—they were edged with holly).

"Crikey! Look at him!"

He stared down at the figure that had just climbed out from the passenger seat. A taxi was in itself a remarkable phenomenon in St Saviour's Street, but the passenger himself was so exotic as to be a yet more rare spectacle. Edward could already see other faces appearing at other windows like pale blossoms suddenly opened.

"Where—what?"

She peered past him—and shrieked.

"Oh! Oooh! Denis, come quick!"

Mr Flack threw down his newspaper and joined them at the window.

"Where? Oh. Rum-looking fellow that—where's *he* going? And in a taxi!"

"Rum?" shrieked his wife. "It's him! It's Alfred!"

"What? That's not Alfred. Can't be."

"Look at him! Just look at him! And in a taxi! A *taxi*! He's gone mad. I told you, Denis, I told you last night after he'd rang— ooh, and there's the Bakers looking and the Farrands and— oooh!"

The little man looked up then and met their gaze and his face, despite the contradictory flamboyance of his attire, was as Edward had pictured it—pale and nervous and short-sighted-looking. It was an anxious face, even in the lamplight, a face uncertain of welcome.

"Oooh!" moaned his mother again. "Whatever'll we do?"

She waved then, and the small figure in its enormous beaded waistcoat half lifted an arm to return the salute and the glass between them mercifully saved him from hearing the words that went with the wave.

"He's gone mad!" she said again flatly. "What*ever* does he think he looks like? And look at his shoes!"

"Like dinner plates," agreed her husband, craning. "He could've gone barmy, Lily. People do."

"Not in my house, they don't," she said grimly. "You get down there, Edward, and open the shop door for him. If my mother was alive and could see him now, it'd kill her. And what— oh—that taxi driver—*he's* waving! Whatever—?" her voice died away.

Downstairs Edward pulled back the bolts and opened the door cautiously. Uncle Alfred was more astonishing at eye level than he had seemed from above, even. His face was made hollow-eyed and staring by the light from the street lamp, and the wind blew his beads and fringes in little mad dances, and his feet were seen to be, indeed, dinner plates. Almost as amazing was his companion, a giant of a man with white face and wild red beard and a hand on Uncle Alfred's shoulder as if he owned him.

"H—hallo, Uncle Alfred. I'm Edward. Mum said would I let you in."

The little man looked suddenly frantic and glanced quickly

63

back up at the window above and made a movement as if to bolt. The other man's grip on his shoulder tightened.

"Easy does it, now," he said softly. "Better anything at all now, than dead. Anything or anywhere, that's what we said, wasn't it?"

The other nodded.

"And a fine nephew, bejam, that you never told me of," went on the Irishman, "and if I had a nephew, the living picture of what I'd be wanting that nephew to be. Good evening to you, boy."

"Good evening," replied Edward, mesmerised. Was this the taxi driver? And surely his mother would never let Uncle Alfred bring in all the luggage piled in the back of the car?

"Won't you come in?" he said. Uncle Alfred nodded, but made no attempt to move.

"Supper's ready."

"Supper!" cried the Irishman. "D'ye hear that, Alfie?"

And next moment both he and his companion were inside and the door blew shut with a furious jangling of the bell and almost simultaneously there was a loud bang.

"Oh!" The fringe on the waistcoat leapt as Uncle Alfred jumped.

"Fireworks," explained Edward. "Guy Fawkes tonight."

"Remember remember the Fifth of November." The Irishman was surveying the room. "And this a tidy bit of a shop indeed, Alfie, and a credit to your sister, and she to you."

Edward led the way upstairs. Almost at once there was a cry and a scuffle, and he turned to see the Irishman clutching his uncle under the armpits, and he dangling loosely like a rag doll.

"Be leaving your shoes here," advised the Irishman sensibly. "Or carry them, in your hand."

And so Uncle Alfred walked into the Flack living-room barefoot and carrying his giant mocassins. Mrs Flack, who had obviously made an effort to compose herself, faced him across the festive table.

"Well, Alfred," she said firmly. Her eyes were fixed carefully on his face, as if she dared not move them to take in the true awfulness—or madness—of the rest of his person.

"Hello, Lily." He spoke with an effort, and cleared his throat almost immediately, as if dissociating himself from the remark and any offence that might be given by it.

"It's been a long time," she observed, and gave Mr Flack a sharp dig. He was making no effort at all at social grace, and was literally boggling at the two visitors, first at one, then at the other, a thorough head-to-toe inspection, as if there were a prize at stake.

"Eleven years," said Alfred, relieved that he could make a mathematical statement. He even embroidered it. "Eleven years and a half."

"Must be." Still she did not move her eyes.

"Been keeping well, have you?" put in Mr Flack, prompted by a further nudge.

"Oh yes. Yes." He cleared his throat again. "Yes."

Pause.

"Have you?"

"Oh yes, yes!" cried Mrs Flack, a trifle hysterically. "Haven't we, Denis? Very well."

"Oh yes," he confirmed. "Yes, we have."

The state of their health having been thus established, the groups stood motionless, as if in tableau, and Edward began to think no one was ever going to speak again.

"Ye look well," said the Irishman suddenly, as if he had been inspecting them too, and this, at last, was his considered conclusion. Everybody jumped, and Mrs Flack, at last, managed to move her gaze from her brother's face. "Picture o' health, all of ye!"

She stared.

"Have you—?" She turned back to Alfred and leaning forward over the table between them said in a stage whisper, "What's he waiting for? Haven't you paid him?"

"Oh no," said Alfred. "I haven't paid him."

The Irishman let out a delighted cry.

"Paid! D'ye hear that, now? Exactly the same mistake she's fallen into as ye made yourself, Alfie lad! It's a marvellous thing, is the power of a word! Deceive the devil hisself you could, wit' a word. Tell me, now"—addressing himself to the gaping Mrs Flack—"tell me if ye wasn't after thinking that car down there to be a taxi, and meself the driver of it?"

"I—I—of course I was!" she snapped.

"I knew it!" He slapped his thigh and hooted triumphantly. "Another of ye—right into the same trap, every one of ye! Taxi!"

"If it isn't a taxi," interrupted Mrs Flack acidly, "with TAXI wrote all over its roof, then I should like to know what it is. And what you are, for that matter!"

The Irishman bowed with a flourish.

E

"That, ma'am, is neither more nor less nor anything but—a motor car. And I—Patrick Finn, ma'am, at your eternal service, and proud to say so!"

"And what've you to do with him?" she demanded, meaning Alfred.

"Everything," replied Finn simply. "Everything. And isn't that so, Alfie man?"

Alfred nodded.

"It is, Lily."

"What do you mean, everything?" she cried. There was a loud crack right by the window and Edward, turning, saw a brief flare of red in the dark, and his mother shrieked,

"Those MacKays—I'll kill 'em!"

"It is Bonfire Night, mother," said Mr Flack. "Legal, tonight."

"It's been Bonfire Night on this Street every night for a month! They want locking up, the whole pack of them! And let's have some *sense*, shall we, or I shall go clean off my head, what with banging and flashing and talking in riddles and you—" and now, at last, she turned on Alfred, "*you* Alfred Graves, arriving here on my doorstep with hardly so much as a by your leave, looking—looking—looking like—oh!"

She sat down abruptly and Edward gave an apologetic look towards his new uncle, who was cringing as if struck, huddling into his overpowering suede waistcoat like some hunted animal.

"Now then, Lily," began Finn easily.

"And don't you call me Lily!" she flashed. "Not Lily to you I'm not, nor ever shall be! And if I'm not wrong, it's you that's behind this whole thing, *you* that's done this to him!"—another stab of the finger towards Alfred, still trying to make himself invisible.

"Look at him!" she went on. Nobody did.

"Like a—like a—" tonight, words failed her as never before. "No shoes!"

"Which is not a crime," put in Finn gently, but she seemed not to hear.

"And hair all anyhow and not shaved and wearing that—that horrible thing!"

She pointed at the offending waistcoat with its brave beads and embroideries and jaunty fringes. In the silence that followed Edward felt that he would die of shame. He actually edged a little, just fractionally, nearer his uncle, to demonstrate his sympathy with him, waistcoat, bare feet and all.

"I'll go." It was Alfred barely audible.

"I'll go." A little louder this time, and then, from his sister,

"I think you had better, Alfred. There's nothing to be gained by your stopping."

"Nothing to be gained," he agreed mechanically, and half turned towards the door.

"The letter, Alfie," prompted Finn.

"Oh. Oh yes! The letter!"

"He'd like to take it with him," Finn explained.

Mrs Flack was all at once on the alert, as if suspecting a conspiracy.

"And that's another thing! What about that letter? What *about* it?"

"You didn't open it?"

"I did *not* open it." She pursed her lips. "I was requested not to open it, and I did not do so. It is there, Alfred, on the mantel. But when that letter came, I had no reason to think my brother had gone clean off his head. Suspected, mind, suspected when I got that funny phone call yesterday, didn't I, Denis? Didn't I say he sounded mad?"

Mr Flack nodded, but reluctantly.

"Now," she continued, "I shall keep that letter, which is my rightful property, delivered to me by the GPO, and when it suits my convenience I shall open that letter, and see just what madness and devilment is in it that there's such goings on about it, as if it was the crown jewels, or something."

"Ma'am," said Patrick Finn softly, "that letter is not for opening. I swear it on my eternal soul." He crossed himself and Mrs Flack gasped. "And may I rot in hell and everlasting damnation if it's not the truth I am speaking." He crossed himself again.

The following silence was awesome. Hell and damnation, eternal soul—such words had never been heard in the Flacks' living-room before, and they fell now like stones into the mouth of hell itself.

A great red-tailed rocket rushed within feet of the darkened window and exploded somewhere above the roof and Mrs Flack screamed again.

"Get out—get out! Go on—shoo! I won't have it, I won't, I won't!"

"But the letter, Lily," said Alfred desperately. "The letter— *please!*"

"No!" She rushed to the mantel and snatched it up and held it

67

behind her back. She faced them. "*My* letter! Mine by law! And my house!"

Alfred let out an anguished groan then, but Finn took him by the shoulder and turned him towards the door and led him out. The Flacks stood and listened to their footsteps receding down the wooden stairs. Edward, still staring at the spot where they had been, caught sight of a single gigantic mocassin.

"He's left this!"

He had snatched it up and was out the door and after them before he could be stopped. He caught up just as the shop door jangled and the smell of night and fireworks came rushing in.

"Here!" He thrust the shoe into his uncle's hands. "Look—wait! I'll get that letter—at least I'll try—she might put it down somewhere—she won't open it yet, I'm sure she won't, and it's supper-time."

"Can ye?" asked Finn.

"Oh do, do!" begged Alfred, and clutched at his sleeve. "Please!"

"I'll do it," Edward promised, half fearful and half aware of the rewarding, expansive glow of heroism.

"Or die in the attempt," he added solemnly, seeing their tense, watchful faces, and longing to impress them with the seriousness of his intention.

"Good lad! And where'll ye fetch it to us?"

"Go down there," he pointed down towards the crossroads. "Wait round the corner, behind the church."

Alfred was nodding feverishly and even shivering, and Edward could hardly guess what might be the contents of the letter.

"It must be a matter of life and death, whatever it is," he thought.

"I shan't be out for a bit," he warned them. "I'll probably have to have supper first." Then, "I wish *you* were stopping—both of you. And she'd done a stew specially for you. She was going to let you stay, you know. She was even quite glad you were coming. She said—she said you and her used to get up to tricks when you were little."

Alfred smiled wanly.

"Tricks!"

"Course ye did, Alfie man! And will again. *Full* o' tricks ye'll be, afore ye're done. Now let's you and me be getting off round that corner, and the lad off up to get that letter afore that sister of yours gets her fingers into it."

Edward watched them climb back into the taxi and as he stood felt rain on the wind blown on his face, and thought about the mammoth bonfire on the waste ground by the church.

"Use petrol to get it lit," he thought.

There had to be a blaze tonight, because it seemed to him that there was an undercurrent of suspense and excitement that had been building up in the Street for days now and that must be discharged, somehow. Before going up he fetched out his hoard of fireworks from under the counter and helped himself to a box of matches.

He entered the living-room, and stopped. His mother sat at the table. In her hand was the letter—opened.

"You've opened it!"

"Be quiet now, Edward," warned his father.

"Yes I have!" She was pink and flustered. "And a good thing too! No wonder he didn't want it opened—no wonder! A nice thing—a *nice* thing!"

"What? Why, what is it?"

"Now be careful, Lily," began Mr Flack.

"In it? I'll tell you what's in it. That precious brother of mine was going to have gone and *drowned* himself, that's what! *Not* that I believe a word of it, him turning up mad as a hatter and the whole Street seeing him and saying goodness knows what at this very minute. Sent it to annoy, that's clear enough to see. And what if I'd've opened it and dropped dead of a heart attack? That would've been a fine joke, that would."

"Didn't *sound* like a joke, Lily," said Mr Flack incautiously. "Sounded like it was meant to me."

"Meant? Meant? And him turning up next day dressed like the Shah of Persia and not a care in the world?"

Edward took a deep breath.

"You shouldn't've opened it! He asked you not to."

"Don't you go telling me what I should or shouldn't do!" Her neck was fiery red now.

"You shouldn't, you shouldn't!"

He was not being a hero now, braving her wrath, but ordinarily and humanly furious.

"And stop keep calling him mad—he's not, he's not! And it was rotten of you opening that letter when he'd asked you not to, and now he'll——"

He broke off, saw them both gaping at him, turned, and raced back down the stairs. The door jangled furiously and he was out

69

in the cold and the rain drove on his face as he ran. He ran by the graveyard and under the shadow of St Saviour's without even thinking of the dark. He turned into St James's Street. The taxi was there, right under the church wall. He saw the pale blur of their faces in the rear compartment. The door swung open and Edward scrambled in and shut it after him. He sat gasping while the others watched him.

"Got it?" enquired Finn at last. "Got it, lad?"

"She's opened it!" His fury still had not left him. "The beast, she's opened it!"

He heard Alfred let out a long shuddering sigh. The rain was whispering and pattering all about them, they were cocooned in the rain and dark.

"Was it true?" Edward forced the words out. He had to know. Alfred nodded slowly.

"You were really going to?" He was filled with awe.

"I did," replied Alfred simply.

"*Did?* But——?"

"He saved me. Jumped in. Pulled me out."

Edward turned his gaze now to the pallid smudge that was the face of the Irishman. Again the rain came into its own, soft and insistent, rain in the dark, voices.

Edward did not speak. The moment he had set eyes on the fiery-headed giant he had registered, however briefly and without even putting the thought into words, the larger-than-lifeness of him. Samson, Perseus, Hercules . . . The stature, the head, hair and beard of a hero—ancient as myth but modern too, with battered taxi for chariot and beaded mocassins for thonged sandals. He stared at the Irishman and saw the outline of his head framed against the long silver needles raining aslant against the street lamp, and unbidden the words of old Mister Rudge came back:

"Last night, the entire sky was strung with steel . . ."

The night was yet to come, he thought, the bonfire to be lit, the rushing rockets to be loosed into a skyful of steel birds. St Saviour's was mysteriously become something strange and other. It had cast off its workaday ordinariness and dissolved into a place of dark, a no man's land. And most marvellous of all it had, in the person of Patrick Finn, a hero.

CHAPTER NINE

¶ *What Happened In St Saviour's When The Real Fireworks Began And How Patrick Finn, Having Gone Through Water, Went Through Fire To Prove Himself A Hero*

Edward went home to supper after all. There were two hours before the bonfire was due to be lit, and once the taxi had driven off there was no point, he told himself, in hanging about in the dark and wet. Finn and Alfred had promised to come back later for the fireworks.

"Get some supper, see—fish and chips, and then back for the fire," Finn had said.

Edward was delighted, for more than one reason. The MacKays, having been so often screamed at by Mrs Flack during the past weeks, would almost certainly run amok tonight, and if they needed a target, Edward himself would be the obvious choice. But Edward accompanied by an uncle and a towering red-haired Irishman (whose temper the MacKays would certainly respect, being Irish themselves) would be a different matter. An even stronger reason was his curiosity about the oddly matched pair and his certainty that Finn was not so much a person as an agent of sorcery, who would put St Saviour's into a crucible from which it would emerge changed, never to be the same again. Finn even blotted out thoughts of Mister Rudge in Edward's mind, and actually in some curious way seemed a natural sequel to the strange meeting earlier in The House. One strange meeting followed on after another almost as a matter of course, a link in a chain.

Edward stepped out into the back yard and the windy darkness. The rain had stopped but you could still smell it where it lay cold on slate and paving and in silvery puddles. He lifted the latch of the yard gate and went into the alley. There was a sputter and a flash and he danced back as a fire cracker sprang up, kicking its heels in the dark. There were yells of triumph and derision and beyond the cracker he saw the MacKays, four of them, capering like mad things and drunk with devilment.

"Edward Flack, Edward Flack,

Got his mammy on his back!"

Edward glanced nervously up and saw the outline of his mother against the light and then the curtains closed.

"Yahoo! Yahoo! Bang! Bang!" came shrieks from the darting silhouettes that were the mad, bad MacKays. There was a brief flare and then the derisive gesture of a rocket, right over the Flacks' roof, curved by wind.

Then the MacKays turned and ran and Edward ran after them and out on to St James's Street to the waste ground by the church. The bonfire was not yet lit. The MacKays would light it, Edward knew, by unspoken consent. The MacKays had begged, borrowed and even stolen for the makings of that huge pile, and their two guys topped it, the hard-working MacKays' guys that had ridden on barrows through the streets for the past month or more and were now, at last, to have their brief glory.

"Where's Brian Hill?" yelled Dave MacKay. "Where's that petrol?"

"It's here." Edward recognised the voice. Mr Standish who ran the Youth Club and coached boxing. "And when I'm ready, I'll use it."

The MacKays stopped dead, baffled.

"Any chucking of petrol, and I'll do it!" he half-shouted into the racketing of the wind. "And any letting off of fireworks on this patch'll be let off here—" his shadowy arm indicated a raised concrete platform nearby. "And anyone who starts any monkey business'll get the benefit of this? Clear?"

It was—abundantly. The MacKays stared at the clenched fist and saw that their reign over the night was finished before it had even properly begun.

"So let's get this lit, for a start, shall we?"

Mr Standish took the petrol can and moving to the windward side of the bonfire began to splash it methodically. Edward felt a sharp blow under his ribs and Mike MacKay, dancing back, put up his fists. Edward lunged at him, missed, and there were yells of scorn from the brothers. They circled him, all four of them, making little darting jabs, four to one under cover of the darkness.

"Ye're barmy, Edward Flack!" hissed one. "Mammy's boy's barmy!"

"There's one!"

"Look out—another!"

"Whose friends wi' Mister Rudge? *We* saw ye!"

72

"Mind he don't *murder* you!"

"Feed you to the birds!"

"St Francis!"

"Old mad fool!"

"Feed the dicky birds—cheep cheep! Got any crumbs for the dicky birds, mister?"

All this in a hissing chorus while their shapes circled him. Edward stopped trying to fend them off. He simply stood at the centre and said furiously,

"He's not mad! It's you that're mad, crazy Irish idiots!"

At that they closed in again, and then there was a whoosh and they were lit with a wild orange light and a cheer went up and drowned Edward's yells. He fought furiously, and they yelled too.

Then a tall figure was in among them and Edward gasped as two out of four of the MacKays were lifted right off their feet by their collars. He heard tearing cloth and then, quite distinctly, the dull knock of their heads together before they were dropped, to reel sideways as if rendered boneless by shock. The other MacKays were almost simultaneously dealt cuffs that sent them staggering after. Above the yells and the cracking of the bonfire and banging of fireworks came the mighty roar of Patrick Finn,

"Out! Out o' here, ye devil's spawn, afore I crack the skulls o' ye to powder!"

The MacKays miraculously found the use of their legs in the instant and shot away across the area and into the road. There they turned at bay to see Finn standing by Edward, hands on hips, watching. They started to swear and curse and Edward caught fragments on the wind, and so too did Mr Standish because he, too, turned, and seeing this the cheated and furious MacKays turned and fled again to disappear behind the hulk of St Saviour's, lurching in the flamelight.

The fire was all ablaze now, gigantic. Edward felt its warmth, blown on his face. He looked up at Finn to see him shaking his head.

"If you take on four," he said, "and good luck to ye if you do, you mustn't do it that way, lad."

"I didn't. They took me on."

"Did they now? Did they?"

"They're all right sometimes. Just mad because old Standish wouldn't let them light the fire. Chuck crackers about, and that."

"All right, are you?"

73

Edward noticed his uncle for the first time, at Finn's elbow. Even in the glow his face was pale. He jumped nervously as a rocket blew skyward.

"Course. Hallo, Uncle."

"Birthday party for him," said Finn. "The very thing."

"Is it your birthday?" Edward was appalled. Had his mother not realised, when she turned him out?

"Not really." Alfred jumped again.

" 'Tis too," insisted Finn. "Really. First day of the rest of his life, this is, and—whoops!"

A rocket provided an exclamation mark.

"Will ye look at them guys, now?"

Edward did look, and felt sorry for the MacKays. The guys who leaned and writhed in their bright nest of flames were theirs, really.

"They'll murder me for this," he thought. Tilting his head back he looked up in time to see a thin tracery of scarlet dwindling into the dark, but faraway, distant, not the tail of any St Saviour's rocket.

"Last night the entire sky was strung with steel . . ." He heard again the voice of old Mister Rudge, and looking to his right just then glimpsed a rain of silver threads beyond the roofs, right over where The House stood.

"Could it—was it true?"

He stood buffeted by wind and light and noise and his mind reeled with the sudden overwhelming vision of a hail of steel birds. He saw them clear and glittering. They came swiftly, in straight lines. They invaded the whole Street, The House, the church, the little slate roofs. They hissed as they came and they struck savagely with their beaks.

"While we're asleep, all of us—what're they doing? What're they *after*?"

He shook his head and opened his eyes, only then realising that he had had them shut. He was looking straight into the eyes of his uncle, who was pulling an alarmed face.

"All right?" he asked in little more than a whisper. "All right, lad?"

Edward nodded. Terror gave way to annoyance. His uncle had thought he had shut his eyes because of the fireworks. He felt impelled to some kind of heroism. He walked over to the fire without really knowing what he would do.

"Here—you—Flack!"

"What, sir?"

Mr Standish was pointing to Edward's pockets, filled with fireworks.

"Come on, now, you heard what I said. You'd better clear off out of it if you can't keep rules."

"But I—I didn't have time. I was going to put them with the others——"

"Go on. Out. And take your squibs with you. And just make sure you don't blow your eyes out while you're about it."

"Oh, he won't be doing that, oh no!" It was Finn, again miraculously there at the crucial moment. "I've let off more fireworks in my time than Old Nick himself, so we'll be getting along and making our own hell where the fancy takes, shall we?"

Next minute he and Edward and Alfred were themselves behind St Saviour's, the noise and light of the fire cut off, and back in the dark.

"That told him," said Edward. "Old swine."

Mr Standish might coach boxing, but once put at the side of a real hero in the person of Finn, he had looked merely badtempered and squash-nosed, properly cut down to size.

"Dangerous, o' course," remarked Finn.

"What is?"

"Walking here and there with pockets full o' squibs, and sparks about blowing thick as bees in June!"

Edward said nothing. They rounded the corner by the church and met the wind again head on, and halted dead. Over the road were bangs and sputterings and shrieks fractured by wind, and the hammering of an iron knocker.

"Come on out, old madman, it's Judgement Day!"

"Be a sport, old guy—sit on the bonfire!"

"This'll give the birds a fright!"

The MacKays, thwarted and cheated of their rightful sport, were now baiting their own bear. A smoky green glow went widening out under the tree and streamed among the boughs and made a wreathed ghost of The House. Pressed against an upper window Edward glimpsed a pale face, and guessed at the terror of the old man, and was over the road and in among the MacKays before he had even considered a properly heroic course of action.

"Stop it! Leave off—let him alone!"

"Yah!" screamed the MacKays, hugely delighted and capering

and dancing to such effect that there seemed twice as many of them as there actually were, an illusion they were curiously often able to create. In the yawning flare of a snow-white light they were doubled yet again, and darted foot-linked with their shadows, a dozen MacKays all hell bent and slippery and turning into thin air wherever Edward aimed his furious blows.

There was nothing airy about the punches he received in return. He seemed to be hammered front and back and sides with hard MacKay knuckles and was forced himself to dance until at last, backing away, he tripped and fell. A cheer went up and all four MacKays struck matches and lit a firework each to celebrate his overthrow. As the touchpapers glowed and one by one the fireworks leapt to life the MacKays seemed to forget Edward altogether, and whooped and danced and shook their fists in an instinctive tribal unity.

Edward lay on the wet leaves. He could smell their damp, rotting odour, and saw the whole scene with a queer, heightened brilliance, as in a nightmare. And as in a nightmare, he lay powerless. The MacKays danced their mad dance in their ring of windblown light and shook skinny fists at the pale blur at the upper window that was the face of old Mister Rudge.

Then Finn was there. The two largest MacKays were taken, jerked back by their collars. They were swept out of the gate and over the road and Edward, scrambling to his feet, saw incredulously that Finn had swung one already over the high spiked railings of the graveyard and was in the act of lifting the other. Not a sound did they utter, but crouched where he had dropped them, boggle-eyed behind their bars like stunned animals.

The two smaller MacKays, themselves shocked into silence, stood rooted while they watched. Finn swung back toward them and with high screams they shot through the gate together and fled. Down the Street they sped, made quicksilver by terror. Edward himself cheered then, but was halted in mid-jubilee by a sudden lighting of the path where he stood. He turned. A weird light showed behind the stained-glass panels of Mister Rudge's door. A pane cracked, glass fell, and

"Fire!" yelled Edward. "Quick—fire!"

He was thrust aside and Finn's long arm went in through the broken pane, there was a rattling of chains and the door was flung open. Finn held an arm over his face and was inside and lost to view behind the tall flames and gusty smoke. Edward hesitated only for a moment. He put his own arm over his eyes and made forward, but felt his other arm seized and found himself wrestling with his new-found uncle.

"No, no!" cried Alfred. "Don't—you mustn't."

"I must, I must! Oh, let me *go*!"

"Finn'll do it! He'll—oh!"

The two fell back together as the flames flew out, then dipped with a fierce hissing. Edward glimpsed Finn with a pail before he disappeared again, but now the flames were lower, almost subdued, licking in a little wavering ring.

"There!" Alfred was triumphant. "What did I tell you?"

Another stream of water hit the fire and it was dead in the instant. The sudden dark and silence was almost as much a shock as the fire itself had been. Finn's giant figure was all at once stripped of detail, reduced to a shape. His face was shadowed and unreadable, so that he was transformed into an image, a symbol, a cipher—a hero. Whether or not from the smoke, Edward actually felt his eyes water.

"I'm looking at a hero," he thought. "I actually am. A real hero."

"Your hands!" Alfred moved towards him. "You've burned them, you must have!"

Finn spread his hands and as he did so a light went on behind him.

"They are! Look—the blisters! Get something, quick!"

This last to the old man who was slowly descending the stairs. Old Mister Rudge was white and mazed. He seemed hardly to see or to hear.

"Quick! Can't you see—he's hurt!"

"Don't, Uncle—let me." Edward went through the door and on to the black, wet mess of the fire.

"Mister Rudge," he said gently, "it's all right. It's me, Edward Flack. These are my friends—they put the fire out."

"The whole sky is afire," said Mister Rudge. "And perhaps it is for the best. The sky ablaze, to burn those accursed birds. A melting pot. Yes, it is good."

"Those are fireworks, Mister Rudge. It's firework night, remember."

"Remember, remember," he murmured. "Who did you say you were?"

"Edward—Edward Flack. You spoke to me this morning. And this is my uncle, and this is Patrick Finn, who put out the fire.

77

Your whole house would've burned down if it hadn't been for him, he put his hand through the door right in among the flames, I saw him, and undid the chain and went straight through the fire and——"

"Here!" interrupted Finn. "What tale is it you're telling? Happy to know ye, Mister Rudge, for such I take your name to be, and Patrick Finn at your service!"

Edward, watching this strange encounter between two strange beings, was sure that he saw a kind of recognition pass between them, an instant understanding one of the other.

"You must come in," said Mister Rudge. "I see now that there has been a fire—a real one."

"Oh, nothing so real it couldn't be put out," said Finn, "and naught but a brace o' rascally Irish lads to blame for it."

Edward remembered the MacKays and looked back over the Street. They were still there—they had to be, because even a cornered MacKay could not vault a six-foot spiked railing. They crouched among the leaning slabs and pallid crosses, their arms wrapped about themselves for comfort. Right up against the bars they pressed to be the nearer to the light and the farther from the haunted blackness behind.

"Oh, let us out!" came a thin voice. "Please, mister. We di'n't mean no harm."

"What's that?" Mister Rudge crept to the open door and looked out. "Boys. The boys that bang on my door and call names and set my house afire."

"The very same," nodded Finn. "And thinking the better of it, I promise ye, at this very moment. You stop there a bit!" he called. "And be thinking on what ye've done, ye heathen brats o' hell."

"Not hell," murmured Mister Rudge. "Surely?"

"Don't leave us here all night!" The voice went up on a high wail. "We're sorry now we done it, true and sorry we are and'll never do't again, we swear to God!"

"Oooh, yes, we're sorry, we are!" confirmed the voice of Pete MacKay.

"Ye can't be sorry enough, not yet," returned Patrick Finn. "Ye can't be sorry enough in five minutes for the like o' the mischief ye've done here tonight. You sit there an hour or two, and then we'll talk about sorry."

The MacKays' voices rose desperately in unison, but Finn's own roar silenced them.

"Quiet, will ye, and remember where 'tis ye are! Wake the dead, will ye?"

And with this he slammed the door.

"I shall park me taxi right outside," explained Finn. "And the man that'll come through your door in the night'll be having to get by me first, and heaven help him then, an' all!"

"That is very kind," said Mister Rudge. "But will you not lose money by it?"

"Money?"

"You said—a taxi."

Edward was by now prepared for the roar of delight that followed.

"Oh—taxi! Oooh—I shall die of that word yet! D'ye hear that, Alfie? The very same mistake ye dropped into yourself—and your sister as well! Oh lardy!"

He wiped his streaming eyes on the back of his hand, smudging the soot on his face to a pattern yet more devilish and grimy. His teeth and the whites of his eyes flashed out and Edward, at least, wished that he would never wash his face again, and go on forever looking what he was—a man who had gone through fire to save another. Mister Rudge sat and watched patiently, waiting for Finn's mirth to subside.

"It says TAXI on it, see," he said at last. "In red letters—T–A–X–I—and there's the joke of it! Oh lardy, the times it happens!"

"What happens?"

"It's the *word*, see. They see the word, and they think—taxi! And they're wrong. 'Tain't a taxi at all—least, 'twas for a few hours, I daresay, while I tried it out, but 'tain't a taxi, not now, nor ever will be!"

"Then what is it?" asked Mister Rudge.

"It's a car. A perfectly ordinary four-wheeled and easy vehicle. It's a car, d'ye see, wit' the word TAXI writ in red on the roof and living witness to the power o' the word."

There was a silence.

"To the lying power o' the word," amended Finn.

Another silence.

"A word can lie," observed Mister Rudge, "but it takes words to tell the truth, too. And just as a lying word can be mistaken for truth, so the truth can seem to be a lie."

79

"And if that isn't true, bejam!" cried Finn. "Words are the rarest tricky things to deal in, whichever way round you turn 'em!"

"I deal in words. They are my business, and I have spent a lifetime learning how to use them. And you and I, my friend, have come in the end to the same conclusion, though for very different reasons. You have found that a single lying word is taken for truth wherever you go——"

"And *that's* true!" interposed Finn. "Never fails!"

"Whereas I," went on Mister Rudge, "have always told what seemed to me to be the truth, and no one has ever listened. They took it for lies, you see, or at any rate, not a truth to be reckoned with. The room we sit in is full of words that I have written. But I do not send them out into the world, because I know now that it is useless. And I do not even *speak* words, now, unless I can help it. I live in silence. Whatever words I have spoken in this Street have been taken as lies, and now they have come to call me mad. Isn't that true, boy?"

Edward nodded, avoiding his eyes.

"*I* don't!" he burst out then. "*I* don't call you mad. And you *do* tell the truth, however mad it sounds. What you said about those birds . . ."

His voice trailed away.

"I told you that. I had forgotten . . ."

"What birds?" Finn asked. "What birds are these?"

"The birds of steel!" Edward told him. "They run through the sky on wires, in straight lines, hissing—I've heard them! I've seen them! I saw them tonight!"

"*What* birds?" asked Finn again. "*Steel*, ye say?"

"*You* tell them!" Edward turned to Mister Rudge. "Tell them what you told me. They'll believe you!"

Finn and Alfred fixed their eyes on the old man.

"It is only I who see them," he said. "They come at night, cutting the dark like scythes. They come down straight and terrible and I hear their hiss as they pass. They peck at the roofs under which the people lie sleeping, and I do not understand why they seem so terrible, or what their business is. But it has come to me, lately, that perhaps their purpose is invisible—just as they themselves are invisible to any eyes but mine."

"And mine," added Edward, but silently.

"I have come to think," said Mister Rudge softly, "that it is upon men's dreams that they come to feed . . ."

80

The silence now was a long one. Four pairs of eyes looked four different ways, avoiding the difficulty of encounter. In the end it was Mister Rudge who spoke again.

"And now," he said, "you, too, think me mad. I should have kept my silence."

"No no! I promise ye, man, ye've spoken right, and among the right people. 'T's just—only—the queerness of it all, and me *used* to queerness, and still left foxed. Ye're talking in a way we're not used to, and time to take it in is what we're needing. Isn't that so?"

He turned to the others, who hastily agreed, and Alfred, amazingly, said,

"The truth's not a thing I've had much to do with in the past, or not knowingly, you understand. But what you've said tonight, sir, sounded to me like truth. Even if it *isn't* true, d'you see?"

Mister Rudge did not reply and Edward himself thought his uncle's remark paradoxical, to say the least. He was still trying to work it out when Alfred, seeing that he had not improved matters, floundered on.

"I was brought up in a different way from you, and used to dealing in black and white—in figures. Something you could get hold of. And what you've said, first sight, it sounds impossible to me. And in my world, the impossible must never be allowed to happen. And if by any chance at all it *should* happen, then it must be explained and made possible. Immediately."

"Ah, yes!" said Finn. "But what ye're talking of, Alfie man, is your *old* world!"

"I suppose it is," he agreed.

"And ye've *done* with it!" Finn was alight again now. "Born anew, isn't it, this very day, and forgetting your birthday already!"

"This morning seems a very long time ago," said Alfred, though even as he spoke he saw again a swift vision of that drenched and glittering morning and felt the first cold touch of the dew on his timid fingers. "Funny thing, time . . ."

"That's what *you* say, don't you, Mister Rudge?" said Edward eagerly, trying to bridge the chasm of misunderstanding between themselves and the old man. "He doesn't even have any clocks," he explained, "let alone calendars. *And* he doesn't believe in space either—that's why there are no mirrors. He says time and space are anchors, and that he's trying to cut adrift from them."

"Oh!" said Finn. "Does he, bejam?"

In the silence that followed Edward saw that he, too, should

F

have held his peace. The others, already struggling with the near-impossible vision of steel birds, were now to wrestle with the enormity of a world with neither space nor time.

Alfred cleared his throat.

"I think it's time we were getting along," he said, "—if you'll excuse the expression. Time, I mean. It just slipped out."

"Of course." Mister Rudge rose and stood waiting. Edward longed to say something to him, but could not find any words. Mister Rudge seemed already to have retreated from them, to be back again in his own dimension of thought and silence.

They left quietly. Even Finn was subdued. As they went up the path, Edward heard him say softly to himself,

"Not impossible, indeed it's not . . ."

Edward, knowing what he meant, shivered.

CHAPTER TEN

¶ *What Edward Flack Wrote On The Night Of November 5th In An Exercise Book On The Cover of Which He Had First Written:* The Chronicle Of St Saviour's As Recorded By Edward Flack

This is to be the first entry in this Chronicle. I only decided to start writing it this morning and already there is a lot to say. I do not mind this as I mean to stay awake very late tonight for various reasons.

The first big thing I have to tell, and what really made me decide to keep this Chronicle, was going to see Mister Rudge this morning. I think this is possibly the most heroic thing I have done so far. My knees really shook when I banged on that knocker but I stood fast.

But the really funny thing is something I have noticed before, which is that what you think are going to be the worst things that could ever happen to you often turn out to be the best. Mister Rudge turned out to be a really nice man but when I say nice I do not mean in the ordinary way, because he is very unordinary and I suppose I must admit I can now see why some people say he is mad. I ought to describe his house which seems very dark because of the trees I suppose, and a kind of queer greenish light goes in there and there are lots of shadows and things glinting in them like treasure in a cave. There are a lot of books in there and things that Mister Rudge has written himself. There are no mirrors and no clocks though I must admit that I did not notice this myself until Mister Rudge told me it.

The reason for this is that he does not believe in time or space, or at least I think what he really means is that he does in a way, but he also believes in another kind of time and space. At least, I *think* this is what he means. I must say that he does rather talk in riddles, rather like a soothsayer or an oracle, but this is only to be expected. And I certainly think it is worth while working out what he is trying to say, though I can just imagine what Mum would say if I told her all that stuff about clocks and mirrors.

But now for the important part. He told me about these birds.

He told me in a very queer faraway voice and described them so that I could really imagine them. I can feel an absolute shiver even just to write about it, but he sits there every night and he sees these birds, not real ones but of steel and running on wires he says, in straight lines and coming down on to people's rooves. One thing he said keeps running over and over in my mind, "Last night, the entire sky was strung with steel", and I shall remember those words until the day I die. And the thing is this, last night when I could not get to sleep I kept hearing these creaking noises on the roof and naterally thought this was the TV aerial in the wind. But I am now sure that this was the birds pecking on the slate with their fierce beaks, like the eagle tearing at Prometheus's entrails. And tonight at the bonfire I am *sure* I saw the steel wires he was talking about, sort of silvery against the sky. Of course normally I would have thought that they were just caused by a firework, but with being told about the birds only this morning I realised what they really were. It just goes to show how you only really see what you expect to see. (We have been doing optical illusions at school so I already knew something about this.)

Anyway that was the most important thing about going to The House. But today there has been another really incredible event, which is that I have actuerly met a Hero in real life which I had begun to despair of ever doing. His name is Patrick Finn and he is a friend of my Uncle Alfred's. At first sight you would not take him for a hero as he looks rather untidy and he drove up in a really old taxi which is not in fact a taxi at all, as he keeps saying. But when you really look at *him*, not just his clothes etc, you see that he is in fact the absolute image of someone like Hercules or Jason. He is of very great stature, about six foot three I should think, with mighty shoulders and a flaming red beard in curls and a mane of fiery locks. He laughs loudly and with a kind of roar and everyone near him looks small and pygmy-like. He looked too big for our living room when he came up with Uncle Alfred. Mum did not like him at all though to tell the truth I think she was as much frightened by him as anything, never having met anyone like that before. It was his joke about the taxi that really set her off though, and she really flew at them then and said horrible things to Uncle Alfred and then cast them both out of her house, never to return.

Needless to say Patrick Finn was nothing daunted and strode out with his head held high. You can see that Uncle Alfred absolutley worships him and I do not blame him. He told me later that Patrick Finn had saved him from drowning the day before. This of course explained his funny way of dressing with everything miles too big for him, especially his waistcoat and shoes because he had obviously borrowed them. I think it was really his appearance that upset Mum and why she carried on the way she did. She is afraid that the Street might gossip and they certainly will especially after tonight. But I do not think she should judge her own brother by his apearance even if she does not approve of the modern way of dressing with beads and jeans and so on. Tidyness is not everything.

The day I have just lived through is the most important in my life so far, and so it is hard for me to sort out what is important to put down because in a way every little moment of it is important. But for instance at the bonfire when the MacKays were fighting me four to one, Patrick Finn came and banged two of their heads together with a mighty thwack and it is as if he always arrives where he is needed at exactly the right time. He could not have known that Mister Rudge's house was going to catch fire, but when it did he was there at the very minute it happened and the way he strode through those towering flames was the best thing I have ever seen in my whole life. It was at that moment that I relised that he really was a Hero, up to then I had only been suspecting it.

Even now I can hardly believe it is true. I really had begun to despair of any heroes being still alive in this day and age, let alone acterly meeting one. I am now hoping and praying that he will stay in St Saviour's long enough for me to really watch him and how he behaves, as this is a one in a million chance for me. He is staying tonight, in fact I have just got up to look and make sure the taxi is still there and it is. And Mister Rudge's light is on. Just now as I looked I could swear I saw some shining streaks in the sky again. Of course, they *could* just have been some fireworks but I doubt it.

I was terrified when Mister Rudge first told me about those birds and I still am in a way, but in another way I am glad about them, as I think they will be a reason to make Patrick Finn stay on in St Saviour's. What I think is that he has turned up so that he can pit himself against the steel birds in mortal combat like St George with the dragon and so on. I am sure that this is correct. If he does not stay we shall all perish.

This Chronicle will record his mighty feats for posterity. I shall keep it hidden in my Monopoly set on top of the wardrobe until I can think of or devise a better hiding place. The main thing I shall have to watch is that I keep my bedroom really tidy now as otherwise she will come in and start rumaging and throwing things out as she did last holidays when she threw out all my back numbers of Puffin Post, not to mention my old cricket bat which may have been a bit chipped but still came in.

It is really important that this Chronicle is not destroyed or lost. When I first decided to make it this morning, it was before I had even met Patrick Finn and it was to be about Mister Rudge and the steel birds and my own exploits such as they were. But now a real Hero has come to St Saviour's it will be a document of even greater importance and I resolve to keep it faithfully.

My hand really aches now. I was going to stay awake much longer than this, until the very last light went out in the Street, except Mister Rudge's, and wait for the evil birds of steel. But I now think I have enough evidence that they are there and so will go to sleep after all. I think I have acheived enough for one day. And even if the steel birds are out there, so is Patrick Finn who will defend us all from evil.

I set my siganature upon this as a true and faithful record.

Edward Flack

CHAPTER ELEVEN

❡ *How Alfred Graves Had Yet Another Strange Awakening
And Was Introduced To Higher Mathematics*

It was definitely red. It was a clear rose red—nothing to do with
blood, he registered with relief. He now saw that it was green
too, a lovely lit olive it was true, but so emphatically not the
right colour for his own hand (at which he had been staring for
the past few moments, it being only a few inches away from his
nose) that Alfred sat up suddenly, his blankets slipped and he fell
right off his makeshift bed. He struck his head, hard.

He lay there half dazed and found himself looking, astonish-
ingly, straight up into a great vault of stone lit by a pale light.
Alfred caught his breath. He tried to order his thoughts but was
prevented by the overpowering rush of feeling inexplicably
roused by the sudden sight of those beautiful curved arches and
bridges of stone. It was as if, paradoxically, they contained in-
finity itself. His whole field of vision was one of perfect symmetry
and Alfred's mathematical soul stretched, soared and actually
seemed to leap up and be lodged up there, like a bird.

"Oh!" He wiped a hand impatiently over his eyes because the
perfection of the lines was becoming blurred. He lay there and
stared and stared and felt the stone in his own heart melt at the
sight of this other stone. He lay for a long time because bliss is
a state difficult to part from. He would have lain there forever,
had he not become aware, gradually, of various aches in joints, of
cold, of a pain in his head. His view of the vault was framed, like
a picture, with wood.

"I am lying on the floor of a church," he told himself. "I am
lying on the floor of a church and have just fallen there from this
pew, on which I must have been sleeping."

He shut his eyes for a few seconds, then opened them
again.

"Alfred Graves," he told himself carefully, "you cannot possibly have slept on a pew in a church."

A smile passed over his lips as his eyes went straight up to the
high vault again.

"Alfred," he warned. "Something queer is happening to you. You be careful."

But the new Alfred, the one who had been born again less than forty-eight hours before, and who was already beginning to take on a life and mind of his own, did not agree. The new Alfred just lay there and smiled beatifically at his old self, like a friendly drunk.

He began to remember the night before and realised that he *was* in a church, because Finn had tried the heavy iron ring and the door had swung open and Finn had said that it was as good as an invitation. At the time Alfred had protested a little, partly because of the sheer unthinkableness of using a church as an overnight hostel, and partly because the idea frightened him. What was vault now, and flooded gold, had been fathomless shadow then. And there had been the dry, unmistakable church-smell of old wood and flags and centuries-old dust. The smell had brought with it the instant memory of Sunday morning hymn-singing and droning voices and the sharp elbow of his mother, sitting between himself and Lily to stop whispering. It had seemed to Alfred that if he were to sleep in a church his mother would turn in her grave—and as likely as not, come looking for him, with an elbow bonier than ever.

"Better not, Finn," he had ventured. "I'd just as soon sleep in the taxi. Getting to seem like home, that is."

"Not slept in a church afore, ye understand," Finn's whisper had come out of the dark. "But oh, man, I like the feel of it in here. I could sleep sweet and easy as a child in here, I could. And the door opened, Alfie, remember. And if a door opens, ye go in."

"B—but the old man!" Alfred whispered back, looking for loopholes.

"Ah—safe as houses!" Finn had given the heads of the two petrified MacKays a final crack together before releasing them from the graveyard. "Them two devil's spawn'll not be back. And something else. The birds, remember, Alfie, the birds!"

A slow soft thrill of terror ran along Alfred's spine as he did remember. And without further argument he had helped Finn carry the bedding into the church, had chosen a pew, lain down, and after one long frightened straining into the darkness, had shut his eyes and slept.

"Where is he?" he wondered now.

He began to raise himself but his head buzzed and throbbed

88

and in sitting upright he lost sight of the vault. He was back in the ordinary world again. With difficulty he half got to his feet and looked about and saw Finn, only two pews away, still asleep. His face was softly washed green and gold. Alfred lifted his eyes to the stained-glass window that was making the colours but the sun streamed into them and made him dizzy again. He gave a groan and sat down. The creak of the pew rang through the church like a pistol shot. Finn's head appeared startlingly above the back of his pew.

"Whatever . . . ? What—? Alfie, man!"

He was there in an instant.

"What is it? However—? Not—the *birds* . . . ?"

The last spoken in a suddenly hushed voice that set a hiss of echoes about them.

"What?" Alfie was dazed still.

"Your head!"

Alfred put his hand to where the pain was and looked at it and for the second time that day saw it red. This time, the red *was* blood.

"I fell," he said weakly. "I fell off the pew."

Then he fainted.

CHAPTER TWELVE

¶ *What Mrs Flack Said The Morning After And How Edward Flack Began To Be Aware Of Signs And Portents*

"Luckily," said Mrs Flack, neatly disengaging a curler, "there's no one knows he's my brother. Yet."

"Nor any reason why they should, Lily," Edward heard his father say.

"At least, I think they don't know." Edward could see his mother through the half-open door, and hesitated still. "There's no one *yet* come in the shop and said 'I hear that's your brother, Mrs Flack, that's going round looking like the Shah of Russia and goes round trying to burn people's houses down in the night!' Not yet, they haven't, but if *I* know this Street, they will."

"But he didn't!" Edward did go in now, immediately, without thought of heroism.

"So you're up!" she said. "Didn't what?"

"Uncle Alfred. Try to burn Mister Rudge's house. He *saved* him—at least, not so much him as Finn. You should've seen him —he went right in through the flames and——"

"Here!" she interrupted. "Here! What d'ye mean, *seen?* You mean to tell me *you* were there, Edward Flack, and after all that was said? You never said so last night when you came in at goodness knows what hour, you——"

"I was tired," Edward said. "I wanted to go to bed. But I was there. I met Uncle Alfred and Finn at the bonfire, and then we just happened to be going past The House when we saw the MacKays——"

"*Them,*" she half screamed. "Don't you go telling me *they* were mixed up in it! Oooh, I'll give it you, my lad, if all this doesn't stop. Times I've told you——"

"I wasn't *with* them, Mum. We saw them—I keep trying to tell you—and they put a firework through Mister Rudge's letter box and it went up in flames and the glass cracked and——"

"Oooh!" She sat down suddenly. "I knew it. Oh, my poor head! The police. That's what it's come to now, the police. And the way I've struggled to bring you up right!"

90

"No police," he said patiently. "There's no need—they'll never even know about it. I told you—Finn put it out. *And* he gave that Mike and Pat MacKay something to think about."

He warmed at the recollection of those two wan faces pressed to the thin bars.

"Finn fixed them, all right!"

"Finn? Who's this Finn you're on about? It's never that red-haired half-baked Irishman your uncle's got in with?"

"That's him. Patrick Finn."

"*Mr* Finn to you, my lad," put in Mr Flack, evidently not wishing to seem lacking in his share of parental sternness.

"Finn," repeated Edward obstinately—to himself.

It was the way he already privately thought of the Irishman. Who could imagine a "Mr Perseus" or a "Mr Robin Hood" or a "Mr Hercules"? A hero's name was title enough in itself. Finn. No room there for a "Mr".

"Make some more tea, Denis," ordered his wife. "It's just come to me what's happened. It's *them* that've about been taken off to prison. Arson, that's what the milkman said, plain as the nose on your face, he said. Oooh, the shame of it! My own brother! Prison!"

"They *haven't*!" Edward was exasperated.

"Then where are they?" she demanded. "Where've they gone?"

"There!" He went to the window and pointed out to where the taxi still stood outside The House. He knew it was there. He had already looked several times from his own window.

"Still asleep," he thought, seeing no sign of life.

"Car's there!" She joined him at the window. "But they're not. Where are they?"

"They're——" He broke off. There was no need for his mother to know that his uncle and Finn slept in the taxi, that it was home to them, as well as vehicle. "Perhaps they've gone into The House. Yes. That'll be it. I bet Mister Rudge asked them in for breakfast."

His voice tailed off. He could see the thinness of his explanation even as he gave it.

"For breakfast? Him? That old madman?"

Edward was silent.

"Never had breakfast in his life, that one hasn't," she went on. "Night for day, day for night, burning lights till all hours. If he *had* breakfast, it'd be at ten o'clock at night!"

91

"A cup of tea, then," he suggested. "After all, they did save his house from burning down."

"And *that*'d've been no great loss!" she snapped. "Where's *our* tea, Denis?"

"Coming, Lily."

"I think I'll just go out for a bit," Edward said.

"You'll do no such thing! You'll sit down there and have some breakfast like any other self-respecting mortal. I'll have no turning days into nights at *my* house. You get down to the shop, will you, Denis, and open up while I have my tea and some aspirin. My head'll crack right open, I swear it will."

Even on Sundays the shop opened, between half past nine and twelve. Mr Flack's feet clattered away down the stairs and Edward envied him his release.

"And when you've *had* your breakfast," she shook a furious spray of cornflakes into his bowl, "you get off into your room and get it tidied up. Do you hear?"

"Yes, Mum. I hear."

He did tidy his room, he felt bound to, in case it did not come up to her expectations and she set upon it herself, sweeping all before her—including the Monopoly with its precious Chronicle concealed inside the folded board. From time to time he peered from the window and each time he saw the apparently lifeless taxi, and he grew uneasy.

"They can't still be asleep! They *must've* gone inside The House, whatever she says. It's the only place they could be!"

By the time he did make his escape—and it was, quite literally, an escape, down the stairs, past the open door of the shop into the stockroom, out through the back door and across the yard, it was nearly ten o'clock. He sped down the alley, calm and quiet now and smelling of rain from the night before, and as he ran heard the Sunday bells ringing sweetly far away in the distance from another part of town. The St Saviour's bells, the ones he had grown up with, were silent now.

He raced over the vacant lot, littered with spent fireworks and the blackened remains of the bonfire, still smouldering. Along St James's Street, past the high, boarded windows of the church, and he was on the corner and could see the taxi, still in front of The House, only forty yards away. Slowly he approached, his eyes fixed not on the taxi but on the windows of The House itself. Were that strange trio in there, at this very moment, breakfasting? He stopped dead opposite and stared between the branches of the elm.

"There are no birds about," he thought. "Perhaps Mister Rudge doesn't throw loaves out on Sundays?"

It seemed, however, a strange exception to make. The situation was so curiously unreal that when Edward *did* hear the organ music it did not at first strike him as anything extraordinary. He even found himself listening to it as it stole out, muted yet rich, into the still sleeping Street. It seemed to fit the situation perfectly, as if it were a musical accompaniment, written specially as for a film. The deserted Street, the empty taxi, the still blank windows of The House and the mystery of the vanished pair—it fitted. A van turned into the Street and went past, tyres hissing softly on the wet surface, and Edward found himself following it with his eyes as if it, too, had a place and a meaning. He was on a blank film set, waiting for the action.

When it came, it was from an altogether unexpected source. It came from within himself in the form, at first, of an uneasiness, a sense that something was not quite right, did not fit. The organ music swelled, rolled from behind the closed door and boarded windows until it became, finally, something to be reckoned with, a theme that was no longer background but insistent, forcing itself on Edward's blankness.

"Oooh!" He let out a soft gasp and wheeled slowly to face the closed door of the church.

"They can't be!" he thought. "It's been shut over six months!"

He went into the cold, stone-smelling porch and willed himself to heroism.

"Who, then, if not them?"

A Catherine wheel spun in his head of gorgons, stone heads, cyclopses. Their classical clarity lent him classical strength and he put his hand to the thick iron ring and turned it. The organ music flowed past him twice as rich and strong and with his heart thudding he stepped inside and closed the door behind him. He turned instinctively to the left, the source of both light and music.

"They left a window in," he thought fleetingly.

He stepped forward, turned down the side aisle and saw Uncle Alfred. It was the soles of his bare feet he really saw first, and with real shock in this hushed, ecclesiastical setting. Uncle Alfred was rolled in blankets. He lay on his back with his hands folded across his chest like an Elizabethan effigy. His lips were smiling faintly and his eyes, wide open, fixed on something above him.

"He's dead!" was Edward's first thought. But he was not—even a few seconds' closer inspection showed that.

"Seeing a vision!"

The possibility, with that music roaming the arches, very soft now, pulled thin and ghostly, was hardly less terrifying.

Slowly Edward lifted his own eyes. The roof of the church was a catacomb of arches, meeting and interlacing and soaring on. He himself had always thought it rather a plain roof, as church roofs go, sadly lacking in imagination, and had often in the past mentally decorated it up a little, to pass the sermon. He had put a good many non-biblical characters and creatures at the various interstices and was conscious, even as he scanned the vault, that if he were to see one of them now—a cyclops, say, with its one eye beaming green fire—it would be no more than he deserved.

But he saw no such thing, and looked back again to his uncle's face for further clues. With relief he saw that his eyes were now closed. Softly he went on and at the pulpit turned right towards the chancel steps. There he looked up to the organ loft and saw, as he now expected, Finn's head and shoulders behind the uncurtained brass railing, and his pale face reflected greenly in the old mirror. The last notes crept about the pillars, searching out the echoes.

Edward heard Finn sigh, quite plainly, and then he got up from the bench and saw him.

"Good morning!" in a strong, delighted whisper. He put his finger to his lips as if to caution himself rather than Edward, and came down.

"How did you get in?" Edward whispered.

"Tried the door—turned the ring, and—the door opened!"

"That's queer. This place has been empty for months. They're going to pull it down, you know. Build a supermarket."

"If a door opens," said Finn, "then you enter in."

"Oh yes. I don't blame you. After all, anyone's allowed in a church. It's a sanctuary, you know. Even if the king's men were hammering at the outer door this very minute, you'd still be safe here."

"Oh I know, I know," nodded Finn, as though that very emergency were in fact likely to occur at any moment. They were advancing now up the centre aisle towards the still prone figure of Alfred.

"What's the matter with him?" Edward reduced his whisper further for the question.

94

"Mazed," replied Finn briefly.

"Oh."

"Fell off his pew, and banged his head. Blood all over. There's water still back there, and I bathed it clean right enough. He'll pick up. He can stop there on his back for a day or two and'll be as right as rain, never you fear."

"A day or two?" Edward was poised between delight and alarm. "Stop in here, you mean?"

"Where better?" Finn made an expressive gesture about him as if to indicate the absolute desirability of the surroundings. "Quiet. Comfortable. And he likes it here. Lies there good and quiet as a babe, and opens his eyes and stares up and smiles as if it was his mother's face itself he saw hanging over him."

He crossed himself hastily.

"Not," he added, "that there's the least likelihood o' *that*, ye understand. 'Twas just a manner o' speaking."

"Yes. Oh yes."

"Right as rain we'll be," went on Finn. "Water laid on an' all. The Lord will provide. I shall bring me little lamp and that and set up back yonder"—with a jerk of his head in the direction of the vestry.

"You're going to—*camp* in here?"

"Oh, better—*much* better," affirmed Finn. "Ye can't be tending a sick man in a taxi. Oh no. And I told ye—he likes it here."

"Yes, but, I mean, are you *allowed*? It's consecrated ground, isn't it?"

His eyes travelled fearfully back in the direction of the light and he noticed, for the first time, that the altar was missing.

"It's gone! The altar!"

"Of course," nodded Finn. "And the altar being gone there being no risk o' blaspheming, d'ye see. The saints above—" with an upward roll of the eyes— "know well enough there's nothing further from my thoughts, heaven defend us!"

"Oh no. No. Of course not. It's just—well, you know, the idea of it. Getting used to the idea."

"Oh I know," agreed Finn, though with no suggestion of similar difficulty. "And now I'll get me stuff moved, if you'd like to bear me a hand. Egg and bacon I fancy, and I daresay ye'll join me?"

"Well—I—all right!"

Finn and Edward made several trips to the taxi and then tiptoed down the nave past Alfred to the little vestry behind the pulpit.

Their preparations complete, they shut the vestry door and proceeded to make themselves comfortable and to converse in normal voices again.

"Pity the hassocks have gone," remarked Finn, upending a wooden fruit box to serve as table. "Could've made something more comfortable for your uncle. But there. Mustn't grumble."

"It's funny," Edward said, "how you can smell an organ. Even if I shut my eyes I'd still know there was an organ about. You play it well. Marvellously."

Finn had lit his stove and now began to throw bacon and lard and sausages into his frying pan. Soon the delicious smell of frying mingled with the strong, dry odours of the vestry and at last overcame them entirely, as if any living smell were more powerful than a dead one. To Edward, sitting on a box with a plate balanced on his knee, bacon and egg had never tasted so good. The sharing of the meal, the dimness (the little vestry window was on the street, and was boarded too) and the general air of conspiracy, made for intimacy. Between every mouthful Edward raised his head to look at Finn and remind himself that he was breaking bread with a hero.

"I wonder how Mister Rudge is this morning," he said.

"I looked." Finn bit hugely at a crust. "Quiet as the grave."

"Did you—did you believe him? About those birds?"

Finn carved off a piece of bacon, chewed it meditatively and swallowed.

"I believe him," he said simply, and set about one of his eggs. Edward followed suit.

"What I say is," Finn went on, "that there's no doubt at all about it. If the old man says he sees those terrible birds, then there's no doubt whatever but that he does. It struck me as truth."

"Oh, it did me," Edward agreed.

"Poetical truth, even," he murmured, half to himself. He lifted the kettle and poured the boiling water into the waiting billy-can. "There being, ye see, no higher form o' truth at all."

"Oh no," agreed Edward again.

"The question then being," the fork poised in mid-passage from plate to mouth, "the steps that are to be taken."

"You mean," Edward controlled his voice with difficulty, "you mean you're actually going to do something about it? Save us all from destruction?"

"Oh, undoubtedly. It being entirely my line of country, you understand."

96

"Oh, I do, I do!" Edward was almost beside himself. He had been right! What else could Finn have meant by those last words? He was a hero, and had come to St Saviour's, summoned by some mysterious call, perhaps even been roused from a hundred years' slumber by an echoing horn in some distant and misty Irish cave of sleeping heroes. With difficulty he restrained himself from asking Finn, then and there, his origins, begging him to relate some past bold and mighty exploit.

"I mustn't let him know," he thought. "Not yet. Let him think I don't realise. He's obviously got himself up in disguise deliberately—that old taxi, and his clothes and everything." A thought struck him.

"I wonder where he keeps his sword?"

The suit of shining armour he was willing to forego, but a sword there must be, of that Edward was certain. A hero without a sword was unthinkable.

Finn wiped his lips at last and poured three large mugs of tea, adding milk and sugar with liberal hand.

"Take one along to Alfie, better," he suggested. "See how he is."

Taking two of the mugs he went through the vestry door and Edward picked up the third mug and followed him down the nave, blinking in the stronger light. Alfred still lay with his eyes shut.

"Alfie," said Finn softly. "Alfie, man!"

Alfred's eyes opened and fell first, wonderingly, on Edward.

"Hello, son," he said weakly.

"Oh, I'm not your *son*!" Edward cried, alarmed by such signs of confusion. "I'm your nephew, remember—Edward!"

"I—I didn't mean it like that," said Alfred, and he closed his eyes again and turned away his head. Suddenly Edward understood.

"Oh, I'm sorry! I didn't—I thought you were thinking that I——"

Alfred's eyes opened again.

"Hello, lad."

"Oh, thank goodness you're all right! You hit your head when you fell. You'll be all right—you're going to stop here a few days and rest, and Finn and me'll look after you. Look—we've brought you a cup of tea."

"Here, Alfie lad." Finn moved up then beside him and lifted his head gently and Edward saw the wound, the dark bruising

G

where he had struck the side of his forehead. Finn raised Alfred's shoulders and supporting them with his arm he held the mug to his lips and let him sip from it like a young child.

"That's—nice."

"Of course it is! And put new strength into you, man. Ye'll just bide here a bit like the young feller says, and ye'll be as good as new."

"Better, I daresay." Alfred smiled faintly.

"And Edward here'll be helping us. Won't ye, son?"

He spoke the last word deliberately and Edward felt his face burn to the roots of his hair.

"Of course."

"You could maybe get hold o' some good bones and a few carrots and that—a good broth'd be the very thing."

"Of—course." Edward was watching the halo surrounding Finn's head. The sun shafted through the one rich window and ringed Finn's head with fire as he crouched there between the pews.

"It's like a sign," he thought. Then, aloud,

"I'll get some from home—it'll be easy. And there's lots of stuff in the shop. Fetch it now, shall I?"

Finn nodded.

"The sooner the better."

"Right, then."

Edward started off. At the door he turned for a last look. They were both watching him and Edward glowed with the realisation that they were relying on him, would be awaiting his return. He raised an arm in salute, and went.

The air was very damp and fresh and he snuffed it in appreciatively. As he paused for a long look at The House the great elm was a-glitter with moisture, lit by a million tiny beads of light. The whole drab length of St Saviour's Street was suddenly itself seen to be wet and lovely and he stared at the puddles, the shining road, the sun striking on the grey slate roofs. At moments like this it always seemed to Edward that he was so bursting with energy that there was something more that he should be doing about it. It was not enough simply to feel, there was something he must actually do. But he did not know what. The urge for action was so strong that he started to race, putting up his hand to his mouth and whooping like an Indian. The spurt lasted only a few seconds.

He saw something lying on the pavement and stopped just

beyond it. He turned back to look and saw that it was a bird. It lay limp and glossy, only newly dead. There was no telltale marking of the feathers on the throat, or any other sign of violence.

"Cat didn't get it," Edward thought.

He almost turned it over to see if the evidence of how it had met its death was there, but could not bring himself to do it. Going on in his mind was not so much a thought as a series of images, of steel birds raining over the Street all night long, of an early bird walking on the roofs in the slow dawn, and then the sudden stunning plunge of a metal beak into those innocent feathers. He heard a voice, too,

"It seems to me that the lovely feathered birds of the day are dying out, slowly . . ."

Edward straightened and scanned about him, looking for a bird, because he had a sudden awful suspicion that perhaps last night all the birds in St Saviour's had met the same fate. He saw a pair of sparrows squabbling, a starling on a roof, pigeons in the road in the far distance. Then his eyes were drawn back to the other bird, the quiet one lying by his feet.

"It's an omen," he thought, and shivered. Slowly he began to walk on. "An omen of doom . . ."

CHAPTER THIRTEEN

¶ *In Which Mrs Flack Hears About The Birds And Goes Visiting In Order To Hear More*

The storm broke at dinnertime over the roast pork. It broke when Edward walked in from his second trip to the church just as Mrs Flack was taking the roasting tin out of the oven. She straightened up when she heard him and banged the tin on the draining board.

"Where've you been?" she demanded.

"Oh, nowhere. Just out."

"Just what? Just what? *I'll* tell you where you've been, my lad. *I* might be blind to your comings and goings and carryings on, and'd be blind forever if there wasn't more people than enough ready and willing to *tell* me what's going on!"

He said nothing.

"It's come to a nice thing," she continued, "if I've to wait on the likes of that good-for-nothing Marth MacKay to come into my shop and give notice of my own son's goings on. You'd think she had enough on her plate with her own seven, without ferreting into my affairs, but there you are!"

Edward stared at the crackling and held his tongue.

"Been down that church, haven't you? Haven't you?"

"Yes," he admitted at length.

"And they're in there—that red-haired Irishman and that brother of mine. In a church. On a Sunday, of all things. Is he still got up like the dog's dinner? Is he still wearing those horrible clothes?"

"Yes," he said. "I think so."

"*Think* so?" she shrilled. "Is he or isn't he? What do you mean, you think so?"

"I couldn't really see. He was rolled up in a blanket."

She stared, speechless for a moment.

"He's walking round rolled up in a *blanket*?" she managed at last.

"Not walking round. Lying down."

"My own brother," she said bleakly. "Lying down. In a church. On a Sunday. Rolled up in a blanket."

She sat down suddenly, her joint forgotten, to work it all out.

"He's hurt himself, Mum. He really has—you ought to see his head."

"Wants his head examining, all right!" she flashed. "Told *you* that, I could've."

"But he hit it. He fell off the pew and hit it, really hard. It's no joke, falling on a stone floor. I think it knocked him out."

"If he's had a bang on his head," said Mrs Flack heartlessly, "then all I can say is I hope it's knocked his brains back where they belong. And *now* what's he going to do? Do you know?"

"Well—not really." He hesitated, to give himself time to think. How much ought he to tell? "I think they're stopping there a day or two till Uncle Alfred's better."

"They—*what*?"

"Stopping there. It's all right, Mum, they're not doing any harm."

"They're doing me harm," she retorted. "Never be able to hold my head up in this Street again, I shan't, if this goes on much longer. All very fine for him, I daresay, lying there rent free and without a care in the world. Quite apart," she added righteously, "from the actual rights and wrongs of the case. It's not right. There's nobody going to tell me that churches was meant to be slept in and fried bacon and egg in. I ask you! Bacon and egg! I wonder it didn't choke them. *You* didn't have any, I hope?"

Edward, trapped by the directness of the question, admitted that he had. At the same time he wondered who had told her about the breakfast in the vestry—who had been spying.

"Then you can go straight to your room and have no dinner!" she cried. "I'll give you cooking meals in churches! There's *one* Christian left in this house, I hope, and up to me to learn you better—*teach*, I mean!"

Edward turned. If he was to have none of the roast potatoes and gravy, the sooner he stopped looking at them the better.

"And when your father'nd me have had *our* dinners," she said, "I shall ring up that vicar. Oh yes—*I* know where he's gone to, and I shall find his number and ring him up. It's my plain duty and'll serve the pair of them right. He'll soon have them out!"

Edward opened his mouth to protest, then closed it again.

"Is dinner coming up, Lily?" came Mr Flack's voice from the other room. "I'm on at two!"

"Coming!" she shouted back. "Here—you take him the meat through to be carving."

Edward took the plate. His father shook his head at him.

"Upset her proper, you have," he said in a low voice with a jerk of his head towards the kitchen.

"I'm sorry. I didn't mean to."

"But don't go taking too much notice. More Alfred she's taking on about than you. Own brother, you see."

"Yes," said Edward. Alfred was Mrs Flack's own flesh and blood.

"Always—well, gentlemanly he was, you see," he whispered hoarsely. "Proud of him in her own way Lily was, and—oh my word, *that* looks good!"

The last in a suspiciously hearty and overloud voice that caused his wife to glare at him through the steam rising from the plates she carried.

"Yours is in there," she told Edward, and put the others loudly on the table.

Edward fetched his dinner. He rejoined the others and sat down. He was wise enough not to thank his mother for letting him have dinner, after all. At any display of kindness or affection she put out all her spikes like a threatened hedgehog. It was as if she only felt safe surrounded by prickles. If ever she was kind, she took care to disguise her kindness as its opposite, as nearly as possible, as if ashamed of her own weakness.

"These roast potatoes are great, Mum," he did allow himself, however, just to let her know. She merely snorted and tackled her own as if they were sworn enemies.

Mr Flack ate rapidly and it was a silent meal. As he scrunched the last piece of crackling he looked at the clock and said apologetically,

"I shall have to get off, Lily, I'm afraid. No time for pud."

"There *is* no pud," she returned tartly. "I wasn't in the *mood* for making pud."

"No," he agreed. He rose and picked up his green bus-driver's hat.

"See you later, then." He went out. Edward heard him whistling as he banged the shop door and set off down the Street. The silence was made all the more awkward by his absence and Edward hastened to finish his own meal. Glancing sideways he saw that his mother, after her initial attack, had eaten hardly anything.

"It's no good." Suddenly she pushed back her plate. "I can't eat it."

She looked genuinely miserable. He put down his own knife and fork and said again,

"I'm sorry, Mum. I really am. I didn't mean to upset you."

"Oh, *you* wasn't to know, I s'pose," she said surprisingly. "You didn't know your Uncle Alfred, how he used to be. Never did I ever think for this to happen. I really do think he's gone mad—even Denis says so."

Edward suddenly realised that much of the performance she had just given in the kitchen had been for his father's benefit, to show how thoroughly she disapproved of her re-born brother.

"Denis says I should just ignore him," she went on, "just go on as if he wasn't there. But it's all right *him* saying that—not his brother, not his own flesh and blood."

"No," agreed Edward.

"Was he hurt bad?" she enquired. "Not that I care, but I suppose he is my own brother."

"Quite bad," he told her. "There's a horrible bruise and a cut on his forehead. Finn says he was knocked out."

"It's downright ridiculous!" she said. "Sleeping on pews! Folks that sleep on pews deserve to get knocked out. Did he ought to go to hospital, do you think?"

"Finn doesn't think so," he said. "He——"

"Finn Finn Finn!" she cried then. "Finn this, Finn that! Who *is* this Finn, I should like to know!"

The temptation to tell her was almost unbearable, the urge to say,

"He's a hero! A real hero, summoned from a cave of slumbering heroes to save St Saviour's from destruction!"

But instinct warned him against such a revelation. He had already seen for himself how out of place Finn's very person had seemed in this neat little living-room. Number Forty-seven St Saviour's Street was not the place to accommodate heroes.

"He's just a friend," was all he said. "And he saved Uncle Alfred from drowning. And he saved Mister Rudge from the fire."

"Did he now? Quite the hero!"

Edward jumped at the unexpected sound of the word and this time the cue was so tempting that again he nearly told her.

"He's certainly brave," was all he allowed himself.

"And what does he do for a living?" she asked. "Nothing, I'll be bound."

"He hasn't actually said," Edward told her. "But he's definitely not a taxi driver."

"And that's another thing! What's he doing going round with TAXI writ all over his roof in red if it's *not* a taxi?"

"It's—it's a kind of joke," he said carefully. "He does it to show that things aren't always what they seem to be."

"Things aren't *what*?" she repeated incredulously.

"What they seem to be. And it's true, Mum, when you think about it. And Mister Rudge thinks so as well. He agrees with Finn."

"And now it's Mister Rudge! My head's spinning, it really is. And he's as mad as a hatter, that one, the whole Street knows it. You've gone and got yourself mixed up with a nice lot of lunatics, Edward, you really have."

He said nothing.

"He's throwing whole loaves out to the birds, that one is," she went on. "Whole white sliceds! He *must* be mad."

"He's got a reason," Edward mumbled.

"Reason? What reason?"

"It's for the feathered birds, of the day," he told her, because a sudden heroic impulse had made him decide to make a clean breast of it, to dare her wrath.

"Feathered birds? Of the day? And what other kinds of birds are there, pray?"

"There are the steel birds," said Edward. "Of the night."

She stared. Her mouth dropped open ever so little.

"They come swooping down in the darkness on wires," he told her, and shivered even as he spoke. "They come hard and straight and they peck on the roofs with their iron beaks, and they are evil!"

"Such nonsense!" she said, half-heartedly, still staring.

"And I've heard them, Mum! I'm sure I have! I heard them the night before last, and last night I actually *saw* them, just for a minute. At least, I didn't actually see the birds, but I saw the silvery wires in the sky, among the fireworks!"

"Oh, my good gracious!" she said blankly at last. "You're not making all this up, are you?"

"No, I'm not, I'm not! Mister Rudge sees them—that's why he's up at nights, to watch them. And he says they're getting more, and he says the birds of the day are dying out. At least, he *thinks* they are. And that's why he's feeding them!"

She was shaking her head now and Edward could see that she, too, had caught the terror of the thing.

"Do the police know?" she asked.

"Police?" The idea had never occurred to him. "Oh no, I shouldn't think so."

"Then they ought to be told! I shall go and ring them up and tell them. We could all be murdered in our beds!"

"It wouldn't be any use," he said with certainty. "They'd think you were mad. They wouldn't *see* them. *You* might not be even able to see them. Even I haven't seen them properly, not yet. They're invisible, with invisible purposes!"

"Oooh, you're frightening me to death! And now I come to think—*I've* heard some queer noises on the roof, these last few nights. And I thought it was the TV aerial, in the wind! And to think it was them horrible birds, all the time! Pecking, on the roof, right over our heads!"

She shuddered.

"I know," said Edward solemnly. "I felt just the same, when I found out."

"What's to be done, then?" she asked.

"We must leave it to Finn," he said. "He'll find a way."

"Finn? Why Finn?" she asked, bridling again.

"Think, Mum, he's a kind of saviour. He saved Uncle Alfred from drowning, didn't he?"

"I s'pose so," she agreed reluctantly.

"And the very next day, he saved old Mister Rudge from burning. That's two people he's saved in two days! And now he's going to save us all, from the steel birds. And that's another queer thing—I've just thought of it—it's *called* St Saviour's, this street. Don't you see? It all fits in!"

"I s'pose it does," she said dubiously, "if you look at it like that. But he doesn't *look* like a saviour. Scarecrow's more what he looks like."

"Ah, but that's just a disguise! Like the taxi! I told you—things aren't always what they seem!"

"It does begin to look like it," she agreed, frowning. "Though it wasn't what I was brought up to think. Those birds—he didn't happen to mention—I mean, they wasn't on anybody's roof in *particular*, was they?"

"Oh no," he assured her. "They came raining down over the whole Street, Mister Rudge says, and the entire sky was strung with steel!"

"Oooh, stop it!" she shrieked. "I can't stand it! What's behind it all, d'you think? Are they from outer space? Oooh, it's horrible. Does Alfred know?"

He nodded.

"He was there last night, at The House. Mister Rudge told them."

She got up suddenly.

"Come along. Help me clear this lot. Look sharp!"

Edward obeyed. He started to carry the dishes through into the kitchen and his mother ran a bowl of hot water and began washing them.

"He might have gone off his head," she remarked, whisking up the lather. "But he is my own flesh and blood."

"I don't think he really is mad, Mum," he said. "In fact, I'm sure he's not."

"P'raps it's only temporary," she went on. " 'Balance of the mind temporarily disturbed'—you read that in the papers. And that bang on the head might've done some good."

Edward thought that the wound on Alfred's head had certainly not looked as if it had done him any good, but did not tell her this.

"I think I know what my duty is," she continued. "Goes against the grain, but there you are. So do a lot of things in this life."

"Are you—are you going to see him, Mum?" Edward suddenly thought he had caught her gist.

"I shall visit him, certainly," she said primly, "same as I would if he was in hospital. Only pity is he's *not* in hospital and everything fair and square and above board, not skulking in churches making an exhibition of himself."

"Oh, he will be pleased!" Edward was jubilant. "He really will! I think he was really upset when you told him to go yesterday."

"I only did what I thought right." She tipped the bowl. "Anyone else'd've done the same. Will he be pleased, do you think?"

"Oh, I know he will," he assured her.

"See if *he* can tell me anything about these birds of yours," she said, thereby giving away the mixture of her motives. "Get down to the shop, Edward, and weigh out a pound of apples, while I get myself tidied up."

"Apples?"

"To *take*," she said, annoyed at having to look good-hearted. "You don't go visiting people that's sick without taking something, even if they don't deserve it."

"Right!" He made off.

"And might as well take a couple of oranges as well!" she called after him.

By the time they left, Edward was carrying a bag in which were a pound of apples, two oranges, a bunch of overripe bananas that "wanted eating up", and a book of his own called *Myths and Legends of Ancient Greece*. Mrs Flack was wearing her best coat and hat and walked the hundred or so yards with an air of conscious virtue because it was Sunday, and she was going to church, and visiting the—undeserving—sick. She held her head very high and looked straight ahead because she was convinced that everyone in the Street was watching from behind the curtains. Edward, who had no such inhibitions, guessed this, and looked to see if they were. He saw no one.

"All having a nap," he thought, "after Sunday dinner. *She* would be, usually."

"Ugh! Look out—mind!"

Her arm clutched at his sleeve and he looked down to see the bird. By now it looked thoroughly dead, dulled and sprawling. Edward shuddered.

"Dead bird!"

She walked on and he realised that the significance of the thing had escaped her. He decided to say nothing. It was too soon. He glanced over at The House as they approached and saw that the broken front door had been boarded over. He also thought for the second time that day that the garden seemed unusually cheerless and silent.

"But it's afternoon," he told himself. "Don't sing so much in the afternoon, birds don't. More in the morning, or evening."

"Here we are, then!"

She stepped into the porch, patted her hair and hat, and turned the iron ring. They were met by a strong savoury smell. Edward sniffed at it, then almost laughed aloud with delight at the incongruity of it—bone broth, in church. He restrained himself. His mother was going to put bone and vegetable broth in the vestry into the category of blasphemy, and he had no wish to be included in her censure.

"I never did!" she exclaimed, sure enough, in a loud, churchy whisper, and advanced. At the sight of Alfred's feet—admittedly now encased in lemon socks, and so much the more acceptable— she stopped dead.

Alfred's eyes were open, and gazing above. His face wore an

107

expression of beatific peace. Edward saw his mother raise her own eyes slowly and fearfully, as he himself had done earlier. He wondered what *she* expected to see up there.

"His mother's ghost, probably," he decided. "After all, it'd be her mother, as well."

Mrs Flack, after a thorough suspicious raking of the vaulted roof, dropped her eyes and advanced with renewed confidence.

"Alfred!" she said sharply.

He seemed not to hear. Still his eyes were fixed above. She even took another quick look upwards herself before repeating, more loudly,

"Alfred!"

This time he did hear. Reluctantly he pulled away his eyes and saw her.

"It's Lily!" He half raised himself, and as he did so the wound on his head became clearly visible and she leapt forward.

"Lie down! You lie down this minute!"

Obediently he lay back and stared up at her as she stood over the pew staring back.

"Now they're *properly* meeting," thought Edward with satisfaction. "Not like yesterday. A real reconciliation. Like Ceres and Persephone."

"Well, Lily," said Alfred faintly at last. "It's nice to see you."

She sat on the pew by his feet.

"That's a nasty head you've got," she said.

"It doesn't hurt. Hardly at all. In fact I like lying here. I feel as if I could lie like this forever."

"You're not delirious, are you?"—suddenly alarmed.

"No. Not delirious, Lily."

"Well, that's something. You'll be up in a day or two, I expect."

"I expect so."

"And you won't lie *here* forever, wherever you lie," she told him. "Going to be pulled down, this place is, next year."

"No!" He did raise himself up then. "On no!"

"Whatever—?" She pressed him firmly down again. "You'll not be here—I told you. Up in a day or two, you'll be."

"Pulled down!" he repeated to himself.

"For a *supermarket*, would you believe! What the world is coming to I don't know. A supermarket! It's blasphemy, of course. That's what I told Denis, when I first heard. 'It's downright blasphemy,' I said, 'to pull down a place of worship to make way for cut-price soap powder', and he agreed with me."

"It *is* blasphemy," agreed Alfred, and his eyes went back to the soaring vault again, and stayed there.

"*Not*," she added, "that what you're doing now isn't blasphemy, for that matter, or very near to it. Whatever got into you, Alfred?"

He did not reply.

"It isn't blasphemy, Mum," put in Edward. "Finn says so. He says that once the altar has been moved, it can't be blasphemy."

"*He* seems to know a lot about it," she snapped. "Goes *in* for blasphemy, does he? Crossing himself and going on!"

"He's a good man, Lily," said Alfred, with unexpected firmness.

At this she tossed her head and pursed her lips as if to indicate that she knew better, but that she was not going to argue with a sick man.

"And now, what's all this about birds?" she demanded.

Alfred turned his eyes toward Edward, who blushed and nodded.

"I thought she ought to know," he said. "I mean, really everyone ought to know."

"Have you seen them, Alfred?"

"I—almost have," he replied.

"Almost? So far as I know, you either see a thing or you don't. Have you or haven't you?"

"The only thing I can think of to say is 'almost'," said Alfred. "Perhaps my head is still a little blurred. What I mean is, that I wouldn't swear that I had, but then I wouldn't swear that I hadn't, either. That's what I mean."

"And no kind of an answer at all," said Mrs Flack.

"If you were to ask me if I *believe* in them," said Alfred, "then I should be able to give you an answer."

"Well, do then!"

"I do believe in them," he said. Then he turned his head aside as if to indicate that he was tired and wished to be left alone.

"We've brought you one or two things," she told him. "Some fruit. It'd have gone bad anyway, if it'd been left in the shop much longer."

"Thank you, Lily. Thank you very much."

"Oh, don't thank me," she said, "I'd have done it for anyone, I hope. And get it eaten up quick, like I said, or it'll go off."

"I will. Oh, I will, Lily."

"And I brought a book," Edward told him. "Though I don't suppose you feel like reading yet."

He propped the Myths and Legends on the pew, like a hymn book. Mrs Flack, evidently viewing this as a minor blasphemy, snatched it up instantly and put it down on the pew by Alfred's yellow feet.

"Where's the other one?" she demanded. "That Irishman?"

"I don't know. I have been asleep, you see."

She hesitated, then began to march up the aisle.

"Come along, Edward," she ordered over her shoulder. "It's my plain duty to see what *is* going on in here."

He hurried after her, overtook, and reached the vestry door first. He pushed it open, calling softly,

"Finn! Finn—are you there?"

He looked about. The groceries and utensils were all neatly stacked, a covered pot was simmering gently on the stove. At the other side of the room was another door, slightly ajar. He could see grass beyond, and stone.

"Well I never!" he heard his mother exclaim. "Would you credit it?"

Edward crossed to the other door and pushed it wider. Before him was the graveyard, bounded on three sides by walls and on the fourth by the high railings on to the Street. The grass was knee-high and whitened with moisture, the stones were formal and marble, many of them black. He had never been into the grave-yard before. It was disused, had been for over fifty years, they said. Was Finn here, in among the cold crosses and leaning slabs?

"Finn! Finn!"

He rose then, his red hair startling in among the pattern of green and white and black. He was like a figure on a medieval tapestry.

"Hello, there!" He strode forward. "And brought your mother to see Alfie! Glad ye came, ma'am!" and he gave a half bow and flourish that might have been mocking, and might not.

"And what did ye think to Alfie, ma'am?" he enquired.

"I thought Alfred was as well as could be expected," she said. "Considering."

"And the better, I dare stake my life," said Finn gallantly, "for a sight of you!"

Mrs Flack refused to be pleased.

"Is that your soup?" She jerked her head back toward the vestry.

"Indeed it is! And oh—the smell of it! It'll put the strength o' ten men into your brother, will that soup, when it's done. Can I offer ye some? Will you stop and try it wit' us?"

She shuddered.

"No, thank you," she said. "And I'm bound to say, whether it is my business or not, that if the good Lord had intended there to be broth boiled in vestries, then it would have said so in the Bible, or somewhere. I cannot stand by and see a vestry made into a soup kitchen without speaking my mind, Mr Finn."

"Of course not!" he cried, as if of exactly the same mind, "and I take off me hat to you for saying it, ma'am!" (with a doffing of an imaginary hat).

"And I give ye my word, ma'am, that never until this very day did it so much as cross my mind to be making broth in the church. Oh no. But then the door *opened*, d'ye see, when I tried it. And then your brother fell and hurt his head, and the most natural thing in the world, it seemed, d'ye see?"

Mrs Flack evidently did not see, and while Finn was talking had actually been peering past him at the graveyard, as if for signs of further blasphemous activity.

"I was looking about out here," said Finn, noticing this, "there being an idea I've had, and the churchyard being likely a very handy place indeed for what I have in mind."

"What idea?" Edward asked. "Is it to do with the birds?"

Finn opened his mouth to reply, but was forestalled by the inquisitorial Mrs Flack.

"And that's another thing! These birds. What's all this I hear about tin birds on the roof of a night-time?"

"Not tin, Mum—steel, or iron."

"Ah!" said Finn softly. "The birds. Shoals o' silver fish all afloat in the sky . . . swimming in nets o' steel . . . the stars caught in their meshes . . ."

"*You've* seen them?"

Finn shook his head and smiled.

"It was a manner of speaking," he said. "It's how *I* see them, you understand. In the mind's eye . . ."

"It's a pity," she said, "that someone don't take a photograph, and let's see what we're up against. Something to show to the police, that'd be, and let them do something about it. Police job, that is, to protect law-abiding citizens from tin birds or steel either, for that matter."

"Oh no," he said. "Not the police. Nothing at all to do with the police, this isn't. Oh no."

"It's *somebody's* business! *I* ain't sitting still with my tiles being meddled with night after night, and Lord knows what else to come! From outer space, if anyone was to ask me!"

"Aye," agreed Finn slowly. "Ye might say that, I suppose. Outer space . . ."

"Oooh! You're setting me off again!" she cried. "It's downright horrible, the whole thing. I doubt if I shall ever sleep another wink. There's something got to be done, and quick!"

"That's the spirit, ma'am," applauded Finn. She looked briefly gratified.

"And I shall do something," he announced. "Of that you may rest assured. Patrick Finn has the matter in hand."

"And nobody," thought Edward, "could ask for more than that."

CHAPTER FOURTEEN

¶ *The Letter Mrs Flack Wrote To The* Haunton Post *And Which The Editor, Having Glanced First At The Signature, Then At The First Two Sentences, Dropped Into His Wastepaper Basket With The Two Words:* "Her *Again!*"

Dear Sir,

I am taking the liberty of writing to you again because of the goings on in connection with St Saviour's Street which I feel you and your readers should know about. It is already known that it is proposed to pull down St Saviour's Church and replace it by a supermarket, and my views on this are already well known and agreed with by every right-thinking citizen.

But it is now my opinion that this blasphemous action is being paid for by the wrath of heaven, or worse. It has come to my notice that there are millions of tin birds coming down from the sky every night when it is dark and pecking on the roof, TV aerials, etc with their beaks. I have not in fact seen them myself yet, but I have certainly heard them, although at the time I put this down to the wind as I had not yet been informed of these dreadful birds. They come down on wires and are obviously either from outer space or the work of the devil (who I expect has been encouraged by the pulling down of a House of God to make way for a supermarket).

It is a disgrace that innocent ratepayers should have to put up with this kind of thing and I am writing this letter to bring the situation to the notice of whatever department is concerned. My health is already beginning to suffer as a result of all this and my own husband says I am becoming a bag of nerves. (Another reason for this being the way certain people have been letting off fireworks in the Street for the past month with not a thought for the welfare of others. The fault, of course, lying entirely with the parents who cannot control their own children, and teach them to swear and steal, let alone let off fireworks from Easter till November.)

But to return to my main complaint, I think it is a disgrace in this day and age that this kind of thing is allowed to happen, and it certainly makes you wonder where it will all end. We are all paying very high taxes and rates and expect some service in return. (I myself have had to buy two dustbins owing to the irregularity of the dustbinmen.) I therefore demand that immediate action should be taken against these birds by whatever department is concerned. At the same time saying that if planning permission had not been given to put up a supermarket in place of St Saviour's Church, I feel quite sure none of this would ever have happened.

Thanking you in anticipation,

Yours faithfully,

Mrs L. Flack

Part Two

CHAPTER FIFTEEN

¶ *What Mister Rudge Said On November 7th*

It seems to me now that the world is growing stranger, day by day. I even begin to weary of it. When I look out from my window I see that everything is grey—road, church, roofs, sky, all grey and with the colour gone, bleached out as it is by moonlight. And it is this that makes me wonder whether it is true that our days are being changed, slowly and surely, into nights. Of course, it is winter, I know, and the days must shorten. But those terrible steel birds thrive and thicken in the dark. Last night I saw them in hosts, bearing down in ranks. They are like spears.

And now I am not the only one who knows of the birds. I have told a boy, Edward Flack, though I did not mean to. And I have told two others, though I did not mean that, either. They listened as I spoke, I remember, and their look was serious. They did not mock. The boy even said that he had already glimpsed the birds, and heard them. And this seems possible, because children have a certain way of seeing through what is familiar and finding truth beyond it. A child does not expect anything. In a sense, everything that he sees is strange, he is living in a foreign country.

But then there are the other children, the ones who came to burn my house. I looked from the top windows and saw them in a wild ring and they pointed their fingers up at me and jeered and called me mad. I had been straining into the sky for a sight of the birds, but my eyes were tired with watching tails of fire streaking over chimney pots and dizzied by falling sparks. And so I did not realise my house was burning until I heard the crack of glass.

This burning of my house has made me afraid. I believe that it is to do with the birds. Those boys are sleeping every night under roofs where those iron beaks are grazing. In the mornings I look down over the Street and I do not see broken tiles. It is almost certain that those birds are invisible to all but a very few and so I believe that their purpose, too, is invisible. I believe that it is evil.

This morning I found a dead bird on my step. It was a sparrow. There was a little blood on the down of its head. The line between day and night is becoming more difficult to draw as winter comes on and so the steel and the feathered birds are more likely to meet at dawn. And a tiny sparrow can be killed at a single blow from an iron beak.

I wept after I had found the dead sparrow. The combat between innocence and ruthlessness is not a fair one. Afterwards, I climbed back to my room and consoled myself with a daydream. It was so clear and joyous, the picture that I saw, that I laughed aloud. A daydream is, after all, simply a way of keeping in mind what is possible but which does not yet exist. And in a curious way I think that my daydreaming was a defeat for those steel birds on their inflexible paths.

In it, first of all it was night, and the sky was strung with steel, tight and hard. Those terrible birds were driving down like hail. But as I watched the sky began to lighten, minute by minute. I saw St Saviour's thronged with birds, real ones, the feathered ones. They gathered and soared and made each his own separate pattern in the air and in my dream the day was not overcast but sunlit, and all the brown birds thronging the sunlight and singing its celebration. Their wings broke the bright blue in fragments. And up and down the Street the people went, quite peacefully and with glad faces. The birds flew about their heads and it seemed to me like the beginning of all time. And best of all, suddenly there came the pealing of bells and as they rang out the people threw their hands in the air and cheered because there had been a victory, and the steel birds had been driven from the sky forever.

They stamped and cheered and danced one with the other and as I watched in my mind's eye, I laughed aloud and at the same time felt my cheeks wet, and thought what foolishness it all was. I am an old man to be living alone. Old and impossible I am and they all say it and keep away as much as they can. And perhaps they are right. I am old, and perhaps I am even a little mad. I have no way of telling. I simply follow my own mind wherever it takes me, and this is the only thing I know how to do. I have done it ever since I was a child. And that is what a bird does, too, so perhaps it is no bad thing, after all. I have no way of telling.

CHAPTER SIXTEEN

¶ *Being Extracts From The Chronicle Of St Saviour's Made By Edward Flack*

November 6th

It really seems as if my whole life has changed because of two things. The first thing was going to see Mister Rudge (my most heroic deed so far) and the second was the arrival of Finn. Usually nothing much happens in my life and what does would certainly not be worth writing in a Chronicle. But now I have got so much to write about a single day, that I do not even know if I will get it all done tonight. Still, there is school tomorrow so there will not be so much to report then. (Not that I am complaining.)

The first big thing that happened today was discovering that Uncle Alfred and Finn had gone to stay in the church. They are using it as a sanctuary. I was rather worried about this at first but Finn says that once the altar has been taken out of a church it is all right. (I wonder if a church still counts as a sanctury when the altar has gone?) The main reason why they have decided to stay is because Uncle Alfred has been sorely wounded on his head. He fell off a pew and hit it. I think this may have made the balance of his mind temperary disturbed, as he keeps gazing up at the ceiling as if he was seeing a ghost or something. It really gave me the creeps when I first saw him especialy as there was some wierd music being played. Finn plays the organ really well much better than Mr Standish used to.

Anyway Finn has put all his cooking things etc in the vestrey and it is really homelike. He tends Uncle Alfred as if he were a babe, and has made some smashing broth. Which brings me to Mum and what a fit she had when she opened the door and smelt it. She said it was blasphamy but as I have already explained it was not. I was really amazed when she said she was going to see Uncle Alfred and she even took some fruit to him. She pretended it was only because it was going off, but it was not. She really has a kind heart under her rough exterior. I could give many examples of this, for instance her saying I could not have any dinner and then letting me have it after all. Dad says she is really fond of Uncle Alfred in her own way and I think this is true. I like him very much myself despite the fact that he does not say much and seems to be in a world of his own at the moment which I suppose is only nateral after first nearly drowning and then being so sorely wounded on the head.

It was not the only reason Mum went to the church to see Uncle Alfred. She wanted to find out more about the steel birds (which she keeps calling 'tin', which is really irritating because this makes them sound just silly instead of dire and vengeful). I told her about the birds partly because I knew she would stop me going to the church if I did not, and partly because I thought she ought to know. In a way I think everyone in St Saviour's should know, as these birds are threatening the whole Street and not just us. I think we should all band together with stout hearts and stand firm against the foe. With Finn around this may not be neccessary.

He says that he has already got an idea of what to do. I do not know what this is as obviously he did not want to talk about it in front of Mum. He had been looking round the graveyard and that is the only clue I have got at the moment. I did have one horrible thought that he might be going to raise the dead, but am now certain that he will not. A hero defeats the enemy by his own skill and valour and deeds of prowess.

Talking about the birds reminds me of an ill omen I have had today. I saw a dead bird on the pavement. Obviously it might just have died a nateral death or even the MacKays might have got hold of some catapults again (although they have been actuerly warned by the police about this). But I do not think so. It lay in my path limp and lifeless and a shudder passed through my frame.

Talking about the MacKays though reminds me of something else that I should record in this Chronicle before I lay down my pen. Mum already knew about Finn and Uncle Alfred being in the church and what is more about them frying bacon and egg. There is obviously a traiterous spy at large or, in my opinion, more than one spy. I think that the MacKays are very likely hell bent on revenge because Finn dealt them a mighty blow last night and imprisoned them behind the graveyard railings. They were certainly scared stiff and kept yelling to be let out and I had a job not to laugh. But the point is I have not seen them once all day and I think that this is obviously because they are lurking.

The MacKays are not easily beaten which is one good thing you can say about them. I certainly expect there will be a punch-up or a fray at school tomorrow. But I shall not flinch from a bloody encounter though I do think that three to one (and sometimes four to one) is a bit much. But if David could face Goliath I should be able to face three (or four) MacKays, and if Mr Gray sees them fighting in the yard he will stop them anyway, as he is always on at them about this.

I will now conclude my entry. I have just got up and looked through my window. All is quiet. It soon will not be, however, as it is nearly closing time. Mister Rudge's solitery light burns aloft. Will he see the sky strung with steel tonight? I have a feeling that whether the birds come or not I will not see or hear them as I am really tired. I do not worry about this, as Finn will keep us safe from harm. He is our champion.

I now lay down my pen certifying that this is a true and faithful record.

November 7th
I now pick up my pen to record that I now know Finn's plan to defeat the birds of steel. Like all great ideas it is very simple. He says that he got the idea from something that Mister Rudge said, but this is only his true modesty befitting so great a hero.

When I got back from school (where by the way I had a bloody encounter with Dave and Mike MacKay and got my shirt torn) I went straight to the church. I could hear the sound of banging and hammering and my first thought was that the police had turned Finn and Uncle Alfred out and were boarding up the door. But my fears were unfounded. It was Finn in the graveyard and he had some wire netting and was making sort of cages out of wooden fruit boxes. It made me think of Vulcan the Smith though obviously he did not have a fire and bellows. (Uncle Alfred was still lying on his pew staring up at the ceiling but was not so wan as yesterday.)

Finn is going to get thousands of birds! Perhaps not exactly thousands but as many as he possibly can and of course they will go forth and multiply of their own accord. We are going to breed them in the graveyard and they will be pigeons, mostly, though Finn says there are other kinds we could have as well. I have always wanted pigeons but Mum always said they were too much trouble and now we are to have hundreds of them! I shall help Finn to look after them and feed and water etc. We shall have to

121

keep them up at first but later we shall be able to let them fly free and they will then find some of their own food and not be so expensive to keep. (Uncle Alfred by the way seems to be quite rich.)

Finn says he got this idea from Mister Rudge when he said about how he thought the feathered birds of the day were graduerly getting less. Obviously they do get less in winter but even allowing for that there do seem fewer birds about when you really notice. (Not to mention the dead one I saw.) Anyway I think the idea is absolutley marvellous, the true thought of a hero.

I remembered about my ill omen yesterday and told Finn and he nodded and then told me that Mister Rudge had found a dead bird on his doorstep as well! Finn said that this bird had a mark on its head as if it had been stabbed by an iron beak, and that Mister Rudge had been very distrort about it and I should think he was. He also said that Mister Rudge had been in one of his faraway moods and had told him about a daydream he had had. I asked Finn what it was but he would not tell. He said that if Mister Rudge wanted me to know he would tell me himself and that it was not right to go about telling other people's dreams. From the way he talked about it I suspect that it was not so much a dream as a vision. As I have mentioned before Mister Rudge does seem to be rather the soothsayer type, and I expect this is what he is, really.

I then left Finn at his labours as I did not want to be late for tea and make Mum mad. She asked me if I had been to the church so I said yes, and then told her about the birds. At first she scorned the idea and said she did not see what good it was going to do to have the Street plagued by birds by day as well as by night. So I then told her about the two dead birds and of course *she* then became distrort and when Dad came in told him everything and asked him what he thought we should do. He had had a hard day he said and only really wanted his tea, and the only thing he said was had any damage been done to the roof and of course Mum said no, as far as she knew. He then said that when damage was done that would be the time to start worrying and he told Mum quite definately that he did not believe in outer space. They were still arguing about flying saucers etc when I went out again.

I have a feeling that Mum does not really understand about the steel birds. She thinks of them as a kind of nuisance and I suppose she might be just a bit scared as well. But she does not grasp the full horror of them, they do not chill her to the marrow. I think that if she met Mister Rudge in his dark old house and heard him talk about them in that queer faraway voice he sometimes has, then she would be gripped by foreboding as I was and Finn and Uncle Alfred for that matter. As for Dad I think it all went like water off a duck's back. Half the time he does not really listen to what Mum is saying, not that I blame him for this as I try to do the same (though obviously I have not had so much practice as him).

I went out and did my daily feat of daring round the alley etc but now think that this will not do any longer and I shall have to think up some truer test of courage. I mean now that Uncle Alfred and Finn are in the church I no longer think of it as a place of utter darkness and terror in fact look forward to going there even when it is dark. It is quite spooky in there at night of course because Finn has only two oil lamps but it is impossible to feel fear in the presence of a hero. He looks very awesome by lamplight because his face looks very shadowy and hollow-eyed, a figure of mystery.

I have toyed with the idea of telling Finn about my daily feat and asking him if he has any suggestions for a new one. I expect he would understand, even if he did not do them himself when he was a boy. I am pretty certain that he did not have to train himself to be a hero as I am doing, but was actuerly born one (like Hercules for example).

One idea I have had for a feat would be when I go to bed to turn off the light then open the window wide and actuerly *invoke* them (the steel birds I mean). It would certainly be a true test as I feel quite creepy even at the thought of it. I mean, what if they actuerly did come? What would I do? On second thoughts I do not think this a good idea as it would endanger others as well as myself. Also, if I met my doom doing this I would not be able to help Finn and Uncle Alfred. I will try to think of something else.

Meanwhile I will lay down my pen and lay me down to sleep in the testimony that this is a true and faithful record.

November 9th
I take up my pen yet again to record the events of this day being the ninth of November. In actual fact there is only one main event which unfortunately I missed through being at school but which Finn narrated to me.

The old vicar came to the church today. Someone in the Street must have become distrort at the thought that there was blasphamy going on with the frying of bacon and egg etc. Someone had rung him up but he would not say who. I do not think it was Mum in fact I am sure it was not as she is now resigned to them being in there and actuerly sent them some more fruit and a packet of digestives. Also I think she realises that Finn will save us all from destruction and therefore is glad he is so handy. So the question arises who rang up? In a way it could have been anybody as there are certainly some funny people on this street, but my own suspicion is that it was the MacKays. Motive—revenge.

Anyway if it was meant as revenge it did not succeed as Finn got on very well with Mr Owen (the vicar) who being a vicar naturally knew that when the altar had gone there could not be any blasphamy. Finn says he told him about Mister Rudge and the vicar told him that he and Uncle Alfred could stay there as long as they liked and even gave them a key to the church door! He said that it was him who must have accidently left the door unlocked and agreed with Finn about it being Providence. I always thought he was quite a good sport in spite of being a vicar and this is what he has turned out to be. Also, being a vicar and knowing a lot about David and Goliath etc it is possible that he realised Patrick Finn is a true hero. If so, no wonder he gave him a key to the church as even vicars do not meet people like this every day.

Anyway this is one of our main worries dealt with and our dreams need no more be haunted by fears that they would be cast out and banished, as obviously the vicar has the last say in matters like this. Finn says that Uncle Alfred is very upset about the church going to be pulled down and that he asked the vicar if it could be saved but he said no unfortunatly not. Finn said that Uncle Alfred then said that he would give his right arm to save it, which was strong language for him I think. It is almost as if some of Finn's heroism has rubbed off on him. (I hope some rubs off on me.)

The only other events I have to record are that Finn has nearly finished making the cages and is actuerly going to get some pigeons tomorrow! Also Uncle Alfred's progress. He is definately not so wan now and his wound has almost healed. He still does a lot of staring up at the ceiling but seems a bit more talkative and is quite excited about the pigeons. When I told him about always wanting some he said that *he* always wanted some when he

124

was a boy as well but that their mother would not let them. He said that *Mum* always wanted some as well, which struck me as quite funny! He said that it was like a dream come true for him and that Finn was the best person he had ever known with which I heartily agreed. I have not said anything to him about Finn being a hero as I think such a revelation might have bad consequences in his state. It could even be a fatal shock. His heart could crack open within him.

I will now lay down my pen. This is a true and faithful record.

November 10th
I pick up my pen to record that we have got the birds! There are three pairs of pigeons, absolutley smashing with really lovely feathers all bluey grey and smooth and gleaming. Their eyes are very bright and inquisative and they keep peering out at the graveyard and tapping their beaks against the wire. Uncle Alfred got up for the first time today and came out to look at them. He leaned on Finn's mighty arm looking very wan but much better really especially when he saw the pigeons.

And then Finn told me that I could pick names for the birds and it came to me all in a flash what I could do! I could name them after heroes. Not the females of course as there are no such things as female heroes, only heroines which is not the same thing. The real difference I suppose is that heroines tend to do just one noble deed and have finished whereas heroes just go on and on doing them. So I shall call the females after goddesses or sometimes heroines. So one pair I am calling Hercules and Joan (after Joan of Arc), one pair David and Bathsheba (which fits quite well) and the last pair Theseus and Grace (after Grace Darling). It just shows that heroines are not the same, by the way you have to give their surnames as well before people realise who you mean. Though Grace Darling certainly was a real heroine I admit.

Their names really suit them and I think they are beginning to know them already. Finn likes the names and slapped his hand in the way he does and said "Perfect, bejam!" which made me wonder if the reason why he aproved so much was that they are his fellow heroes. It may even have given him the first hint that I know who he really is, though he has given no sign of this. He said that I had better get a list of more names ready for when they breed and I have plenty of ideas for this.

Appollo, Beowulf, Florence (Nightingale), Persus, Bellepheron, Jason, Hereward the Wake, Bordicea, Achilles, Hiawatha and at a pinch Moses though no doubt I shall have thought of a lot more names by then. I would also like Robin Hood but this does not seem a very suitable name for a pigeon.

I wish I did not have to go to school and could stay with Finn all day and look after or tend the pigeons. They look to me as if in a way they *are* heroes or warriors bred to combat the terrible birds of steel, but perhaps this is only my imagination. But they are certainly noble and beautiful birds and as far as I am concerned I do not mind giving every bit of my pocket money towards feeding them. However Uncle Alfred seems to have quite a lot of money and Finn went to a bank to get some out for him today. He says that he wants some new clothes and tomorrow Finn is going to go and buy some for him. The ones he is wearing are much too big for him, being Finn's, and he will not put on his old suit and told Finn to cast it into the fire and destroy it, or at any rate to get rid of it.

I told Mum about the pigeons and she said she might go along and have a look at them herself. I think she is trying to hide the fact that she is pleased about this, as if it is true that she used to want pigeons when she was a girl this must be like a dream come true for her as well, even if she will not admit it. She did not approve of the names I have chosen however and said they were too much of a mouthfull and that if she had a pigeon she would call him Pretty. Why on earth she should want to call a pigeon by that name I do not know, the only thought having occured to me being that this was a name she chose when she was little and did not know any better. And of course she is proberly forgetting that these birds are meant to be warriors, in a way. You cannot have a warrior bird called Pretty.

Having now seen the pigeons and become fond of them there is one thing that worries me. Do these birds really have to be warriors in the meaning that they have to actuerly do battle with the steel birds? If so, I am not sure that I agree with this, in fact, I do not. In a combat between these two types of birds it is obvious that the steel birds are going to win as they have the advantage of being made of metal so that they cannot sustain wounds. On the other hand they would have the power of dealing deadly blows with their cruel beaks (as in fact they proberly already have done to those other two birds).

I think we ought to go and see Mister Rudge again and get this cleared up. After all there is nothing to be ashamed of in consulting the oracle in fact heroes did it all the time. What I think is that if we raise enough birds they will drive out the others by sheer force of number. As I see it, it is really a battle between day and night and between good and evil, and if the balance is weighted on the side of the day birds then they will be victorious. This would certainly fit in with various stories I have read. And what is really encouraging in the things I have read is that good always does overcome evil, and I believe with all my heart and strength that this is what will happen in St Saviour's. The dark will never vanquish the light.

If ever I get a chance to get one of those MacKays on his own I will really give him a bashing. They know about the birds now and keep yelling things like "Quack quack Teddy Flack!" after me, and "Coo—it's Flack—coo!" and so on. I suppose they think this is funny. They had better not lay a hand on those pigeons that is all. I will bash them to hell if they do however many of them there are. I will shed their blood.

CHAPTER SEVENTEEN

¶ *In Which Mrs Flack Jumps To Conclusions, And Becomes Lil Again*

The television van was standing outside the shop when Edward arrived home from school. He had come straight home so that he could have an early tea and then have an hour with Finn and the pigeons before doing his homework. The whole weekend would then be free before him.

"I'm sure the days *are* shortening," he was thinking. "I mean, more than they usually do at this time of year. Soon I won't get any time at all with the pigeons, except at weekends."

Seeing the van only reinforced his fears. His eyes went straight up to the roof and the aerial in the vain hope of seeing actual proof of his suspicions. He went in through the shop. Only his mother was there, weighing out butter.

"Edward! The telly's gone wrong! Oh—there you are!"—this last to the man who was just descending the stairs. "What is it, then?"

"Looks like the aerial, I'm afraid," he said.

Mrs Flack's hands flew up.

"I knew it!" she gasped. "Oh my good lord!"

"Not my job, I'm afraid," he said. "Have to send someone out to look at it. Won't get it done today, I'm afraid. Something special you wanted to watch, was there?"

But the prospect of missing possibly a whole weekend's viewing hardly counted with her.

"The aerial!" she repeated. "I knew it."

"Funny thing," he said. "Third aerial we've had round here in the last day or two."

"Oh!" she moaned.

"All these high winds we've been getting, I reckon." He did not seem to notice her dramatic reaction. Or perhaps, Edward thought, some people did behave dramatically when they found out they were going to miss Sports Report or something?

"High winds?" she repeated. "High winds?"

"Well, there have been a lot lately," he said. "And some of

these aerials are getting a bit dodgy. Ever thought of getting a new one?"

"A new one? I thought that was what we were coming round to! And how much would that be may I ask?"

"Oh—about ten. With fitting."

"Ten? Ten pounds? *I'm* buying no new aerial. There's nothing the matter with the one that's up there. And it'd be just the same if there *was* a new one, with those blessed b——"

Edward held his breath. She stopped just in time.

"Anyway, you tell that man to come and put this one on properly," she finished. "If it'd been put on properly in the first place, it wouldn't come loose in the first wind that blew."

"Not exactly the first, Mrs Flack," said the man. "Been up ten or fifteen years that has, I should guess."

"Bad workmanship," she snapped. "And you can tell him I said so. And mind you tell him I want it done quick. Don't want all weekend without a thing to watch, tell him."

"Phew!" Edward let out a whistle when he had gone. "I thought for a minute you were going to tell him—about the birds, I mean."

"Did nearly let it out," she admitted. "But I wasn't having him think I'd gone barmy. Tin birds on the roof indeed!"

"*Steel*, Mum. Birds of steel. With iron beaks. But I thought you *believed* in them!"

"P'raps I do and p'raps I don't," she returned. "But even if I did, it'd be because I'd got proper reason to. But to go and say that to an *outsider*—I *would* want my brains examining! Enough to get you put away. Especially with a brother going round looking like Alfred does—has he changed out of those horrible clothes yet?"

"Yes," he told her.

"Looks all right now, does he? Respectable?"

"His things certainly fit him."

Edward chose his words carefully. He did not think that his mother was going to approve of Alfred's new outfit, which was very like the one he had taken off, except that it was a better fit. Finn, when making his choice, had tried to take into consideration Alfred's heretofore clerkly personality, while at the same time leaving plenty of scope for its future blossoming into something freer and more joyous (signs of which were already apparent). He had therefore struck what seemed to him to be a modest balance. There was just a hint of subdual about the waist-

I

coat (which although it was well-fringed did not run quite so extravagantly to beads) and the embroidery on the flared blue denims was merely two-tone, instead of multicoloured.

Alfred himself had been very pleased with them, and also with the open-thonged sandals Finn had bought so that if they were not a good fit it would not matter so much. Alfred wore the yellow socks under them for warmth and said they were the most comfortable pair of shoes he had ever had. Clearly Mrs Flack was going to be less concerned with the comfort of Alfred's feet than with the impression they made upon other people, and Edward felt sure that the sandals would score low on respectability, to say nothing of serviceability.

"He's feeling a lot better," Edward went on, to prevent further discussion of Alfred's appearance. "And he got up yesterday, to look at the pigeons."

"Oh, he's seen them, has he?" She sounded ever so slightly peeved, like a child who has missed a treat. "Always was daft about pigeons."

Edward forbore to reveal that he knew the same to be true of herself. He said,

"And you can come, can't you, when the shop shuts? It'll be dark, I know, but you can still see them. And then you could have a proper look tomorrow—half-day closing."

(Mrs Flack closed her shop half day on Saturday on the principle that by so doing she ensured a brisk trade on Sunday mornings.)

After tea, and when Mrs Flack had closed the shop, she did put on her coat and hat.

"You can run down for some chips when your father gets back," she told Edward. "Better go and see how that brother of mine's going on, I suppose. There's plenty wouldn't."

Edward was glad that her first view of Alfred's new clothes would be in the half light of Finn's lamps. As it turned out, she was so overcome by the warmth of Finn's welcome that she had no time to make a critical inspection.

"On his feet and right as rain!" he greeted her. "And the vitamins he's had from the fruit ye sent him cured him entirely, I'm sure of't! Ye're a good woman, Mrs Flack, and proud to have you to friend!"

Mrs Flack, who had never heard herself described as "good" in her life, and had certainly never thought of herself as so, expanded despite herself, and answered,

"I do my best, Mr Finn. It's no more'n anyone would've done."

"Indeed it is!" he cried. "And don't I wish I had the luck of such a sister meself!"

"Oh well," she said. "Alfred and me've always been close."

Alfred gaped. She saw this, and added defensively,

"We *were* close, Alfie, when we were kids, you know we were! Ma used to say we ought to've been twins. Don't you remember?"

"Oh, I do, I do!" Alfred said fervently. "And oh, Lil, you called me Alfie—just like you used to. When we were on our own—do you remember?"

"Ma wouldn't let us call you that," she nodded. "Said it was common. 'Lily and Alfred you are,' she'd say, 'and never mind your nasty common Lil and Alfie!' "

She giggled. Now it was Edward's turn to gape.

"And we had that den, do you remember, behind that shed by the canal?"

"Till she found out—ooh, the row there was—and when she found out we'd been making fires!"

"Beat the daylights out of us," agreed Alfred. "Used a slipper."

There was silence.

"She was hard on us," said Alfred.

"People were, in those days." Mrs Flack seemed to come back to herself again—or almost. "Now, what about these pigeons I've come to look at? Pigeons I've come to see, Alfie Graves, not you. Don't you go getting that idea!"

"Come along, Lil," he said happily. "I'll show you. We shall need a lamp."

In the graveyard they all crouched in the damp grass in their new-found intimacy and stared through the lamplight at the sleepy pigeons, who crooned softly and stirred in the straw. One of them blinked his eyes right open.

"That's Hercules!" whispered Edward. "Look, Mum, he's looking straight at you!"

"So he is!" She actually knelt now and leaned forward, forgetful of her coat in the mud and of the marble cross in danger of nudging off her felt hat. They stared at one another in the dim light, the middle-aged woman and the bright-eyed bird.

"He could be yours!"

Edward was seized by a sacrificial impulse that was near-heroic. Hercules was his favourite hero.

"Couldn't he, Finn?"

"Could he?" She spoke softly and put a finger to the netting.

"There, there, silly old boy. It's all right—only me!"

The pigeon tilted his head consideringly, then settled back down into his feathers again, at ease.

"He knows," she whispered. "He likes me!"

"*Course* he does!" came Finn's encouraging whisper. "And why should he not, bejam?"

"And who's the other?" she asked. "Who's that little beauty there with him?"

"It's his wife," said Edward. "It's Joan. Joan of Arc."

"Hercules and Joan," she repeated. "Little beauties."

Edward straightened and stood back a little and watched the others.

"What a queer thing," he thought. "How queer the world has suddenly gone."

His mother was kneeling in damp grass to coax a pigeon in a voice softer than he had ever heard it. Those same pigeons were safe in straw, but strangely housed in among the black crosses and pallid gleam of tombs. The lamp was lighting a faint mist above the ground, and it brushed faces silvery and caught red in Finn's hair and beard. A car went by beyond the railings. It seemed an oddity in itself, seen from that high-walled square of greenery, with its almost country night-smell and silence.

"I can smell dew. I think it's dew. I've never smelled it before."

And he knew that that particular cold scent would fix the scene before him now forever, in every detail. He looked over at The House, and Mister Rudge was there in silhouette at the upper window. He raised an arm, and the old man returned the salute.

"*Queer* old man," he thought. "All that darkness, and all that silence . . ."

And the thought came to him that Mister Rudge too was a hero, though of a different kind. He looked back at the crouching figures, then up again at the lighted window, and was seized by an almost unbearable excitement. Something, he knew, was bound to happen. Patrick Finn and Mister Rudge between them had started a chain of events that would carry them all along now, inevitably. St Saviour's was already in the crucible, the alchemy was at work.

"And the birds. The other birds . . ."

Edward raised his eyes but saw only lit windows, chimney

stacks against the sky, the looming shapes of factories by the canal behind The House.

"Too early yet. But they'll come!"

He caught sight of Mister Rudge again, waving, and saw that Finn had risen and was signalling to him.

"We're coming, old man, never you fear . . ."

He spoke softly, as if to himself. And hearing him, Edward felt a sharp pang of jealousy. Finn had got the pigeons not for himself at all, but for the sake of old Mister Rudge, that his dreams might be the quieter.

CHAPTER EIGHTEEN

¶ *In Which Mrs Flack Meets Mister Rudge And Has A Fit Of Sneezing*

They spoke in subdued voices as they left the graveyard and went back into the even deeper quiet of the church.

"I suppose I ought to be getting along," Mrs Flack said.

"Can I stop a bit longer, Mum?"

"Both stop!" said Finn. "Come along wit' Alfie and me to The House."

"The House? To see *him*?"

Mrs Flack was incredulous. No one in the Street ever visited Mister Rudge—it was almost a law of nature.

"Asked us, see," explained Finn. "And it's my belief he's glad of a bit of company these dark nights. What wit' those birds, and whatever."

"Go on, Lil," urged Alfred. "Come with us!"

She hesitated. There was no danger in going to see the old man, mad or not, with the rest of them there too. And old childhood fantasies about The House and its mysterious inmate rose up again to mingle with plain adult curiosity and make the prospect of actually seeing them almost irresistible.

"One in the eye for the others," she thought. "There's not one of 'em seen it, but Mrs Cottingham."

"Will you, Mum?" Edward begged. He had already begun to sense a change in her, and a visit to The House could only reinforce it, take it further.

"Well—I suppose . . ." she demurred, in a voice that indicated that with a little more urging she was willing to be won over.

"Settled then!" said Finn—and so it was.

At the gate of The House she had to be urged further. She stared ahead under the boughs of the elm towards the boarded door, and hung back.

"Oh, I don't know . . . there'll be Denis back before long."

"And you home in plenty of time and to spare," said Finn easily and took her arm and guided her, helpless, up the path with him. Finn banged the iron knocker. As they waited there were light footsteps and voices in the Street.

"Look at that, will you? And there's *Ma* Flack, as well!"

"Old Lily of the Alley going to the madhouse!"

"Look out—he's there!"—meaning Finn. The MacKays danced like boxers, poised on the balls of the feet ready for off at Finn's first move. He made none.

"Off wi' ye, devil's spawn!" he roared.

They broke and scattered but for only a few yards and then they were hovering again.

"Come here," invited Finn, "and I'll show you something!"

They shrieked nervously and kept on dancing. Then the door opened. Edward felt his mother's hand clutch at his sleeve.

"She's scared!" he thought, and straightened instinctively, being a tower of strength.

"Hello, Mister Rudge," he said rather loudly, showing off his own easiness.

The old man peered forward.

"It's Edward Flack."

"And me—and him—and her!" said Finn. "Good even to ye, Mister Rudge!"

They went in while he held the door. Again Edward glimpsed the stairs turning up into the darkness, the gleam and the richness. Then they were in the big front room with the books. Finn pulled out a chair for Mrs Flack and she sat down. The others followed suit. They sat in a silent circle in the dingy light. Mrs Flack seemed deliberately not to be looking at Mister Rudge (at whom she had longed all her life to have a good look) and to be looking, in fact, at anything *but* Mister Rudge. ("It's not manners, to stare.")

"My word," she exclaimed, being the first to be made uneasy by the prolonged silence, "what a lot of books!"

Mister Rudge nodded agreement.

"Don't you find they collect dust?" she asked. Then, without pausing for answer, "Gives the room a really old-fashioned look, all those books!"

Mister Rudge was nodding courteously but was evidently bewildered.

"Of course!" cried Edward. "You don't know her! This is my mother, Mister Rudge."

"Lily Flack," she supplied. "Pleased to meet you, I'm sure."

Mister Rudge made a little bow.

"I am honoured," he said.

He said it so simply and matter-of-factly and Mrs Flack could see so plainly that he actually meant it, that she was thrown into confusion.

"Oh, so am I!" she cried. "Ever so honoured! And very kind of you to forgive the intrusion—I shouldn't have come, only the others went on at me so. Ought to be going along and seeing about Denis's supper, I ought really, but there you are—here I am!"

Mister Rudge smiled vaguely and Edward saw that his mother spoke in so strange a tongue to him that she stood in need of an interpreter, almost. What did Mister Rudge in his clockless time-less world know of timetables and domestic rhythms, of shiftwork on buses and fish and chip suppers? What did he know, indeed, of anything outside his own head and The House? Edward's gaze travelled to the shelves of books.

"That," he thought. "He knows all that . . ."

Even so, he began to see that Mister Rudge was, in a sense, not entirely flesh and blood, because he lived removed from the world outside where everyone else went about their daily business. He knew, in a way, nothing. He could not for instance, Edward thought, know from a book how it felt to run in new snow, the soft grind under your feet and the dazzling blank ahead. Nor, for that matter, could he imagine the hot-aches that followed, the delicious yet excruciating dethawing. Mister Rudge had never travelled on top of a crowded bus and smelled stale tobacco smoke and wet clothes and wiped a spyhole on the misted glass for a bird's eye view of the town below. He did not know the warm vinegary smell of the chip shop, had never felt the stab of a sharp MacKay fist. Apart from the sights and sounds and smells of the world, he had never *felt* whatever nameless emotions they were that things like this gave you.

"He doesn't feel," he thought, "he only lives in his head." And himself felt an unexpected pity, because it seemed to him that books were a poor substitute for living.

"All right as *well*," he thought, because he read a great deal himself, "but not instead of."

And he wondered whether Mister Rudge had willingly given up the outside world of change and weather to go journeying into the clockless mirrorless country of the mind like an explorer, or whether it was perhaps an escape? It seemed important to Edward to know this. Because a man who could be made excited

136

and joyous and sad by the world, who could enter into it as a flesh and blood man does, could give it all up only if he were a hero. Not a hero of the same stamp as Patrick Finn, but a hero none the less.

"I couldn't do it," he admitted to himself.

He suddenly saw again, fondly, the sleepy pigeons, Hercules and Joan with their round-lidded eyes and sleek heads, and even smelled the chilly dew as he had known he would.

"Never!" he thought, and actually looked at the watch on his wrist to reassure himself that time did exist, for him if not for Mister Rudge.

He came out of his musings to find that the ice had been broken.

"There was a mark, on its head," Mister Rudge was saying, "as if from a blow."

"I never did!" cried Mrs Flack indignantly. "Shame! Whatever chance would a poor little thing like that have against one of those horrible tin things!"

"I wept, afterward."

Mister Rudge had not really heard her. He soliloquised because he was used to holding conversation only with himself.

Mrs Flack stopped in mid-flight, floored. Whatever was she to say to that? What an embarrassing remark! Wept? A *man*? Over a dead bird? She sneezed instead of answering and took out her handkerchief.

"Bless me," she remarked absently as she did so.

"Edward and me saw a dead bird as well, didn't we, Edward?" she went on then, almost cheerfully, determined to bring the conversation back within proper limits.

"I had no bread this morning," went on Mister Rudge, pursuing a line of thought that was at least parallel with Mrs Flack's. "And perhaps it was only that that made it seem that the birds are fewer. Fewer day by day."

Mrs Flack's parallel line of thought took a violent swerve and met Mister Rudge's head on.

"Ah, but they're not!" she cried triumphantly. "That's where you're wrong! There may've been two birds dead, but there's six live birds *more* that I know of, isn't there, Alfie? And six take away two is four, so there's four more!"

This simple piece of arithmetic left Mister Rudge uncomforted. It was doubtful that he even heard it.

"The steel birds of the night do not grow less." Edward felt

137

the now familiar prickle of the beginnings of terror. "They thicken like corn and are growing over the stars. And they hiss, as they come. Like this—"

He stopped, and made a long, loud hissing sound. It was extraordinary. They all sat straightbacked and staring on their hard chairs and watched the old man hissing. He broke off, covered his ears with his hands, and cried,

"They hiss, they hiss like snakes!" He took away his hands. He was talking to himself now. "I dread to look through my window, I dread the sight of them. I can do nothing to drive them off. They are of steel and can do harm, but may not be harmed themselves. They are implacable."

Silence followed.

"Our aerial," said Mrs Flack faintly at last. "I knew it!"

She was actually pale.

"*Now* she knows," Edward thought. "*Now* she is chilled to the marrow!"

"Courage, man!" cried Patrick Finn. "We are a match for the steel birds—you and I and all of us together!"

"I fear not." Mister Rudge spoke with bowed head.

"But we are!" insisted Finn. "Men, we are, and flesh blood, and only a little lower than the angels! And nothing in the whole world at all we cannot do, if we put our strength to't. Oh let us, let us fight 'em, man!"

"Oh yes, yes!" cried Edward, and Alfred echoed his words. Mister Rudge lifted his head and looked at them and the dullness had gone from his eyes.

"I almost begin to believe we could," he said slowly.

"Can," urged Finn. "Can!"

The very air of the room seemed electrified with possibility. Edward, tingling as he was with heroism, thought of the battle to come and remembered his question.

"Mister Rudge—the birds—must we fight them? I mean, really fight? You see, those pigeons—they've all got names, and we really love them, already. I don't want them to get killed."

"They will not be killed, I think," replied Mister Rudge. "They have only to be. That is enough."

"I thought so! I get it now—I really do! And the more of them the better—and the more of us!"

"That is true."

"What about the dead birds, then?" demanded Mrs Flack, in turn bewildered. "The ones we saw? They'd been killed, right enough."

138

Mister Rudge's face clouded.

"That—I do not understand," he answered. "That I had not reckoned on. And it may even be that I am mistaken. You must not think that I know everything there is to be known. No man knows. I know little—very little. It may even be that there will be a battle."

"Then we'll *do* battle!" exclaimed Finn.

"Nothing daunts him," thought Edward, even as he mourned inwardly for his gentle pigeons.

"I don't think I am afraid," said Alfred. The rest looked at him, surprised.

"I might have been, once," he admitted, "but now I would rather do battle with the invaders than go back to what I was before. I would rather *die* in battle."

"There's—there's no one going to *die*, is there?" Mrs Flack was horrified. She sneezed violently and it was as if the sneeze was itself a sign of horror.

"Bless me!" she cried urgently.

"We must all do our part," said Mister Rudge. "I to watch the night sky. I am the watchman, the guardian."

"And us to rear the birds," said Finn. "And we will! We'll see St Saviour's flying wit' birds like snow, bejam!"

"Edward!" said Mrs Flack through her handkerchief. "You remind me that in future all stale loaves out the shop go out to the birds!"

"Yes, Mum."

"*And* cakes!" she added recklessly.

"Yes, Mum." Then he sneezed.

"Bless you! You're sneezing!" she said. "It's to be hoped we're not sickening, the pair of us. Ashoo! Oh, bless me!"

Her eyes were streaming.

"C—could be the dust, I suppose," she went on.

Edward was horrified. He looked at Mister Rudge, who had not even heard.

"You want to be careful," Alfred told her. "You sound as if you've a cold coming on."

"The cold is coming on," said Mister Rudge. "The days shorten, the nights lengthen and the cold is coming. On New Year's Day, if those terrible birds have not gone from here, I shall give my warning."

"Come now," said Finn softly, rising. "Let us be gone and let the old man be."

Alfred and Edward got up and Mrs Flack was at the door before them.

"Goodnight, then, Mister Rudge," she said. "It's been a real treat."

At that moment there was a sharp crack on the window. They all jumped and Mrs Flack let out a little cry. They stared at the window but there was only darkness beyond.

"It sounded—like metal," quavered Mrs Flack.

"It was a stone," said Finn grimly. "I'll wring their necks, I will!"

He made to go.

"Ssssh!" Edward put up a finger. "Listen!"

They stood intent and heard, quite distinctly, coming from outside, a hissing. It stopped.

"Hssssssssss!" Old Mister Rudge still sat, and he hissed softly. "You hear it?"

They were all bemused, thrown into a kind of derangement by hearing the hiss with their own ears, by witnessing a mystery in which so far they had only half believed. They stood and strained and could neither move nor speak nor even think. They stood like statues, waiting. They must have waited for a full minute before Mrs Flack, never made happy by silences of any sort, spoke.

"I heard that!"—half awed, half incredulous. "With my own ears!"

No one contradicted her.

"It was *them*! Must've been! At—ishoo! Bless me! Oh my lord! Bless me!"

"Wait!" ordered Finn, coming to. He sprang to the door, was across the hall in a couple of strides, and flung open the front door. He stood scanning swiftly about. The others gathered behind him, peering past him.

" 'Twas them—I'm sure on it!" he said under his breath.

"Look sharp, Edward!"

His mother gave him a little push.

"We're off now, quick! Goodnight!"

She gave a nervous look upward as they reached the gate, and then was scurrying up St Saviour's Street towards home as fast as she could, sneezing as she went.

CHAPTER NINETEEN

❡ Being Some Of The Dreams Dreamed By Edward Flack Between November 11th And November 17th While He Was In Bed With Influenza

He was in the alley doing his feat of daring when the birds came. They came not in ones and twos but in thousands, hissing in a steel hail, and Edward crouched against the wall and watched while they plunged around him to roof and chimney. He was alone and thought he saw the full white moon behind the hail. A bird came to a wall right by him and he felt his heart hammer hammer hammer and would have screamed but the scream would not come.

Then he was walking in the Street under a brilliant moon. The birds had gone and the sky was quiet again. The doors of all the houses opened and people came out into the Street. It was utterly quiet. There was no sound of footsteps as the people came out straight and fixed and walking in a trance. The hush was so unearthly that it was as if the world had stopped. It was as if time had stopped and the ticking of the clocks. Edward saw faces that he knew but they did not know him or even seem to see him. He ran and ran and ran and was under the great elm of The House. There he crouched and his heart hammered hammered and he watched the people go by in the moonwashed Street absolutely soundless and with eyes straight ahead like sleepwalkers. Edward shivered and knew that they were not the people he knew at all but hollow men and made blind and cruel. He dared not show himself. He saw his mother go by with bleached face and dead eyes and wanted to move, but could not.

St Saviour's had gone. There was a gaping pit where the church had been. And then the whole Street was empty and Edward was alone and knowing that the moon was not a night moon but would shine forever and the houses be empty and the people gone forever and ever.

He came out from under the tree as a hero would and stood full in the light of the moon with a sword flashing in his hand. And he heard a faint hiss and stood fast and held up the sword and it caught a silver fire so he looked upward and saw that they were coming again and blotting out the moon and he ran and ran and ran . . .

He was in the countryside and still alone and the trees and hedges were bare and motionless. He looked about and saw only the dry winter landscape and there were no cows nor sheep nor birds nor any other living thing.

And then he heard a strange chant, a kind of lament, and he ran and hid in a ditch. All the people in the Street whom he had once known were approaching in a ragged file with blank eyes and dragging feet. They wailed and moaned and their voices went up and down in a weird music and their breath smoked in the frosty air. Past him they went in procession and they wore strange robes of greyish blue and their heads were uncovered and their mouths smoked white and he knew them all and yet they were strangers and he could not speak nor stretch out a hand nor make any sound or stir.

He lay in the ditch among the dry sticks and they wound past and up a hill and over the brow and slowly out of sight. He did not know what was over the hill nor why they were going and he dared not follow. The strange music of their wailing faded and there was utter silence.

Edward stood up. He held a sword. The fields were bare and dead. The air was empty. There was no birdsong and as he wheeled about the silence and the emptiness became so terrible that with a cry he flung away his sword in despair and darkness followed.

CHAPTER TWENTY

¶ *How Patrick Finn Became A Grocer For A Week, And How Hercules And Joan Turned Up Trumps*

It was a question, Edward thought, of whether heroes did heroic deeds even when they were ill. He lay racking his brains for an instance of a hero even being ill at all. Heroes did not tend to have things like influenza, they went in more for being sorely wounded or swallowing fiery draughts.

"You can't really do a bold and mighty deed when you're actually lying in bed," he thought, and was distracted for a while by wondering what a hero's bed would look like, as obviously it could not be an interior-sprung divan. He decided on a heap of goatskins and closed his eyes while he tried hard to imagine himself lying on rough fur. It was not easy. It was an effort even to imagine anything.

"I feel sorely wounded," he thought. "All over."

In the end he decided that if an emergency should arise—such as a python emerging from the goatskins or a deadly foe entering with lifted sword—then a wounded hero would deal with it at once. In the meantime, he would just lie there and read and doze like any other ordinary mortal who was sick.

"That's all right, then," he decided, secure in the knowledge that neither python nor deadly foe was likely to appear at a moment's notice at Number 47 St Saviour's Street.

Mrs Flack was being ill in the next room. It seemed to Edward that she was being very noisily ill. She was all the time calling out names, and for the first day or two Edward had himself been so ill that he had called back. He had called back nonsense, but it had not seemed to matter. Uncle Alfred had sat in the living-room, and gone from one patient to the other, soothing and giving hot drinks and straightening beds.

By now Edward was used to the strangeness of Uncle Alfred in the house. When he had first looked up and seen him bending over him in his tasselled waistcoat and pink shirt, Edward had thought it was all part of the nightmare, and once had even clutched at him with the sheer relief of finding himself no longer alone.

Finn, Edward knew, was down in the shop, playing grocer. He knew that he was only playing because of the laughter that kept floating up the stairs, and because the only way a true hero could serve butter and bacon and keep his heroic stature would be to make a game of it. It still worried Edward a little, and from time to time he would make a half-hearted attempt to visualise Hercules weighing out tomatoes or Robin Hood reckoning the till.

"I'm glad I'm in bed," he thought more than once. He did not want to see Finn playing grocer. Mrs Flack, on the other hand, evidently did. She kept shouting advice and instructions downstairs. Almost every time the shop bell rang she would call out,

"Who's that? Who's that?"

Alfred would look, and tell her, and then sometimes he had to carry down messages to Finn, who had no idea of the desperate cunning of his customers.

"Tell him to watch she don't try to give him out of date coupons on Instant Coffee!"

or,

"She'll tell him oranges are only three pence down the market, but you tell him to tell her to go and get 'em there, then! He's not to reduce 'em, tell him. I'd rather they went rotten!"

Edward had already gathered that takings were up since Finn had taken over. He was not surprised.

"If people knew who he was, there'd be a queue right down the Street," he thought, "down the Street and round the corner."

He was just beginning to feel well enough to be amazed how easily both Finn and Uncle Alfred had been absorbed into the Flack household. In the early stages of his illness the whole world had seemed confused and strange and the constant presence of Uncle Alfred and occasional glimpse of Finn had not struck him as out of place.

"Mum'll be grateful to him forever more," he thought with satisfaction. "If she could, I expect she'd shower him with gold and lavish gifts. She'd crown him with garlands."

Almost immediately the glow faded as he recalled the encounters he had had with the birds, the dreams that had not been dreams exactly, because they had had this curious clarity and reality. They had been real and yet unreal—as if a film he had been watching.

144

"Or visions," he thought, half fearfully. He was well aware that heroes had visions, from time to time, and so recognised that his recent experiences might show at least that he was making progress in his training for heroism. On the other hand, he did not feel very heroic when he remembered them. He felt afraid.

Finn's head appeared round the door.

"Asleep?" he asked. "The sleep ye've had, bejam, day and night alike! Better, are ye?"

"Much better, thank you."

"And better still when ye hear the news. Would ye like to hear some news o' the birds?"

"Birds?"

"Pigeons. Two particular on 'em. Guess the news, can ye?"

"Eggs!" Edward sat bolt upright. "They've laid some eggs!"

"So they have," nodded Finn, almost smugly, as if he himself had had a hand in it. "Oh yes. All of three eggs, and as proper and beautiful as ever I saw."

"Which ones? Who laid them?"

"Hercules laid 'em!" replied Finn triumphantly. "Which is to say Joan—Joan of Arc laid 'em, this very day. And ye can lie here and be thinking o' names for 'em, for names they'll be needing in three weeks, more or less."

"It's marvellous! Good old Hercules! I think I could get up now. I feel really well!"

"So ye do," agreed Finn, "so long as ye stop there. You stop there another day, and tomorrow ye shall get up, the pair of ye."

"Is Mum better, then? She sounds it."

"Your mother'll live, that's definite," said Finn. "And by the talk of her ye'd not believe she'd been ill at all. I like the spirit of her, I do indeed."

"Do you? Do you really?" Edward was amazed. That his mother should decide to like Finn was surprising, but that Finn should actually find something to admire in her was astounding. He felt thoroughly pleased, even proud of her.

"She knows what she's doing, all right," he told Finn offhandedly. "And I bet she's pleased about the pigeons—*her* pigeons."

"You'd be thinking she'd laid them eggs herself," affirmed Finn. "Like a mother with a new-born babe she'll be, when those eggs crack."

"She's never had a baby," said Edward. "She's not my real mother, you know."

K

"Is she not?" Finn was unperturbed. "That depending how ye look at it, of course. I'd say she was your mother, right enough, the way she's rearing you."

Edward said nothing, mainly because he was so surprised. He had made for himself such a secret picture of his beautiful and tragic mother, that to replace her once and for all with Mrs Flack was for the moment unthinkable, despite what Finn said.

All the same, he did think about it from time to time during the day, and in the evening he got out of bed and fetched the Monopoly set. His legs were trembling by the time he had done this.

"Weak as a kitten!" he thought. "Like Samson with his head shorn!"

He made an entry in the Chronicle because there had not been one since the 10th, and it was now the 17th, and he did not want to go down to posterity as a sluggard.

November 17th

I lift my pen although my hand is weak to record the events of the past week for posterity. I have been lying on my bed of sickness since last Sunday with a mortal fever which Uncle Alfred says was 'flu. Even now I feel as if I have been sorely wounded from head to foot. My mother was also smitten with this fever but is now much better and talking a lot.

I will first describe what happened last Friday before I fell mortally ill as it is quite important. The first thing was that Mum went to see the pigeons but really she was going to see Uncle Alfred as well. And the amazing thing is that they are now really friendly and call each other Alfie and Lil. They are reunited, like the Prodigal Son. Anyway, I said that she could have Hercules and Joan (of Arc) as her pigeons and she seemed really pleased about this and in fact was quite soppy about it when she actuerly saw them. As I have said before she certainly has a warm heart under her rough exteriour.

Then we all went to The House which is where the really important thing comes in. At first it was just like it usually is and Mister Rudge kept talking about the steel birds in what I call his creepy voice and Mum seemed to get on quite well with him though I do not think she has a clue what he is talking about half the time, not being used to soothsayers and oracles I suppose. But this time it was even worse than usual because Mister Rudge kept making hissing noises to show us the sound the birds make when they swoop down on the wires, and this really was enough

146

to chill anybody to their marrow. Even Mum was obviously chilled to hers and in fact this was when she first started sneezing.

Then just as we were going there was a mighty crack at the window. It sounded like metal and we all immediately thought of the steel birds except Finn who thought it was the MacKays chucking stones. (They were certainly hanging about outside when we went in and yelling names like Lily of the Alley and so on.)

Finn was about to go and see when there was this hissing noise from outside the window. It was really loud and we all stood rooted to the spot with terror and personally I felt the blood curdel in my veins. Only Mister Rudge did not seem surprised (with having heard it before I suppose) and he sat and hissed himself for a bit. When we went out Finn looked round for the MacKays but there was neither sight nor sound of them.

If this was indeed the birds of steel then the danger is increasing as normally these birds do not come till much later at night. I think it was meant as a warning to us. We must beware.

Obviously with lying on my bed of sickness I do not know the rest of the dire events which have taken place in the outside world. As I lay tossing I had strange and aweful dreams of the steel birds except that I do not really think they were dreams at all, but visions. They were visions of doom and I do not really wish to think about them and will not describe them here except to say that what I saw was like the end of the world, only worse.

Patrick Finn, like a true hero, stepped into the breech and has been looking after the shop for Mum. I record this as this is proberly a record. To my knowledge no other hero in history has ever done this before and only a really great hero would stoop to do such a thing. He has won Mum's heart with his nobleness and I am not surprised. He even said he thought Mum was all right and I suppose she is really. My trouble is that I tend to keep comparing her with my real mother who most proberly died of a broken heart after my real father was killed. I see now that this is a bit unfair on Mum.

The really great news I have lifted up my pen to record is that Hercules has laid some eggs though in fact of course it was Joan of Arc who actually laid them. When Finn told me this it almost banished my fears. He says they will hatch out in about three weeks and told me to think of some names which I have been doing. I have almost definitaly decided on Romulus and Remus and Florence (Nightingale). This of course is if there are two males and one female. I hope there are, as for one thing it is easier to think of hero's names than it is heroine's though on the other hand of course heroes cannot lay eggs.

This news has really gladdened my heart and I should think Mister Rudge will be as pleased as punch when he hears. After having had some dire and horrible visions of my own this last week I now know more how he must feel. It is a marvellous feeling to think that all is not lost and that Finn is our champion and that soon St Saviour's will be full of birds of the day. The right is on our side and we shall be victorious.

Tomorrow I can get up though obviously I shall not be going to school (or next week either with any luck) so I will go and look at the eggs and report on them. Who knows, by tomorrow there may be three more! (or even more!)

I now lay down my pen as I am weary to the bone. This is a true and faithful account.

Part Three

CHAPTER TWENTY-ONE

¶ *What Mister Rudge Said*

It is December now, they tell me. It is very cold, that is certain, and the days are dark. The days seem to have grown shorter all at once, but perhaps that is because I have been ill. Being ill was like being away for a long time—away from here, away from myself, even, in a curious way.

I had some terrible dreams while I was ill of the steel birds, but I had some beautiful ones too. I dreamed again that bells were ringing and people rejoicing and birds were flying in St Saviour's. The strange thing was that this time the birds were white. They were perfectly white and gentle and seemed to drift on the air rather than fly. That dream gave me great happiness, it comforted me. Each time I close my eyes I pray that I might have it again.

Since I was ill I have felt very weak. It is an effort for me to climb those steep stairs to the upper room, and yet I must because I am now the self-appointed guardian of St Saviour's and have a duty. The man called Finn is very kind. He and I say things to one another without speaking. While I was ill he often came and sat with me and we were silent together.

Since he has come things have altered. I am still alone and lead my life in my own way but now I feel for the first time that I am a part of the Street. He has brought me many things, fruit and flowers and even hot food, freshly cooked. And when I ask him who has sent these things he smiles and says, "Your neighbours". I like that. It is a good word, neighbour.

Sometimes the boy comes too, Edward Flack, and the other man. The boy gives me hope. His face is bright and shining and he talks to me of the pigeons, which he loves, and of their young that are soon to hatch. I have always been afraid of boys. I was afraid of them even when I was one myself. And the others, the ones who come to set fire to my house and who point and jeer, I am still afraid of them. They have not been lately. Or perhaps I did not hear them because I was ill. Edward Flack is not like these other boys and I have grown to be fond of him and to look forward to his coming.

Perhaps I should not have told him of the birds of steel, perhaps it was not a good thing to fill the mind of a young boy with such things. But he does not seem to be afraid. He believes that we shall be victorious over those terrible birds of the night, and when he is here I can even sometimes believe that myself.

But the days are shortening and the kingdom of those evil birds is widening day by day. I throw out loaves to the birds of the day and when they come, I try to count them, but it is hard to count birds. They do not stand in a row to be counted, and they do not even stay still for very long. And my eyes are not so good now so that I cannot tell one sparrow from another, though I could once. I have always loved birds. And so it is the more strange that my last days should have come to be haunted by those travesties of birds, birds that neither sing nor fly but run mechanically on wires. There is nothing more horrible that I could imagine.

Sometimes I have even wondered if I do imagine them. But if I do, then others have caught the contagion from me. They have heard them on the roofs, they have glimpsed the shining wires. The boy told me that he had seen them even as I have, in a steel hail. He said that it was in a vision, and of course if he spoke of it it would not be believed. But I believe in the truth of visions. The world of flesh and blood is not the only world.

I say this, and yet curiously I find myself now with a kind of hunger for the world of flesh and blood. It is not that exactly. It is *green* I hunger for. The Street is grey now and the elm is picked bare and some days I feel as if I would sell my soul to feed my eyes on green spaces. I long for distances. How very strange it all is. Here I am, having lived my life almost entire within the four walls of The House, and now at the end I long for distances.

Ah, well. I shall not see any, now. I must do as I have always done, live in the mind's eye. I must make my own distances, inside my own head, and my own green. It can be done.

CHAPTER TWENTY-TWO

¶ *How Patrick Finn Spread The Word And How Mrs Flack Began To Spread Her Wings*

"He's a lovely man," said Mrs MacKay with decision. "And though I'm Irish myself I'm bound to say it. A thoroughly lovely man—and never mind what them devil's spawn of me own say, neither!"

Edward, weighing butter and listening, was surprised to hear Mrs MacKay describe her own sons as "devil's spawn" (though admittedly he had heard her call them worse). He supposed that this made Mr MacKay the devil, and while he doubted this, it seemed likely that this was how his wife saw him, judging by the torrential abuse that streamed perpetually between them.

"Ah, well, boys will be boys," observed Mrs Flack judicially.

Edward was equally surprised by this remark, though not so surprised as he would have been a week or two earlier. His mother, there could be no doubt about it, was changing.

"Transformed," he thought. "Transmogrified. Smelted in the fire!"

The reason for the change was equally clear. It was Finn.

"He is bursting her fetters!" he thought. "He bursts everybody's. He's even bursting mine."

Now that Finn had himself served in the shop, and even now came in for an hour or two every day to help out, Edward found that he himself was beginning to enjoy it. Things were not the same. For one thing, at least twice as many people came in than ever before, and twice as often. And when they did come in, they talked—properly talked—not just remarks about the weather or the disgraceful price of eggs, but real conversation. Mrs MacKay was a case in point. Formerly she would not come to the shop at all if she could avoid it, having made widely known throughout St Saviour's her view that the goods were overpriced and that the shop itself had a funny smell. She was now actually sitting on the rickety chair by the counter while Mrs Flack busied herself with the longest grocery list Mrs MacKay had ever written.

153

"He's a lovely man," she said again now, determined that the point should be thoroughly made.

"Oh, he is," agreed Mrs Flack, "and I'm glad you can see it, Mrs MacKay. With him being such a close friend of the family, we like to think he's well thought of."

"Been a friend of the family long, has he?" enquired Mrs MacKay.

"Not altogether long," conceded Mrs Flack, "but very close to Alfred he is. You might almost say he's *part* of the family now."

"And that's another thing," said Mrs MacKay. "The change there's been in your brother, Mrs Flack, is altogether astonishing."

"Oh, it is," Mrs Flack agreed. "And there again, there's plenty might disapprove. There's plenty might say he should've stopped in his office and got on in life in the ordinary way—he was getting on very well, you know."

"Oh indeed, Mrs Flack! *Must've* been! The head he's got for figures!"

"But there's more to life than getting on, you see," went on Mrs Flack, "just the same as beauty's more'n skin deep. I mean, his clothes did seem a bit queer at first, and I don't mind admitting it."

"Oh, I like them!" Mrs MacKay had a distinctly gypsyish appearance herself and did most of her shopping for clothes at jumble sales. "And I'm delighted he's come back to St Saviour's, I am really. Delighted. A family's best to stick together, and even if you've the luck of a boozing, good-for-nothing husband like mine and sons like to turn out as bad or worse!"

"Oh, I don't know . . ." murmured Mrs Flack. "Not that bad, Mrs MacKay."

"Worse!" affirmed Mrs MacKay with force. "And when I heard what them little devils had done that night to that poor old gentleman at The House, I thought I should've dropped dead of mortification!"

Mrs Flack contented herself with tutting sympathetically.

"Tanned the hides off 'em I did, mind," Mrs MacKay continued with satisfaction. "Black and blue, when I'd done with 'em, and'll not be doing *that* again, little devils! I'll not have fellow creatures done harm to at *my* house, thank you very much! And the old gentleman," she lowered her voice, "to think on it! When Mr Finn was telling me I could scarce believe me own ears! To think

154

on it! To think of the way folks round here have treated that poor old gentleman all these years and calling him mad and Lord alone knows what all else, and all the while him a saint straight out o' heaven, more or less!"

"I know," said Mrs Flack. "And to think we might never have known, if it wasn't for him."

"About the birds!" whispered Mrs MacKay in a hoarse whisper. "Oh—when Mr Finn told me about them terrible birds I thought I should've dropped straight down dead. Hot and cold from head to foot I went."

"Heard about them from the old gentleman himself I did, of course," boasted Mrs Flack. "And I'm bound to say he's a thoroughly educated person, and as to being mad, the last thing possible. The *books* he's got—you'd not believe. Oh, he's a gentleman, right enough, no doubt of that."

"It's my belief," confided Mrs MacKay, "that he's got the *sight*! Oh yes. Not a doubt of it—me grandmother herself had it on me mother's side, and the things she saw! Not birds, mind, never heard o' her mentioning birds, but there's not the least doubt in the world that if Mister Rudge can see them terrible, evil, skulking birds on the chimney pots of a night—them birds are there, Mrs Flack. Whether you nor me nor anyone else at all can see 'em, they're there. Oh yes. They're there."

"Oh dear!" cried Mrs Flack. "I know! Oh, you're setting me off again, Mrs MacKay—the thought of it!"

Edward himself felt a slow shudder, and made himself remember the pigeons. In less than a week Joan of Arc would have a brood—Romulus and Remus and Florence (Nightingale). Only a few days later Theseus and Grace Darling would have a hatching—again, of three. David and Bathsheba, for some reason, were slow in coming round to the idea of a family. None the less, within the fortnight there would be twelve pigeons in the graveyard instead of six.

"A real flock," he told himself.

"Wonderful idea of Finn's, o' course, the pigeons," he heard his mother say, as if she too had gone straight to the thought of the pigeons for comfort. "Won't be long now before there's one or two happy events in the graveyard."

"He's a lovely man," affirmed Mrs MacKay yet again. "Only he could've thought of it."

Whether irritated by Mrs MacKay's possessive eulogising of Finn, or by the inference that she herself was a mere passive instrument in the matter, Mrs Flack was prompted to make an entirely unforeseen and astonishing remark.

"Getting a couple of pair of my own, tomorrow, as a matter of fact," she said offhandedly.

"A couple o'—?" prompted Mrs MacKay, puzzled.

"Pair. Of pigeons. Thought I'd keep 'em in the yard—plenty of room. And the more the better of course."

Edward stared dumbly at his mother. Was she serious? He guessed that the remark had been made impulsively, and some instinct warned him that he must not appear to be surprised. He returned his attention to the butter and incised it with the deliberation of a surgeon.

"Oooh!" Mrs MacKay was suitably impressed. "Well—fancy! Should never've thought of you in connection with pigeons, Mrs Flack."

"Oh, I've always had a soft spot for them," Mrs Flack told her.

This, at least, was truthful, and all at once she glowed with pleasure at the thought that at last she was to have some, of her very own, something she would never have dreamed of, but which had all the time been possible—if only she had allowed herself to dream of it. She went on, speaking her thoughts aloud,

"I've plenty of wooden crates that'll serve for nesting boxes and I daresay Edward'll tack me some wire over, and that. And I think I'll have two pair, just to start with, and one pair I shall call Sweet and Pretty—yes, I shall, and the other pair I shall have to think about."

"Perseus and Andromeda!" said Edward instantly, to forestall any further disastrous suggestions of her own.

"Oh, go on!" cried Mrs Flack. "You and your funny names! You'd never *believe* the names he's got for them there birds. Sound more like *Popes* than birds—I don't know where he gets his ideas, I don't really. Anyhow, I shall have the two pair, as I was saying."

"It'll be very nice," said Mrs MacKay.

"Well, it's like I said, the more the better. And it is a bit urgent, you know. Something to do with New Year's Day. It's no good shilly-shallying about. And of course, it's nice to know you're doing your bit."

"Got room in the yard for some meself, come to think," said Mrs MacKay jealously. "I shall have to see what Mr MacKay says."

"Lovely!" cried Mrs Flack generously.

156

She was to have pigeons of her own at last, and begrudged no one else in the world the same happiness.

"That *would* be good of you, Mrs MacKay, if you could see your way to it. Finn'd be thoroughly pleased, I know, and Mister Rudge as well."

"I *shall*, then!"

Mrs MacKay, never slow to kindle, caught fire.

"And never mind what that drunken fool of a husband of mine says! *I'll* have two pair!"

"That's marvellous!" said Edward. "It really is."

"And the first thing I do when I get home," she went on, "I'll set to and find the catapults them devil's spawn've got hid about the place, and break them over their heads, I will!"

Catapults. Edward had a swift picture of the dead bird he had seen on the pavement that Sunday in November, and of the other lifeless heaps of feathers he had found about the Street in the last few weeks. Was it, after all, the MacKays who were responsible, wreaking vengeance on Finn and Mister Rudge? Was it then really impossible for those cruel birds to savage the living with their iron beaks? He did not know. What he did know was that St Saviour's was caught now in a mounting tension between night and day, good and evil, that must be resolved one way or the other by New Year's Day. And he knew that the pigeons were helping, were weighting the balance on the right side.

"Will that be all now?" enquired Mrs Flack. "Or were you wanting me to put something aside again for the old gentleman?"

"Of course!" cried Mrs MacKay. "Poor old man—ill and all, and no one to care. What'd he fancy, d'ye think? A tin of pilchards, d'ye think, what about that?"

"Very nice. Put it down, shall I? He liked the sardines Mrs Farrands sent him Tuesday last. Fond of fish, likely."

"Put down a tin o' pilchards and a packet o' them crackers ye've got on offer," ordered Mrs MacKay recklessly. "And give him my best, will ye, if ye see him, and tell him that if I hear o' them brats o' mine giving him trouble, *I'll* give 'em fire, I'll set fire to their tails, for sure I will!"

"I'll tell him," promised Mrs Flack, while recognising perfectly the unlikelihood of her delivering any such message.

"*Here* he is!" exclaimed Mrs MacKay as the shop bell rang and Finn came in with a gust of cold and winter air.

"Good day to ye, Finn!"

"Good day to ye, Martha. Give a hand, shall I, Lily?"

"It'd be nice," she said, pleased.

"And how're them beautiful birds of yours going on?" enquired Mrs MacKay.

Mrs Flack, seeing her chance of the limelight, stepped in.

"A hand for half an hour'd be real handy, Finn, if you could manage it. Got one or two things to see to, you know. I don't believe I mentioned to you about the birds I'm to have?"

"Birds?" Finn echoed.

"Pigeons. Two pair. In the yard out the back. Edward's to make me some boxes, you see, and the sooner we get on the better."

"Sweet Jaysus," said Finn solemnly. "I take me hat off to ye, Lily Flack!"

"And me!" cried Mrs MacKay. "Two pair *I'm* having!"

"Glory Hallelujah!" Finn threw up his hands.

Then, incontainable, he seized the astonished Mrs MacKay and whirled her about the tiny shop in a triumphant caper.

"Glory Hallelujah!" he shouted again and abruptly letting go he was behind the counter in a couple of strides and going through the same performance with a crimson-faced Mrs Flack.

"She's dancing! In wild abandon!"

Edward, mazed, watched. Mrs Flack, who was proper and strait-laced and knew what was what, was dancing with a wild red-haired Irish giant whose beads and fringes had gone into frenzy, and she was actually crying at the top of her voice (or as near the top as she was able to find after such long disuse),

"Glory Hallelujah! Glory Hallelujah!"

Edward searched for a classical parallel, for the heroic counterpart. He could not think of one. For once, words had failed him.

"Crikey!" he had to content himself with thinking. "*Crikey!*"

CHAPTER TWENTY-THREE

¶ *How Fate Dealt A Mighty Blow And Patrick Finn Proposed A Taxi Ride*

The weather turned from wet to a bitter cold and the wind was in the east. Everyone on the pavements seemed to be hurrying, head bent and shoulders hunched. Christmas was only a fortnight away and the shops were rich and warm and brilliantly lit. Already silver trees glistened in front windows, and the carol singers were out.

In St Saviour's the chief carol singers so far were the MacKays, who peddled their lusty Christmas messages as relentlessly as they had wheeled their guys. They had voices oddly sweet for villains, and from a distance at least were an appealing sight, grouped under some street lamp, hands deep in pockets and mouths rounded in song. They sang Once In Royal David's City and We Three Kings almost non-stop, because their own market research had proved that these particular two brought in more money than any of the others. As Christmas drew nearer they ranged ever farther afield from St Saviour's into the town. St Saviour's had had the MacKay carols since the last week in November, and goodwill was wearing thin.

Edward was not surprised to see them when he came out of the pet-shop in Trinity Walk. He had gone there straight after school to buy special food for the pigeons. Finn was worried about the young—Romulus, Remus, Florence (Nightingale), Hiawatha, Hereward and Helen (of Troy). They were only a few days old and barely feathered and thin. Edward himself had privately thought them a disappointment once the initial thrill of the hatching was over. They did not seem to have the makings of heroic pigeons. A customer of Mrs Flack's who had kept birds as a boy had told Finn that he was probably feeding them wrongly.

"Then we'll feed 'em right, bejam!" he had cried, and so Edward had been sent on his present errand.

It was dusk as he hurried back towards St Saviour's, a heavy paper carrier in each hand. The town was lit and exciting, it actually seemed to smell of Christmas, cold and pungent, yet fruity. It was like chrysanthemums. And overlaying it was the equally heady smell of fog, because the wind had dropped and left an extraordinary stillness into which the mist was stealing. All the people had white smoking mouths. The sound of carol singing made it all even better.

Edward did not recognise the MacKays until he was almost up to them, because they were singing The Holly And The Ivy, which was a new departure for them. Dave MacKay spotted him first and nudged Mike who nudged Pat who nudged Pete, and they all kept singing with their eyes fastened on him. Edward grinned at them, delighted that they were in mid-song and power-less to do anything but follow him with their eyes.

Oh the rising of the sun
And the running of the deer,
The playing of the merry organ,
Sweet singing in the choir!

He was past them now and they pivoted to watch him go, and Pat shook the collecting box hard as they launched into the second verse.

Edward was half-way home when they caught up with him. They came up silently out of the fog and walked along in step, flanking him on either side.

"Please to put a penny in the old man's hat!" Pat shook the collecting box under Edward's nose. "Come on—ten pence—let's have it!"

"Not likely."

"Go on—a penny, then!"

"No, I said."

"Hasn't got one," said Mike. "Or shall we turn him upside down and see?"

"I've got one, all right," Edward said. "I'm just not giving it you lot. Come off it."

"What you got in there, then?"

"Seed. Corn."

"Oooh, for the dickies! Hey—what about it? What about them steel birds—sons of Dracula! Seen 'em, have you?"

"As a matter of fact I have. In a way I have, anyhow."

"*We* seen them!" hissed Pat MacKay, dancing ahead to peer into Edward's face. "Ain't we?"

"All of us," said Mike. "Screeching down like bloody bats!"

Edward kept walking. They were turning on to St James's Street now.

"And hissing—hisssssss!" All four of the MacKays began a loud hissing, thrusting their faces into his, boggling their eyes.

"Pack it in," he said. "And it's not a joke, anyhow."

The MacKays kept up their hissing and Pete began to zoom his hands down to within an inch of Edward's face in imitation of birds, and then actually caught him in the eye so that he blinked, tripped, and was down on the cold ground. The bags flew out of his hands. He lay for a second seeing the corn spreading about him and then the MacKays cheered and began to holler, and jumped up and down on the bags so that the remaining seed spurted out in little jets. Edward reached and grasped the nearest ankle and brought Mike MacKay down on top of him. Edward threw him off, rolled away, and was on his feet, fists up.

"All right! Come on then! You and me—and keep out of it, the rest of you!"

He received the first punch before the words were out of his mouth, but he dealt two swift ones of his own and felt a surge of exultation because he knew this fight was going to be different. Whether it was that heroism had begun to rub off on him from Patrick Finn, or whether it was the memory of Mister Rudge's pale frightened face at the upper window that night in November, or even the spilt corn that slithered now under his feet, he did not know. But he fought as never before, and the yells of the three watching MacKays gradually died off and at last they were fighting in silence but for their own breathing and the soft thud of blows.

"A bloody nose a bloody nose a bloody nose!" Edward's mind was repeating, and then it came—a hard straight right, a yell, and surrender. Mike had stepped back, both arms up to shield his face, and as he took them away there was the blood—seeming even more than there was because the sleeves had smeared it over his whole face. The three onlooking MacKays turned as one and went off, skimming the pavement, and their brother, with a final disbelieving swipe of his sleeve across his nose, followed.

Edward stood panting and watched them as they dwindled into the fog. Then they were round the corner and out of sight and earshot and already the triumph was fading. He looked down and saw the corn, hopelessly scattered and wasted now, and thought,

"They won, really."

He walked on and left it. He suddenly realised that he did not feel any better after winning his first real fight with a MacKay than he had felt on the countless other occasions when he had lost.

L

He felt just as aching, sick and dizzy as he had always done. He went to the church, not just because it was on the way home, but because he wanted a sight of Finn. He thought that if perhaps he told him about the bloody nose he had just given Mike MacKay it would make it seem more heroic, more of a victory.

The minute he stepped into St Saviour's he lost the smell of the fog, exchanged it for the now familiar dust and stone odour and the different cold. He had become used to the space and the bareness and silence, and liked it. By now he even knew the green and gold men among the flowers on the tall stained window, their calm eyes and serious profiles. Tonight they were near invisible in the gloom, there only because he knew they were there.

Finn and Alfred had moved into the vestry now for warmth, though as often as not Edward would find them in the church itself, sometimes alone, sometimes together. Alfred would roll himself in a blanket and lie on his back on a pew, staring up at his roof, and Finn would be at the organ. Both were lost to the world, and Edward would creep up unnoticed to one of the front pews, and lose himself with them.

Today there was no sign of either. He opened the door into the vestry and peered in. He could make out Uncle Alfred, seated in the near darkness on a crate, head buried in his hands. He hesitated.

"Come in, lad."

He straightened and lowered his hands.

"Gone dark," he said. "I can hardly see you."

"Are you all right?" Edward asked. "Is it your head again?"

"No. No, not my head."

"Oh. Good. Is Finn at the shop?"

He nodded.

"Something awful's happened!" blurted Edward. "The corn and that—for the pigeons. The MacKays came at me and the whole lot's been spilt—you couldn't even sweep it up. And it cost a pound—over a pound!"

"I can give you another," said Alfred. "But there's worse than that I've to tell you."

"Worse? What?"

"You mustn't be too upset," said Alfred. "It was the cold, Finn says. That and wrong feeding. Should've found out more about it, I suppose, instead of getting carried away."

"Oh—the pigeons! Not the babies? They're not—?"

"Two of them. Two out of three of the first ones."

"Romulus and Remus," thought Edward dully. He remembered how bare they had been, how tiny their bones through the pink skin. The real Romulus and Remus had survived cold and starvation to be suckled by a wolf.

"I'm sorry about it," said Alfred awkwardly. "I'm sorry for all our sakes, but I know they meant a lot to you. You mustn't be too upset."

"I'm not," said Edward. But he was.

"Found them this afternoon. And I'm afraid—well, we don't really much like the look of the others, either."

"Oh no! Not all of them! Let me look!"

"Here—let me get the lamp. We'll both go."

They took the lamp and went through the other door and into the graveyard. The railings were only faint lines in the fog and a white mist seemed to rise from the ground and wreathed stones, and the chill within those high walls was bitter, piercing.

"It's freezing!" Edward's teeth actually chattered. "No wonder they——"

"The wind, Finn says." Alfred led the way, yellowing the mist. "That east wind that got them. Got a book on it now. Keep well protected from draughts, it says."

"Oh Hercules!"

Edward knelt before the crate and saw the pigeons. The two of them turned their heads and looked into the light and it seemed to him that their eyes were not only woeful, but reproachful.

"Oh damn!" he cried softly and wiped his hand over his eyes. Then he saw something else. It lay in the corner of the box on top of the straw and it was dead. For an instant he was right inside the life of those two silently gazing birds, could feel the cold they felt, almost feel the stab of the sharp straw.

"It was our fault!" he cried. "Oh, I'm sorry, I'm sorry!"

The pity he felt for the pigeons was stronger than that he felt for himself, or for the others, stronger even than the fear. St Saviour's would not be full of flying birds when the tide of the year turned. Their plan, brave and glorious as it had seemed, had failed.

"There's no time now," he thought. "Less than three weeks to go."

He lifted his head instinctively to look for the lighted window of The House, but it was hidden from him by the fog. A sudden thrill of terror ran through him.

"The fog!" he gasped, standing up. "Oh—the fog! He won't be able to see!"

Old Mister Rudge would sit vainly at his window tonigth straining into the dark, and the steel birds would be invisible, their glitter blanketed, their hissing muffled. Tonight there could be an invasion, without warning. The cold and the dark and the deathly hush of fog were all at once too much, and he made back for the door.

They stepped inside just as the door opposite opened and Finn stood there.

"Oh Finn! What shall we do?"

"Poor boy," said Finn softly. "Poor boy, now don't ye be worrying about a thing."

"But it's failed! We'll never win now!"

"Aye, well, that's how it'd seem," agreed Finn. "But then things are not always what they seem to be, d'ye see. The taxi—remember the taxi!"

"But that's different!"

"Oh no," Finn told him, "it's not. It's one and the same thing entirely. Alfred'll tell you. Took a taxi—or thought he did—and stayed alive. Isn't that so, Alfie man?"

"It's true," said Alfred. "You want to listen to him, Edward."

"It's just—I feel so trapped!" burst out Edward. "I think it must be the fog, coming down so suddenly. I feel as if—it seems as if St Saviour's is—oh, cut *off*, as if the rest of the world has gone—disappeared, and there's just us left. And the steel birds—Mister Rudge won't be able to see them, and——"

"Then perhaps they won't come," suggested Finn.

"You don't—but you don't think he's making it all *up*!" cried Edward. "He's not—I know he's not!"

"Oh no," agreed Finn. "Not making it up. But leave things a bit—wait, will ye? Ye mustn't be afraid."

"I'm not afraid. I'm not."

Edward was used to telling himself this even when it was not true. Because even if he did feel afraid, the fact that he denied it at least made him braver, if not exactly fearless.

"And I'll tell ye what," Finn went on, "I've hit on a treat for us all. Altogether time we had a treat, it is. We'll take a taxi out of it for a day, all of us. How'll that be?"

"Your taxi"?

"Mine. All arranged. Your mother'll have Mrs Farrand to see to the shop Saturday, and we'll go and we'll give the old man a real treat—a glimpse of green, for it's that he's pining for."

"Mister Rudge? *He'll* go?"

"We'll go to the country—and glad of a sight of it I'll be meself. And we'll see green and we'll see birds, and it'll put new heart into us, bejam! And we'll have a picnic—aye, that's it— a picnic!"

"A Christmas picnic!" exclaimed Edward, and then he laughed, because he had to.

CHAPTER TWENTY-FOUR

¶ *Being The Letter Mrs Flack Wrote To The* Haunton Post *On December 13th And Which The Editor, Having Glanced First At The Signature And Then At The First Two Sentences, Dropped In His Wastepaper Basket With The Two Words: "Her Again!"*

Dear Sir,

I did in fact write to you concerning the present subject in November and was surprised that you did not see fit to publish this letter in the *Post*. But no doubt you noted its contents and passed them on to the Department concerned. I also regret to say that I have heard nothing whatever yet from any department at all which does lead you to wonder what we are paying rates for.

As you know Planning Permission has been given to pull down St Saviour's Church and erect a supermarket and my views on this are already known. But since this happened the steel birds I wrote you about last month have been getting more and more in number. I have not actually seen them myself, I am glad to say, as I do not think my nerves would stand this being in a very bad state as it is what with one thing and another. (One thing being that I have recently had a bad attack of flu and another being my TV aerial having to be replaced as a result of these terrible birds on the roof, and also by the way several other TV aerials in the area.) But a gentleman who lives in St Saviour's has seen these birds and has warned us that the situation is getting rapidly worse. It has been foggy for the last two days as you know and heaven knows what has been going on in the sky during this time.

However the people in St Saviour's you will be pleased to hear are not ones to sit by and watch things going from bad to worse without taking action. As a result of a suggestion from a friend of my family, Mr Patrick Finn, the residents of St Saviour's have been making an all-out effort to raise as many birds as possible in retaliation. These are pigeons mainly though a few of the Old Age Pensioners have been getting budgies and canaries as being less trouble for old people and also a bit of company. I myself have two pair of pigeons, Sweet and Pretty, and Darby and Joan, who you will be glad to hear are both expecting happy events in the near future.

I think you can say that there is hardly anyone in St Saviour's who is not doing their bit one way or another. There is a very good spirit among us such as there has not been, as many people have been remarking, since the war. We are all pulling together.

But the fact remains that we are up against something really terrible and unknown and do not know what the end of it all will be. What I would therefore like to suggest is that this letter should be published in your paper as a kind of St Saviour's Appeal, the object of this being that as many people as possible should donate birds to help us in our battle.

My brother who is at present not employed owing to his health but is an extremely clever man has said that he will be willing to look after the birds received. He has now read several books on the subject and is becoming quite an expert though obviously we did make some mistakes at first.

The Season of Goodwill is almost here and I feel sure that many of your readers will want to give generously, especially as people are not as often called upon to give birds as they are to give money, the latter obviously being in very short supply at this time of year. They could rest assured that they would be going to good homes and well looked after. Whole sliced loaves, as well as sponge and fruit cakes, scones etc are at present being fed to birds in this area which will give you some idea of it.

Finally I should like to say that in St Saviour's we are still not in agreement with the church being pulled down to make way for a supermarket for which there is no real need. My brother, Alfred Graves, feels very strongly about this although he has no axe to grind whatsoever and has asked me to say that he thinks it would be a crime, not to mention blasphemy, and that he may very likely organise a petition against it himself, despite the failure of previous attempts.

As you will see the people of St Saviour's do not take things lying down and are determined to stand together come what may. Thank you in anticipation of dealing with my request.

Yours faithfully,

Lily Flack (Mrs)

CHAPTER TWENTY-FIVE

¶ *Being Entries Made By Edward Flack In The Chronicle Of St Saviour's*

I lift up my pen with a heavy heart to record what has happened this week in St Saviour's. All the baby pigeons have now died except Hiawatha who must have been stronger than the others. They died partly because we were not feeding the pigeons on the right things and partly because of the east wind as they are supposed to be kept out of draughts. So really it is our fault. But Finn says that we shall now move them into the church itself if there are any more young and even Mum agreed with this though normally she would definately have said this was blasphamy. Her two pairs have both got eggs and if they hatch out sucessfully I only hope she will give them proper names as the ones she has picked so far have been really embarassing.

Dad laughs at her and I am bound to record that really he does not seem to have entered into the spirit of what is transpiring at all. I do not think he believes in the steel birds and he just goes off to the buses as usual and it is really funny to think that Mum turned out to be trumps instead of him. I am bound to say that I am surprised at this. She really does seem to have changed at least in some ways though obviously in other ways she is exactly the same as she always has been like nagging at Dad and me etc.

What I must also record is that Finn has wrought a mighty change in St Saviour's. It just is not the same place. He has elloquently talked nearly everyone into getting birds of one kind or another. The MacKays have got some pigeons and their mother said she would break their catapults over their heads if she found them and I hope she did. Old Mrs Parker has got a budgie and is teaching it to talk. Obviously birds like this would not stand a chance in an actual combat but from what I gather it will not be like this. I am bound to record that I cannot imagine there being an actual combat as the mind boggles at the thought.

Mister Rudge is not at all well and does not say much when you go round there. He seems very far away. I think he tells Finn more than he tells me which is not surprising as no doubt he realises by now that Finn is a true hero. He even tells Finn his dreams. Finn says he is longing for green, and so on Saturday we are all to go in the taxi to feed his eyes on verdant pastures and have a Christmas picnic. He says it will do him good to see all the birds there and also to see that St Saviour's is not the whole world though obviously it must seem like that to him as he has not been out of it for years. We are going to have a picnic and Finn says he will take his stove and fry sausages and things. It will be a feast fit for heroes.

It seems queer to think that it is nearly Christmas as this year there are other mighty happenings in store, you can feel it in your bones. Mister Rudge keeps talking about New Year's Day and obviously he thinks this will be when St Saviour's goes into the crucible to be transformed, and the steel birds must be defeated, vanquished never to return. The thought fills me with dire terror.

Talking of dire terror I have now devised a new daily feat of daring. The point is that obviously I cannot go round the alleys and past St Saviour's etc like I used to as this does not really frighten me enough now to count as an ordeal. But if I am to be honest I am still rather afraid of the dark and so what I have devised is a new route for me to go in the dark. It really is horrible. I go down St Saviour's away from the church and then turn left at the bottom and come back along by the canal. The factories are all in darkness and the water glints black and fearsome and the tall chimneys rise into the sky and of course there is not a human soul in sight. This route would have been bad enough before I knew about the steel birds and the point is that if the birds *did* come, for one thing those tall chimneys are the first thing they would alight on and in the second place if they attacked me no one would hear my shrieks of terror and despair. I would be like Leda and the swan. There is no doubt that this is a real trial of strength for me and the way I can tell this is how marvellous I feel when I come out from the canal path on to St James's again. I feel as if I have been through fire.

Some people might not see any point in me doing all this and I certainly would not tell anyone about it, not even Finn, at least not yet. But if for instance you want to be a pianist you have to do five finger exercises before you can play symphonies and so on, and it is the same if you want to be a hero. The only difference being that I have to make up my own five finger exercises.

But since I have met Mister Rudge and got to know him a

bit (not very well because I do not think anyone could ever get to know Mister Rudge very well, not even Finn) I have had a bit different ideas about being a hero. Which is to say that it is not just to do with being strong and brave in the sense of doing mighty feats of daring but being courageous in another way—more inside your own head, in a way. When I beat Mike MacKay, for instance and gave him a bloody nose (which he certainly asked for) I thought that I would feel absolutely marvellous and triumphant. But I did not. In a way I felt really let down though obviously it was nice to win for once in a way. But Mister Rudge could never have beat Mike MacKay in a fight, that is certain. He would fall like corn before the sickle. And yet the queer thing is that I know for a fact that Mister Rudge is a hero and that Mike MacKay is not. Mike MacKay is just a good fighter (not to mention a bit of a dirty one at times) and that is all. And just being a good fighter does not make a hero. If it comes to that, I have not seen Finn dealing deadly blows in a fray, the nearest being the time when he banged the MacKays' heads together and tossed them into the graveyard to ponder on their misdeeds.

In my opinion, what makes people like Finn and Mister Rudge a hero is more to do with what goes on inside their heads, and I am bound to say that this gives me fresh heart. I am not really a good fighter. But if you are not daunted, if you keep a stout heart and do not count the cost, then this can make you into a hero. Finn was not daunted by Mum for instance, and he won her over, and now he has won the whole of St Saviour's over. And Mister Rudge is nothing daunted by the sky full of birds of steel, even though he sees them night after night and they haunt his darkest dreams. He is not afeared of living alone and going on journeys in his own mind, he has the courage to toss his clocks and mirrors to the four winds and go journeying alone into time and space. And I think that this is what it means to be a hero. It means to have courage to go your own way undaunted even if the whole world is against you.

And the funny thing is that in the end perhaps the whole world is not against you. Take Mister Rudge for instance. Up till last month everyone in the Street thought he was absoluteley mad and called him names like St Francis especialy when he started throwing out whole loaves to the birds. But now people take notice of him and what he says, even Mum says she thinks he is a really marvellous old man and the whole Street looks up

170

to him. They are organising a Christmas hamper for him and everyone is giving things as a surprise for him. I have seen the box Mum is keeping things in and there is ham and Christmas pudding and cake and crackers and butter and mincemeat and baked beans and turkish delight and jelly and even tinned sausages. I bet his heart will really rejoice when he opens it—I know mine would.

I seem to have rather got off the point of the Chronicles of St Saviour's in all this but in a way it has got something to do with it. I think that if you are going to write something for posterity then you have got to write the truth and I can solemnly swear that what I have written above is the truth. I think that I have grown up quite a lot since I first started training to be a hero and writing this Chronicle. I now think that being a hero is more to do with holding fast to good and standing firm against evil than to do with slinging stones, fighting dragons and strangling snakes etc (though I suppose you could say that dragons and snakes etc are evil). Not that I do not think you have to be courageous. I do, and that is why I still do my daily feat of daring. You must pass through the fire to become tempered steel.

No one knows what will transpire in the next week or two not even Mister Rudge although he is obviously a soothsayer or oracle. But even though our brave and glorious plan with the pigeons has failed and come to naught I still believe that we shall vanquish those terrible birds of steel. Even Mum has girded up her loins. We shall not fail.

CHAPTER TWENTY-SIX

¶ *How Mister Rudge Took A Taxi In Search Of Green*

"I thought I'd just warn you, that's all," Edward said. "I've only been with him once, and he might just have been having an off day."

"I'm sure Finn's a lovely driver," said Mrs Flack firmly. "There's plenty about these days don't know how to drive, and I expect it was them getting in his way."

Edward said no more.

"She'll find out soon enough, bejam!" he thought. He peered into the capacious black zip-up bag that was serving as picnic hamper.

"Did you remember the sausages?"

"Yes I did. And there's enough stuff in there to feed an army so there's no need for you to go poking about messing things up. You won't starve."

"They're here!" Edward crossed to the window for the twentieth time that morning just as the taxi drew up with a squeal and a blowing of the horn. The road and pavements were white with frost and Finn's head, poking out from the window, the more fiery by contrast.

"Look sharp then, Edward! Bring that rug and the bag and I'll carry the stool. Look sharp!"

"Have a nice time!" called Mrs Farrand as they passed through the shop.

"Be all right then, will you?" queried Mrs Flack.

"Oh, right as rain. Thoroughly enjoy myself, I shouldn't wonder."

"Well, it's ever so good of you. Bye bye, then!"

And Mrs Flack was out of the shop without a second glance.

"Good day t'ye!" Finn got out and made a sweeping bow. "Take your luggage, ma'am?"

He took it, and with the other hand opened the rear door for a pleased and confused Mrs Flack to get in. Alfred and Mister Rudge were already there, sitting opposite one another, Mister Rudge facing the engine.

172

"We thought for you to sit next Mister Rudge, Lil," said Alfred, "and Edward next to me here."

"Lovely!" She sank back into the seat and looked sideways. "Lovely day, Mister Rudge."

"It is indeed."

Edward climbed in, Finn stowed the luggage, and they were off with a jerk.

"Isn't it big?" said Mrs Flack happily. "And ever so comfy. Ages since I went in a taxi. Ages and ages."

Alfred leaned forward confidentially.

"Don't you worry about his driving, Lil," he whispered. "It gave me a bit of a turn at first myself, but you get used to it. He'll be——"

He fell sideways with a gasp, the sentence unfinished. Finn had executed his first right-hand turn of the day. He made his entrance into the High Street and a chorus of hooters burst into full song. Finn gave a cheery blast of his own horn in acknowledgement and settled back with a loud sigh of contentment.

Edward looked across at Mister Rudge. He was wearing a thick black overcoat that looked as if it went down nearly to his ankles, and his knees were covered by a rug. Round his neck was wound a long grey woollen scarf and he wore a greenish-black hat. His face was very pale.

"He is taking his first faltering step back into the world," Edward thought. "After all those years... For him it's a real feat of daring, like me going into the dark. No wonder he looks white."

They were passing now through the busy Saturday streets of the town centre and Finn was leaving a trail of other white faces in his wake.

"Such crowds of people!" cried Mrs Flack in his defence after a particularly urgent emergency stop. "Why don't they get their Christmas shopping done earlier? That's what Denis always says. He says—whoop!"

She fell right across Mister Rudge's lap as Finn made another of his stylish turns.

"*Now* we're away!" Finn was gleeful. "Straight on ahead now and the open road!"

Edward felt certain that it was unlikely to be quite as simple as this, but was nonetheless glad that the town centre had been safely manoeuvred and the worst was over. He was all at once filled with surprise to find himself travelling out of town on this frosty December day in this amazing vehicle and with such strangely assorted fellow passengers.

"I could never have *imagined* this happening," he thought. "Not in a million years. Mum—sitting right next to Mister Rudge! It's like a dream."

The four of them were cocooned in a strange intimacy in the back of the cab while the white world sped by, remote behind the misted windows. So unusual a situation was it that it seemed to Edward that none of the others was quite real—or at least that they were not the everyday selves he knew. Mister Rudge was the least recognisable. Edward had only ever seen him in the dim quietness of his own house, and now he was out in the open, his face queerly lit by the whiteness outside, his eyes red-rimmed and watering with cold. He was strangely vulnerable, out of his own element, no longer in command.

"Like a fish out of water," Edward thought. "He's moved back into time and space again. I wonder how he feels?"

Suddenly he remembered the purpose of the visit.

"The green!" he exclaimed, dismayed. "There isn't any! It's all white!"

"And the sun struggling like a lost soul!" returned Finn from behind the open glass partition. "If ye'll give it a chance it'll be through that mist like a ball of fire and be eating up the white in no time at all. Oh yes!"

"The green . . ." murmured Mister Rudge. "How I long to feed upon the green . . ."

Mrs Flack looked distinctly startled.

"Yes, well," she began, never one to let a conversation lapse or a remark go unanswered. "I was reading this article the other day in one of my women's papers . . ."

She paused. Mister Rudge was clearly not about to prompt her further, but on she plunged.

"Talking about colours, it was—food—you know. Talking about making the plate look nice for invalids to tempt them. Like if it was something wishywashy, say, like fish, to put a tomato with it for a splash of colour, or a sprig of parsley. Both, for that matter. And what it was saying was that the one colour people really can't fancy to eat, is blue."

No one said anything. Edward stared out at the white fields and wished she would stop.

"I thought it was interesting, myself," she said. "Said it wasn't in nature, blue, and that's why we don't fancy to eat it. And it's

174

true, you know, when you think about it. Nearest you come I suppose is grapes, but even they are more purple. Not a proper shade of blue. But *green*, now—I agree with you there, Mister Rudge. Now that *is* nature, green is."

"Green and distances . . ." murmured Mister Rudge.

"And coming to the very place shortly," said Finn encouragingly. "And if that isn't the sun now, bejab!"

It was the sun, and they all looked out to see it visibly breaking the mist and dazzling furiously on the white furrows and hoary hedges. The world was ablaze.

"That is beautiful," said Mister Rudge. "I do not think I could have made anything so beautiful in my mind's eye. And even if I could, I could not have shared it. I could not have shown it to others. You all see it?"

"A sight for sore eyes!" affirmed Finn joyously.

"Oh yes, Mister Rudge, don't you bother about that," said Mrs Flack. "The window's quite cleared now, and I can see perfectly, thank you. I must say it does look pretty. I had quite forgotten what it was like, the country. Hadn't you, Alfie?"

"Until lately," he answered. "But I shan't let myself forget again."

They were travelling now along a narrow road with hedges on either hand so that when they emerged on to a kind of grassy plateau the view was sudden and astonishing.

"There!" exclaimed Finn triumphantly. He bumped the taxi up on to the grass and switched off the engine, leaving a great quietness.

Finn got out then and stood legs astride and drew in a great breath. Edward, seeing him brilliant in that wintry landscape, saw him again as unmistakably heroic. He too climbed out and his nostrils actually stung with the heady scent of frost and his own breath clouded about him. In the distance he could hear the bleating of sheep and wheeling about he saw them in a lower meadow, grey on white.

"Look!" Finn pointed. "The green! What did I tell you!"

The sun was eating the frost away minute by minute now. Already there were green patches on the hillside, wet and dazzling.

"Come now," said Finn gently, and helped Mister Rudge to climb out, and stood then lending him support on his own arm.

"Is that it?" he asked. "Is that what ye wanted?"

The old man nodded. He looked all about him slowly and wonderingly, not to be hurried, and Edward thought,

175

"It's all new to him! He's just like a little child—or a released prisoner seeing daylight again after half a century in the dungeons. He really never has seen anything like this before. All his life he's spent in St Saviour's and all he's ever seen is the Street—and the birds. The birds of steel. But he doesn't want pity. No hero ever wants to be pitied."

And he watched them, the old hero and the young, the frail old man enveloped in his black greatcoat, and the red-bearded giant in his beaded finery, and knew that this was something he would remember his whole life. The melting frost, the smell and sound of sheep, the feel of the turf, the whole dazzle of the morning and most of all, like emblazoning on a heraldic green, the two heroes.

"Mister Rudge will remember it the rest of *his* life, too," he thought, and suddenly knew why Finn had brought them here.

The whole day had a curious unreality despite the acuteness with which Edward experienced the unaccustomed sights and smells and sounds. At one time, when each of the five had wandered off alone, Edward looked up to see the others up in the distance placed against the now all green turf, and thought,

"We are like pieces on a chessboard."

Most of the day Mister Rudge sat in the taxi, wrapped in his rug and content simply to gaze. Mrs Flack was the most difficult person in the party, because she was so determined that they should all enjoy themselves. As it happened, they all were, in their own way, but Mrs Flack thought that enjoyment should necessarily be visible, energetic and even a little noisy. Her own voice was ever so slightly raised all day, her laughter an unnatural degree louder and longer, her step determinedly spry.

The picnic lunch was probably the only time when the party did come up to her expectations.

"Isn't it lovely!" she cried, as the sausages went into the fat, and "Oooh, lovely!" as they came out again. If it had occurred to her, she would probably have brought crackers and they would all have been wearing fancy hats.

"You wait!" she said mysteriously at one point when the conversation had lapsed. "It'll all turn out all right, you'll see! Been writing one or two letters, I have."

"Letters, have ye, Lily?" prompted Finn courteously.

"*Oh* yes. And to the right quarters. Lily Flack can get an idea or two of her own, you know, once in a while."

"As if we doubted it!" cried Finn. "And what idea is this, then?"

176

"Oh, there'll be a bird or two in St Saviour's before I'm done," she said. "Could be a hundred, could be a thousand. Could be *more* than a thousand."

"Great saints above!"

"She's gone barmy," thought Edward, and reached for another sausage.

"You'll see, anyhow," she said smugly. Then she reached and patted Mister Rudge on the knee. "Don't you worry about a thing, Mister Rudge. I'll see that you get your birds. You just leave it up to me."

He nodded and smiled vaguely before returning his gaze to the scene about them.

"Never the twain shall meet!" thought Edward.

All day the birds were about them. No one remarked on it. But as hour followed hour a certain reassurance came to them all because the winter day was perfectly as it should be and the birds were pattering the air and going from leafless hedge to tree all unawares and careless.

In the afternoon a sudden chill set in again and all at once the sun was a red disc over the hill and a white mist was creeping up. By mutual consent they made their way back to the taxi. Mrs Flack came pink and breathless clutching a bundle of twigs and berries. They all stood for a last look about them and as they did so there came a beating of wings.

"Look!" Edward pointed. A flight of white birds were winging overhead—gulls.

"The birds—the white birds!" gasped Mister Rudge, and even began to take stumbling steps after them in vain pursuit. By the time they had disappeared into the gloom he was quite separate from the rest of the group, forty or fifty yards away. He stood for what seemed a long time still facing after them. They waited patiently.

"Be getting in, will ye?" said Finn quietly. "And I'll fetch him in a minute."

They did so, and Edward, sitting inside the taxi again and looking out, had the extraordinary thought that it seemed quite possible that they should all drive off and leave the old man there alone in the dusk, and that it would seem quite natural, a fitting end.

"What a queer idea!" and he pushed it away.

They waited. He watched Finn walk slowly to where Mister Rudge stood and then stand for a time there with him. Then he saw Mister Rudge half turn, stop, then stoop to pick up some-

M 177

thing from the turf by his feet. They came back then, their features by now indistinct in the deepening dusk. Silently Finn handed him back into his place and wrapped the rug about his knees. The door slammed.

Mister Rudge sat quite motionless, staring down at his hands above the rug. Edward looked down. Mister Rudge was holding a long white feather.

"Oh lardy!" thought Edward, shocked into Finn's own jargon. "A sign! An omen!"

Finn switched on the engine, the headlights of the taxi flooded on and the whole landscape was blotted out at the turn of the switch.

CHAPTER TWENTY-SEVEN

¶ *In Which Mr Flack Voices His Doubts And Is Duly Put Down*

"I don't get it," said Mr Flack. "You can't believe it, Lily. You can't."

"Ah, but I can. And I do. And so'd you, Denis Flack, if you'd seen and heard half what I have these last few weeks."

"Look," he said, "you reckon there's these birds, tin birds——"

"Steel," interrupted Edward.

"These steel birds, coming down out the sky, on wires, every night. Right?"

"Right."

"And that old man Rudge's seen 'em, Edward here and Alfred think they *might've*, you've heard 'em—or so you reckon—and that's about the lot. What it is, Lil, is the old gentleman—and I think none the worse of him for it, and there's no offence meant—has gone right off his head, and is seeing birds!"

"And what about the rest of us?" she enquired. "Gone right off our heads, have we?"

"No. Now, I didn't say that. All I say is, your imagination's run away with you. You got carried away."

"And when've you ever known my imagination run away with me?"

"No—well, that *is* funny, I grant you. No, I've never known it happen before, not where you're concerned, it's a fact. It's mostly to do with that Irishman, I shouldn't wonder. Gift of the gab he's got, and no mistake."

"Finn hasn't seen them, Dad," said Edward. "Any more than you have. But he believes in them."

"Look," Mr Flack said, "if there's all them wires coming down out of nowhere night after night like the old boy says, how come there's been no accidents?"

"Accidents?"

"With aeroplanes! You can't have skies full of wires and not get one tangled up in 'em sooner or later."

"It's no use your going on, Denis." Mrs Flack saw no immediate answer to his challenge and sidestepped instead. "And it's no use your going on saying Mister Rudge is mad. Come to that, I don't know how you can say such a thing when you've never even met him."

"*You* used to," he reminded her. "And you hadn't met him, either."

"He's a very educated man"—she was sidestepping again.

"But he doesn't live in the world, Lily! Lives cooped up in that old house all on his own year in year out. He doesn't live in the world. If I told the lads down at the station about them birds of yours, they'd think I'd gone clear off my rocker! They work, see, and they've got wives and families, and watch football, and television and that, and they know very well there's no such *things*!"

"He knows a good sight more than those mates of yours down the buses!" retorted Mrs Flack.

"Ah, I daresay. But where does he get it from? Got a lot of books, has he?"

"Hundreds. Thousands, I shouldn't wonder."

"There you are, then. Lives in a world of his own. Reading books day in and day out—it's turned his head. Stands to reason. I tell you he don't know what real life is."

"I think he *does* lead a real life," said Edward. He could remain silent no longer.

"Oh yes? Goes out on night shifts does he?"

"Yes, he does, in a way!" He stood his ground. "And he leads a real life, whether you can see it or not. He lives it inside his head."

There was silence.

"And that's where those birds of his are," said his father at last. "Flapping round inside his head. And you'll go the same way yourself, my lad, if you don't watch it. I've always said you read too many books—stuffing your head with rubbish. And you've said so, Lily, yourself."

"Well, yes, I have," she agreed, "but I don't suppose it does any real harm."

"I've just thought of something," said Edward suddenly. They both looked at him.

"I bet Mister Rudge doesn't believe in *your* life!" he said. He really was excited by the idea that had just struck him.

"I bet if you were to go in there and tell him what *you* think the world's like, he wouldn't understand a word you were saying.

All that stuff about buses and football and television. I bet he'd think you were as mad as you think *he* is!"

"You *what*?" Mr Flack laid down his knife and fork.

"Edward!" reproved Mrs Flack.

"I mean it! And it's true! You've got no right to go round saying you know what's real and what isn't! You don't! Nobody does! And I tell you Mister Rudge's birds are as real to him as your buses are to you, and *I* believe in them, I do! And I wish they'd come down now, this very minute, right through the roof and straight on to this table, and then you'd see!"

He threw down his spoon and fled. In his room he switched on the light and swiftly drew the curtains. He threw himself on the bed, trembling, partly because of the things he had just said and partly with terror, because what he had said at the end had amounted, really, to an invocation. On many nights he had dared himself to make one, but had always ended by postponing it. Could those few careless words really have set in motion whatever awful machinery drove the birds of steel down the sky?

"The wrath of the heavens could descend!" he thought. "Steel birds could fly like darts to wreak vengeance!"

After a few minutes, however, it became clear that the steel birds were not to respond to his invocation, and equally clear that his parents were going to leave him alone—perhaps till morning—to cool off. He got up and found the Monopoly set, then seated himself on the bed again, leaning against the wall.

December 22nd
I lift up my pen though my hand is shaking with emotion to make a further record of events in St Saviour's. The first thing I shall record is not exactly a mighty deed or anything but I wish to get it off my chest, to unburden my bosom, as this is partly why my hand is trembling. I have just had a row with my father about Mister Rudge and the birds of steel. We do not see eye to eye and it is at times like this that I realise that we just are not flesh of one flesh and blood of one blood and never will be. He just will not understand about the birds of steel, it is as if he was blind, like a brick wall. He tries to set us all at nought. He sets Mister Rudge at nought and also Finn and Uncle Alfred and me and Mum—all of us. Not to mention practicly the whole Street.

Though if I am to speak truth I think it is really only Finn and me and Mister Rudge who believe with all our hearts and souls and strengths, and out of us three it is quite true that only

Mister Rudge has seen the birds in their full and dire terror. It is really as if Mister Rudge has had a dream, or rather a vision, and has told it. And the rest of the people believe he has had this vision all right, but don't believe it deep down. Whereas I do believe it deep down, because this is what a vision means, something that only appears to one man or a few (usually heroes, prophets etc) and which the rest of the world disbelieve at the time but which turns out to be true.

If I am to be a hero I must learn not to mind what the world says and saying what I thought to Dad just now was the first step towards this. I must be undaunted and stand fast and keep my own counsel. My great hope is that I may have visions of my own one day (I have decided not to count the dreams I had when I had the mortal fever) and that is why I must train myself now as hard as I can.

I have hardly had time to do my air-force exercises this last month or two and I now think this does not matter much as I am definately coming to the conclusion that true valour is not a matter of muscles etc. In actual fact as I have mentioned before (though I do not of course record this as a mighty deed for posterity but am just mentioning it) I beat Mike MacKay for the first time a few days ago but I did not feel at all heroic afterwards. The more I think about it the more I think that true valour is inside your head. It is all right Dad going on about his buses and real life and so on, but in my opinion Mister Rudge leads a much more interesting and heroic life than he does. I bet that Dad would never see one steel bird if he lived to be a hundred. I hope Mister Rudge lives to be a hundred. But I had this very queer feeling about him when we were in the country the other day though I will not in fact record this as I expect that it was only my imagination.

I should now recount our journey on the 17th December into the country. This was so that Mister Rudge could see some green and some distances for which he has been pining. We had a picnic which may sound ridiculous in December but was a truly great and original idea of Finn's. It was better than any summer picnic I have ever been on as for one thing it was truly a feast of heroes and for another there were no wasps ants etc. At first it seemed as if our journey might be in vain as everywhere was white with frost. But Finn said that the sun would come out and melt it—and it did!

He took us to a deserted place where there was no sign of any human dwelling or abode and there were only sheep and birds.

Mister Rudge really did feast his eyes upon the green. He looked much older than I first thought and was very white, proberbly because he was so wrung with emotion. Finn was very quiet (for him). Mum made the most noise of anybody.

Right at the very end, just as we were going, the sun glowed like a big red ball of fire and the mist came creeping up. And some gulls went winging over our heads and Mister Rudge cried out with a loud voice and tried vainly to follow them. Afterwards in the taxi I saw that he had a long white feather in his hands. When he saw the gulls he called something about "white birds" and I am sure this was a sign or omen for him. So what I am now wondering is if he has had visions about white birds and that they are good whereas the birds of steel are evil.

What makes me think this is first the way he tried to follow these birds and second how peaceful he seemed on the way home and hardly took his eyes from the feather.

This has given me an idea. I told it to Finn yesterday and he agreed, in fact he clapped me on the back. This idea is that we should give Mister Rudge a pair of white doves for Christmas. I do not think there is anything in the world we could give him that he would like better, I think it will delight his heart. In fact I can hardly wait to see his face when he first sets eyes on them. (To me, the perfect names for them would be Hero and Leander but of course he will choose his own which will proberbly be even better.)

Tomorrow I am going to the church early as Finn says he will have a surprise for me. I cannot think what this will be and am consumed with curiosity. My slumber will be uneasy, but I think the sooner I lay down my pen now the better. I can hear carol singers in the distance. They are singing Hark The Herald Angels Sing which is one of my favourites and I just cannot imagine the steel birds coming down while it is being sung. This Christmas will be different from any other I have ever had in my life. Already it feels different, much more exciting, as being cooped in with Mum and Dad as usually happens watching television is not all that much fun.

I now lay me down to sleep signifying that this is a true and faithful record.

CHAPTER TWENTY-EIGHT

¶ How Patrick Finn Gave News Of A Party And How Mrs Flack Found Herself Being Constantly Surprised

"A tree!"

"D'ye like it? Straight out the forest, and high as a ship's mast, bejam!"

"It's marvellous! It makes the whole church different. I could smell it the minute I came in."

"Ye can't have Christmas without a tree," said Finn. "Oh no. 'Twouldn't do."

The low sunlight passed through the calm green and gold men and washed the stone flags with colour and tipped the branches of the fir tree.

"Decorations, though! We'll never get enough. It's about fifteen foot high!"

"Oh yes," nodded Finn, "we shall. For one thing—there's this!"

He led the way to the arched vestry door. In there sat Uncle Alfred a-wash in a sea of gold and silver. He had begun to grow a beard and there were strands of tinsel caught up in that too. He looked so wild and outlandish that Edward actually felt his heart lift at the thought that this was his uncle, instead of the dour, mathematical figure he had been led to expect.

"Crikey, Uncle Alfred! Fantastic! What're those?"

"You'll see, when they're stretched out," he replied happily, brandishing his scissors. "Stretch out, they will, when they're hung, like the biggest icicles you ever saw. Got the idea off the television when I was having tea at Lil's last week. Easy as wink to do."

"Can I help? I know how to do lanterns. That red shiny stuff— can I make some lanterns out of that?"

"A thousand lanterns!" Finn told him. "And whatever else ye like! And will ye come now and be looking at these?"

The doves were housed in a box of Finn's own making. They were white, beautiful, and very calm.

"Oh!" Edward gasped. "Finn! They're beautiful! They're— I've never seen anything like them."

"Oh no," agreed Finn. "Not like these. Can't have."

Edward spent the morning squatted on the vestry floor with Uncle Alfred, making red paper lanterns while Finn played carols on the organ. In the corner were the pigeons, Hercules and Joan, Theseus and Grace, David and Bathsheba, with the one surviving offspring, Hiawatha, now feathered and bright-eyed and certain to survive. They cooed softly, filling in the silences. Edward did not notice the cold until he found his fingers too numb to work the scissors. At just that moment Finn gave a final flourish to the last bars of O Come All Ye Faithful and appeared almost immediately at the door.

"If I wasn't forgetting! The rest of them!"

"The rest of what?" asked Edward.

"The decorations! It's a tree, d'ye see, for the whole Street—the tree o' St Saviour's, ye might say. And all to bring shiny things and lights for it, to be dressed properly for the party."

"Party? What party? When?"

Finn held up his hand.

"Party there'll be, sure enough, but I'll not be saying when, not just now. Likely enough it'll be New Year's Eve—but I can't say, not for sure. What we'll do, we'll go along the Street and knock at doors and tell 'em. Tell 'em there's to be a party here, and before Twelfth Night. Oh yes, before then it'll be. And ask 'em for something for the tree if they want to come."

"But how'll they know *when* to come?"

Finn was like a bottomless well of unexpectedness. First it was picnics in December, now it was mystery parties—guess the date.

"We shall tell 'em!" replied Finn. "Easiest thing in the world. Run up the Street and knock on doors and call 'em all out. That's how they'll know."

"Oh. Oh, I see."

"And if it should be New Year's Eve," said Finn thoughtfully, half to himself, "it'd be perfect. Yes, perfect."

"Well, why can't it be, then?" asked Edward. "Think—it all fits. That's the night when—well, I don't really know, but Mister Rudge does seem to think it's important, he seems to have got it fixed in his head as if something must happen then. Almost as if that was the night when we must do battle with the birds of steel and go into the crucible!"

Finn regarded him consideringly.

"You really do think it'll be that bad, then? Ye're truly a

185

strange kind o' boy," he said, "yes, you are, and've got the makings of something quite extraordinary, I swear ye have. But leave it now. Leave it."

Edward's heart expanded, he was almost suffocating. As he left the church he could still hear Finn's words, and the more he heard them the more he thought that only one interpretation could be put on them.

"He thinks I've got the makings of a hero, he must! What else could he mean? Oh, Allelujah, glory allelujah!"

If there had been a dragon to hand, he would have cleft it in twain with a single stroke—if he had had a sword to hand. But he had neither, so he simply ran as if possessed, repeating to himself,

"I speed with winged sandals to bear tidings from the gods! I am Mercury of the winged feet! Tidings of comfort and joy!" He leapt up the stairs three at a time:

"I'm Mercury, I'm Mercury!"

"Is that you, Edward?" called Mrs Flack from the kitchen.

"Yes! It's me! And I bear tidings—I mean, I've got some news! There's to be a party! Finn and Uncle Alfred are giving a party and they've got the most enormous tree and we've been decorating it which is why I'm a bit late."

"A party!" She sounded pleased. "Well, that'll liven Christmas up a bit. When is it?"

"Oh. Well. You see, he's not saying, yet. He's inviting the whole Street, though, just about."

"Well, it is Christmas," said Mrs Flack, not unduly perturbed by this news, as once she would certainly have been.

"And we can all help out with the food and baking. You can't do much baking in a church."

"Don't tell anyone," began Edward impulsively, then paused. This was the first time in his life he would ever have confided a real secret to her.

"Promise?"

"Go on, then. Promise!"

"Well, I'm pretty sure it'll be New Year's Eve. There's a *reason*."

"The birds!"

She lowered her voice, despite the unlikelihood that anyone was eavesdropping in her own kitchen, with the shop shut for dinner. Edward nodded.

"You see, it's something to do with us all standing fast together,

I'm sure it is," he told her. "Though of course if we could've had hundreds of birds it'd've been even better."

"Pity about that." She wiped her hands on her apron and indicated the plates. "Take them in, now. There's only you and me. Yes, pity about the birds. Tried to do something about that myself, but it didn't come off."

"What? What did you do?"

"Well—" now it was her turn to hesitate. "Promise you won't let on? Sounds a bit silly in a way, I s'pose."

"I promise. And I bet it's not silly."

"What I did, I wrote this letter to the *Haunton Post*. Telling them—you know—about those terrible birds and the awful threat we're living under and that. And what I did, I appealed for people to give birds. Thought it'd be something different, and catch people's fancy. Give birds, see, instead of money. And if they'd printed it—and I must say I can't think why they didn't— and people *had* sent birds just think how many there might've been!"

Edward had put down his knife and fork and was staring at her with real surprise, and admiration—and respect.

"Oh, there would've! There could've been *thousands*! What a marvellous idea, Mum! Crikey, fancy thinking of that!"

"Do you really think so?"

"I *do*! Oh, I do! And the *Post* must be crazy, not printing a letter like that. Human lives might be at stake—anything could happen."

They stared at one another, then smiled and picked up their knives and forks again, a little confused by it all.

"I shall go and look at this tree," announced Mrs Flack when the washing-up was done. "I love a real Christmas tree, I do. It's the smell, I think."

"Why don't we have one then?"

The words were out before he could stop them. Their own little silver tree, tarnished by ten or more Christmases, was already in place in front of the window.

"Well, I don't know, now you ask. I suppose I thought it'd be cheaper, in the long run, having the silver and bringing it out each year. And so it is. Still—getting a bit tatty. Could have a real one next year."

"There's something else for you to look at, as well. A surprise," Edward told her as they rummaged in the shop for the best fruit to take down with them.

187

"What's that, then? All these surprises! It's just like—" she broke off, and began to laugh.

"What?" he asked, seeing no sign of her stopping.

"I was going to say—just like Christmas!" she wiped her eyes. "Oh dear—it's just like Christmas!" and he joined in her laughter. They were still laughing as they set off down the Street and Mrs Gray, watching from her window, was moved to remark,

"I don't know what's come over Lily Flack, I really don't! She's not the same woman!"—which was more or less, had she known it, exactly what Edward himself was thinking.

"Lord above!" she exclaimed when she saw the tree. "Trust you to get the biggest tree in Merton, Patrick Finn! Wherever did you get that?"

"Oh, down the market. Too big—nobody wanted it—got it for a song. And MacKay and some of his mates gave us a hand wit' it, see."

"You carried it?"

"Too big for the taxi. Need a blessed lorry for that. Carried it home last night, we did—right under your window we went—did ye not hear us? Singing carols fit to burst—and fit to burst indeed, wit' the weight o' that!"

"I heard you," said Edward. "I think. I didn't know it was you."

"And what's that?" enquired Mrs Flack, approaching the chancel steps. Edward, following, saw something he had not noticed earlier.

"Oh! If it isn't a crêche! A proper little old-fashioned crêche!" and she actually knelt on the lower step to see it the better. "Look, Edward—carved, all out of wood—all the little animals and the kings with their crowns—oh, it's beautiful!"

"Ye think so?" Finn seemed hugely pleased. "D'ye hear that, Alfie man? D'ye hear what your sister thinks o' your handiwork?"

She turned slowly.

"Alfie? You? You made that?"

The part of his face that was not covered by beard reddened visibly.

"Well—got to do something with your hands, you know. There's not much you can do in here at night, with only the two lamps. Passed the time. I used to do a bit of woodwork if you remember, Lily, when we were kids."

"So you did," she said, still amazed. "But this—well, it's

downright beautiful. So this was the other surprise, was it? Surprised me all right, this has."

"Oh no," said Edward. "I didn't know about this myself. There's another surprise yet."

"Another!" Her hands flew up in one of Finn's own gestures. "And I've that shop to open in ten minutes or have the door broken down. The way folks leave things to the last minute! Christmas Eve tomorrow, and half day at that, and they start buying *mincemeat*, I ask you! Where's this other surprise?"

She was led into the vestry to see the doves and was duly ecstatic.

"I think that's lovely, I really do. And he really deserves a nice present, poor old gentleman. I've knit him some mittens myself, that I daresay'll come in handy, but he'll fairly *love* these, and a really lovely idea of yours, Edward. What names should they have, do you think? I think it'd——"

"We're not giving them names, Mum," he said quickly. "We're leaving it for him to choose."

"Better, really," she agreed. "He'll think of something. Give him something to think about, besides them terrible birds. When you think how that poor old man's been haunted by those birds—no wonder he's not well. I wouldn't be, and that's a fact. I shall have to be getting back to the shop, I really will."

"Is there anything I can do to help you?" Edward asked Finn. He grinned.

"You can start knocking at doors," he replied. "You can start at the bottom o' the Street and work to the top—and not forgetting the alleys. And ye tell them all they're invited to a party, and if they want to come, to give somet'ing for the tree."

"*That's* a good idea!" applauded Mrs Flack. "My word. That way, you'll get your tree decorated and know how many to expect as well. Fancy thinking of that."

"I'm off. Everybody I'm to ask—really?"

"Every last man jack," nodded Finn. "It's a big place we're holding it in, and room for all."

"Church won't have been so full for years," said Mrs Flack. "*I* never saw it very full. Come along then, Edward, look sharp! You've a job to do."

Edward went out and was Mercury again, flying with winged feet from door to door bearing a message from a hero. He had to call back at the shop for carriers to hold the decorations he was given at every house.

"One for everybody that's coming," he told Mrs Baker, who lived nearly opposite themselves. "That way Finn'll know how many to expect."

"It reminds me of VE Day, it really does," she said, bringing out a yellowing muslin angel and a shiny bauble, "Had tables down the middle of the road, and flags and buntings—the whole Street turned out. Not that you'll remember that, dear. Weren't born, you weren't."

"I've heard about it," Edward told her. "This'll be better than that. This will be a feast fit for heroes."

"Well, *that* was supposed to be," she said, "but it certainly will be lovely, the whole Street at a party!"

"It's not just a party, you know," he reminded her (though from time to time he was having difficulty in remembering this himself). "It's a show of strength. It's a stand against the enemy."

"Oh dear me yes! Those dreadful birds! *Shall* we get rid of them, do you think? There's not going to be any *fighting*, is there?"

"Time alone will tell," said Edward. "St Saviour's will go into the crucible and emerge transformed—transmogrified!"

"Oh! Oh, I see. Well, we shall all have to hope for the best. Thank Mr Finn for his kind invitation, will you, and tell him me and Percy will be there."

It was much the same at every house. Edward was given so many mince pies that in the end he had to give up eating them and began to save them, instead.

"They'll do for Finn and Uncle Alfie," he thought. "And if they don't want them, there's always Hercules and the others."

He was actually in the alley, and about to turn in at the MacKay yard when he realised where he was. He halted.

"But Finn did say everyone. And he gets on all right with Mr and Mrs MacKay."

He picked his way through the scattered junk and past the hutch where the MacKay pigeons were plucking the netting with their beaks. When he knocked Mike MacKay opened the door as suddenly as if he had been waiting with his hand on the latch, ready.

"Yeah? What?"

"I've come to see if you want to go to a party."

"What party? Yours?"

"No, for the whole Street. Finn's giving it."

"Oh—him! No thanks!"

He made to shut the door but Mrs MacKay appeared and pushed him out of the way.

"What is it?" she demanded. "What's up now?"

"Nothing's up," Mike mumbled. "Ask him!"

Edward explained it all for the hundredth time that day. Mrs MacKay accepted with a great show of enthusiasm and was the only inhabitant of St Saviour's who did not express surprise about the vagueness of the date of the party.

"Perhaps that's how they have parties, in Ireland," he thought. "When they feel like it."

"Only thing is the decorations. Nine you'd be wanting, wouldn't you? It's precious few'll be left on our own tree, but there ye are—Mike!"

"Look, don't bother," Edward said quickly. "It doesn't matter that much—it's only so as Finn'll have a rough idea of numbers. And I've got loads of decorations for the big tree now."

"Aye, well, that's very good of ye. And if only me own seven had your manners me troubles'd be halved!"

Edward, knowing that the MacKays were listening from somewhere behind, wished that she had not said this.

"*That* should be good for a black eye!" he thought.

By the time he had finished his knocking there were six carrier bags of decorations, he had a definite feeling that St Saviour's was a bigger place than he had ever taken it to be, and it was growing dusk. Back at the church he found Finn and Alfred frying sausages and as he came in Finn threw a couple of extra links into the pan.

"One hundred and thirty-two!" Edward announced.

"Lardy!"

"And look—" he delved into one of the carriers and pulled out some decorations.

"Beautiful!"

"And these!" Out came the mince pies, a little crumbly round the edges but none the worse for that.

"Beautiful!"

"There's about twenty or thirty, I think. I started off by eating them but had to give up. Can we decorate the tree now?"

"Tomorrow," said Finn. "Christmas Eve—and the hairs of me neck standing up on end at the thought of it, and if there's one day in the whole calendar I would choose to come back to earth for, when I'm dead and among the blessed saints, that'd be it!"

Edward tried to work out this complicated sentiment. The gist

191

of what Finn had said he understood very well, because he felt the same about Christmas Eve himself.

"Oh, it's rare and magical, Christmas Eve is, and I've a fancy for us to decorate that tree then, and sing carols and draw in the smell of it, and me go back to being a boy again. For why should I not?"

"I've found myself going back to when I was a boy again these last weeks," said Alfred. "Never used to give it a thought—before. It was just as if it had never been."

Edward, who himself *was* a boy, was hard put to see exactly what the pair of them were saying.

"Shall *I* look back," he wondered, "to days like today, for instance, and wish them back again? What a queer thought!"

He was in something of a hurry to *stop* being a boy, to grow up, and had been ever since he had decided to become a hero. Signs of heroism were not generally appreciated in a boy, he had discovered. Many a time he had been punished for feats of daring that would have earned a fully fledged hero a crown of laurels, if not a shower of gold. Besides, until lately, he had never thought St Saviour's a place fit for heroes, and had itched to escape into the kind of landscape depicted in his books of myths and legends.

Recently he had begun to change his mind about this. Finn and Mister Rudge, both indubitably heroes, managed to live and work in St Saviour's, and as far as Edward himself was concerned had actually changed it, transformed it. It had become a place fierce, wild, mysterious, beautiful. It had become a place of possibilities.

Christmas Eve it was when the tree was decorated. In the afternoon Mrs Flack came too, and there was a good deal of precarious wobbling on stepladders, and squealing. There was also much cross-talk of the "You'll never guess what I've got *you* for Christmas!" variety, and in the background was the organ and every now and then the working party broke off their chatter to sing, or listen. Edward could see Finn's reflection greenish in the organ loft and he was almost on a level with the tranquil men of green and gold in the stained window.

They all stood round then to admire their handiwork. Already it was getting dark and the tree was sombre despite the glinting here and there among its branches. It would be tomorrow before they would see it in its full glory. Alfred and Finn were to spend the evening with Mister Rudge. Edward went and gave the pigeons a double ration of seed and a mince pie and they cooed and purred in their shadowy corner of the vestry.

As he and his mother walked back Edward looked up, but as usual saw nothing because of the street lights. You had to go into the alleys to see the stars.

"Or the birds," he thought. He waited, but the familiar terror did not come. "The entire sky was strung with steel." He quoted the words to himself. Nothing.

"I am not afraid," he thought. "Tonight I am not afraid."

CHAPTER TWENTY-NINE

¶ *Being Entries In The Chronicle Of St Saviour's As Recorded By Edward Flack*

December 27th

I lift up my pen to record how Christmas was spent in St Saviour's and also I fear to relate bad tidings. I think however I should relate the moor cheerful things first as after all it is still Christmas and meant to be full of comfort and joy.

Christmas started off about as usual though obviously the minute I lifted my head from my pillow I knew that this would be no ordinary Christmas. We had breakfast as usual and then gave each other our presents. I gave Dad a set of pen and propelling pencil and Mum a red leather purse and a book on pigeon keeping which she seemed very pleased with. From them I got a really marvellous knife with all kinds of attatchments, a model aeroplane kit, some gloves, an enormous tin of toffees and a five pound note. I shall probably spend the whole of this on books as I never get any unless I buy them myself.

Then I went off to see Finn and Uncle Alfred who had been up very early to go to church. I also saw the Christmas tree in its full glory and it really did look beautiful and will not drop its needles as it is so cold in there. They were coming to our house for dinner so the main thing was to take Mister Rudge's present for him. Finn covered the box with a rug to make it look more mysterious and we went over to The House. It was very cold—a white Christmas you might also say as the frost was certainly white though perhaps this does not count though I cannot see why not. Anyway, before we went over Finn warned me that we must not stay long. He had already been over to The House as usual and he said that Mister Rudge was really poorly and really ought to stop in bed but would not.

We went in and there was Mister Rudge sitting with a rug wrapped round him and Finn had made him a blazing fire. I could see a change in him myself though I do not know quite how to describe it. He seemed further away and yet nearer which sounds ridicerlous but is true. In other words, he seemed very far away and yet somehow gentler than before, as if he really thought of you as a person even if you did not belong in his world. Finn and Uncle Alfie and me all started singing We Wish You a Merry Christmas and then Finn swept the rug off the box and there were the two doves!

He just did not know what to say. He just sat and looked. There is no doubt whatever that this meant something really special and that I was right when I said there was nothing else in the world we could give him that would rejoice his heart so much. His own face was about as white as the birds. He just sat and looked. Now that I think, I do not think he even said thank you, and of course immediately anybody might think how bad mannered this was. But it was not rude at all. The way he just sat was better than saying thank you. Anyone can say that.

Uncle Alfie and I went quite soon but Finn stayed on to minister to the sick man. Then Finn and Uncle Alfie came to Christmas dinner at our house and it was the best we have ever had mainly because we were laughing so much the whole time. The food was the usual—turkey, stuffing, sausage, bread sauce, roast and mashed potatoes, peas and sprouts and gravy. Then we had the pudding but I have never seen one lit up before and Finn did it himself and the whole pudding gave a kind of little explosion and was licked up with watery blue flames and it tasted delicious, all burnt and fruity. Finn had forgotten to take the sprig of holly off the top and that all got blacked up and afterwards I took it and am keeping it as a souvenier. Then we had mince pies and afterwards gave presents.

I had deliberately given Finn something I made myself because in the first place I felt like making something for him and in the second I thought it might work like a sort of magic. I thought that if he had something that I had made and carried it about with him, it would be a kind of talisman, and keep us in touch in a way even when apart. Because I have a feeling that Finn will not stay much longer in St Saviour's. Anyway what I did, I got an ordinary key ring and then I made a four-leaved clover with an enamel kit I had last birthday. The point being that wherever Finn goes his keys go as well. He was really pleased with this and kept saying "Lucky Finn! Lucky Finn!" on and off all day and of course he was only joking as a man of his nobleness does not need luck. I gave Uncle Alfred a very brightly coloured scarf. This was to let him know I sympathise with the way he dresses and I am sure he got the point because he winked at me. I must say that when I saw him that first night they arrived I would never have believed he could ever wink at anybody.

Now for what they gave me. Finn gave me a medallion on a chain to wear round my neck and I could not have been more pleased for the reasons stated above. Now, he will have something of mine always with him and I will have something of his. Obviously Mum would not let me wear this over my shirts at school but she will not know whether it is underneath—and it will be! On the medallion is a man with a beard and curly hair who looks like a cross between Appollo and Finn. I shall look at it whenever I need to take courage.

Uncle Alfred's present was a pair of pigeons he had carved himself out of wood—Hercules and Theseus, of course. I have got them on my chest of drawers. Mum thought they were really marvellous and told him he ought to take up wood carving and I would not be surprised if he did. Finn and him had clubbed together to get her a smashing cushion with a peacock on it and you could see she was pleased with it. They gave Dad a pair of slippers (which I am sure Mum must have had something to do with as he needed a new pair anyway). The exchange of gifts was then over.

Now I am afraid I must relate the bad tidings, which are to do with Mister Rudge. Finn came round on Boxing Day and his face was grave and he told us that Mister Rudge was much worse and had taken to his bed. He has a bed in the upper room, right by the window, so that if he is propped up he can see the Street. I expect this is where he kept his long night watches. He was the guardian of the sky. He sat up there alone through the night so that he could warn us of the birds of steel who come to do us harm. He did not flinch. If I could have a grandfather I would want him to be like Mister Rudge. And as I have not got any real flesh and blood of my own I suppose he could be. He has no flesh and blood of his own either. He is alone.

I asked Finn if I could go up and see him but he said no. In a way I was sorry but in another way glad. I have found in life that things you have imagined and thought about a lot are often not up to what you thought when you actuerly see them. I have thought and thought of Mister Rudge up there, right high up, practicly nudging the stars. I think of it as a place of mystery and sorcery. And I would not like to go up there and find it was just an ordinery room with wallpaper and so on. Nor would I like to see Mister Rudge in his pyjamas. It is not right for a hero to be in pyjamas. At least I expect it is as obviously heroes have to sleep sometimes, including Finn, but my imagination just is not strong enough to imagine this.

Finn said that Mister Rudge had asked for the doves to be brought up and this news really gladdened my heart. I am more certain than ever that these birds mean something to him and are a sign.

December 30th

I lift up my pen to record that Mister Rudge is no better and if anything worse. Finn says that he is not in pain but weak and calm. It is a strange thought to me that two months ago I had never even set eyes on Mister Rudge. I can remember that night when I saw him and waved and he waved back and I knew that from then on everything would be different. Going to see him at The House was one of the greatest feats of daring I have ever performed (though now it seems really peculier to think I was ever frightened of him). It was the beginning of all my strange adventures. I will now lay down my pen not to sleep but to lie and think about him. I will imagine myself to be there in that dark top room with him and Finn and the doves and the stars through the window. I pray the steel birds will not come tonight.

CHAPTER THIRTY

¶ *What Happened In St Saviour's On New Year's Eve*

It was already dark in St Saviour's when the word went about that the party was tonight. Edward and Alfred heard first. They were in the vestry with the pigeons when Finn came back from The House where he had spent nearly the whole day. He stood in the doorway and they looked up to read his face.

"He is dying," he said.

Neither spoke. Edward felt a terrible pain and breathlessness, he could not speak. A man was to die.

"It must be tonight. The party."

"The party? Tonight?" Alfred was shocked.

"Never fear," said Finn, "there's no disrespect in what we mean to do."

Again no one spoke.

"And another thing. It's snowing!"

"Snowing!" Edward exclaimed and was immediately ashamed. He went down the church and went and stood in the porch and saw that the ground was already white and exciting and snow falling in great tissue-like flakes. He glimpsed The House through the mazy white and could see the top light burning right up against the invisible stars. The sky itself was dizzy with whirling snow.

"There'll be no steel birds for him tonight," Edward thought.

"He has the two white birds in his room." It was Finn behind him in the shadow and guessing his thoughts.

"I know. You said."

"And tonight, God Willing, the entire sky shall be filled with 'em!"

Edward looked at his face, pale in the gloom.

"Things are not always what they appear—remember? Remember the taxi?"

Edward nodded.

"Tonight in St Saviour's, the very bells o' heaven shall ring for old Mister Rudge!"

"But——"

198

"He had a dream, d'ye see, and our duty to a dying man is to make it true. And easy enough, if we do it right. And here's how we'll do it."

"Go on, Finn." Alfred had joined them in the porch.

"Run up the Street—run up the length and breadth of St Saviour's and bang on the doors and bid them come to a party—a party for the New Year, tell 'em. And tell 'em to wrap up warm, for it's in the Street we'll be dancing tonight!"

"Shall I go now?"

"And tell 'em another thing. Tell 'em to put on all the lights in the house, to leave it full lit when they come—a light at every window!"

"But what—what if—they mightn't——"

"Tell 'em," ordered Finn softly, "tell 'em an old man's going out with the old year. And he'll look out his window and he'll see the Street lit and filled with people. And they'll be dancing and singing and the bells'll ring. Tell 'em that. Tell 'em tonight the bells of St Saviour's will ring for the last time—ring in the New Year!"

"I'll go, then. I'll go now."

He stepped out of the porch and could actually smell the snow and its touch was light and icy on his face. He turned back.

"What time shall I say?"

"Near midnight!" Finn called after him. "Tell 'em near midnight!"

Edward was alone then, cut off by snow. His thoughts were very slow and odd.

"Go home first and tell Mum and Dad. Mister Rudge is dying. Get my other coat and some gloves. It doesn't seem real. I shan't see him again."

The world about him, the familiar Street, were made foreign by the whiteness and he was forced again to look back and search out the high light of The House.

"Old Mister Rudge. Going alone into the dark—or light."

He could not take it in. The only picture he had of the old man now was of him receiving the doves on Christmas Day.

"It was true, then. The white birds were a sign. What is he thinking, I wonder?"

He banged right into someone and yelled with shock. Mike MacKay thrust his face forward.

"Here, you, look——"

"Mike! Mike!" Edward caught at his sleeve. "It's tonight!"

"What is?"

"The party. Listen—the old man's dying. He's dying—Mister Rudge!"

Mike MacKay's face was pinched and distrustful.

"*Dying?* Honest?"

"Honest."

"Christ."

"Yes, he is, he is! And Finn wants to get the whole Street out, the whole Street blazing and everyone out in it and the bells ringing!"

"Bells? Here, listen—have you seen him? Here, you two—Pat, Pete! Here!"

Two further MacKays materialised instantly and wraithlike out of the snow. Edward had been only a few paces off an ambush.

"Listen—he's dying—the old man! Right at this minute!"

They all turned their eyes fearfully towards the speck of light that marked The House. One of the MacKays, the youngest, crossed himself surreptitiously, but the others saw him and followed suit. The snow fell.

"He could haunt us! The things we've said!"

"And done!"

"Never knew he was dying!"

"He wasn't," said Edward. "But now he is. I'm to bang on all the doors in the Street and fetch people out, and get the houses all lit up, and they're going to ring the bells."

"The bells!"

"At midnight!"

"Help me—will you?"

Vigorously the three MacKays nodded and the snow in their hair flew out and shone with the movement.

"Bang on doors!"

"We'll bang—we'll hammer!"

"Ring the bells, can we? *I'll* ring a bell!"

"Christ!"

"Quick—come on!"

"Midnight!" called Edward urgently. "Tell them just before midnight. And all the lights on!"

He ran to keep pace with them, three MacKays gone crazy now with excitement, made mad by the sudden transformation of the world by snow and by the thought of death only a stone's throw off.

"You do the alleys!" he shouted as he ran. "I'll start this end of the Street, you start the other!"

In the lamplight he saw the MacKays kicking up snow at their heels, making head-to-toe haloes for themselves, momentarily sainted.

"Come out, come out!" he heard them yell. Then they were invisible and muffled and he was in at the shop door and up the stairs and faced with announcing his message again, this time in the everyday, untransformed ordinariness of the living-room, where Mrs Flack sat knitting and counting, all unaware. She looked up.

"The time has come," he told her.

CHAPTER THIRTY-ONE

¶ *Being The Final Extract From The Chronicle Of St Saviour's Recorded By Edward Flack*

New Year's Day

I lift up my pen to tell the events in St Saviour's last night. Of all the deeds I have so far written this is the one that should go down to posterity even if all else perishes and I will write it with my best endeavour.

Last night Mister Rudge died. It was this morning really not long after midnight. Finn says that it was like a prophecy fulfilled and I think that it was because of all the other things that happened. Last night St Saviour's went into the crucible never to be the same again.

When the snow came it was as if the whole world had changed in the twinkling of an eye. It was so queer, the Street to be suddenly so white that everything that happened afterwards seemed to be in a kind of a dream. It was as if we all went mad.

If anyone had told me that everyone in St Saviour's would come out into the Street at midnight in the snow and sing and dance I would have thought they were mad. But this is what happened. They did come out, and they even left their lights on as Finn had said and the whole Street was ablaze with snow and light. The MacKays were running round like mad dogs and they were banging and hammering on doors and fetching people out and I would never have believed it possible. Their hearts smote them at the thought of their past misdeeds. It was as if they were looking over their shoulders for the ghost of Mister Rudge.

When midnight came it was still snowing and Finn opened the upper window of The House and leaned out and shouted,

"Happy New Year!"

And everyone stopped dead in their tracks and stopped singing and snowballing and shouted back,

"Happy New Year!"

It went very quiet then because we all remembered Mister Rudge there in the room behind him.

Then Finn shouted in a mighty voice,

"Now are the steel birds gone forever from this place! Now let the bells ring in the new day!"

And my heart stopped within me. He went back in and then the bells began to ring, they really smashed out and you didn't know if to laugh or cry and some of the people were crying. Mum was, for one. And I was still watching and I saw *two* pale faces at the window and knew that Mister Rudge was looking out into the Street for the last time.

Somebody began to sing Old Lang Syne and next thing there was an enormous circle right across the Street and the pavements and everyone joined hands singing at the tops of their voices and the snow was still falling. It was like feathers and I realised that this was what Finn had wanted.

I shall never see such a thing again as long as I live. I have just looked out again from my window and it is already as if the whole thing had never happened. It is very quiet out there. The snow went on falling in the night and covered over all our tracks and left everything white and bare.

Mister Rudge is dead and St Saviour's will never be the same again. The steel birds have been driven forever from the sky. I know that. But I do not mean that they were never really there at all, because they were. How else could all our lives have been changed because of them particularly mine? But I am absolutley sure that now Mister Rudge has gone the birds have too. They have been excorcised.

Finn will go soon, I think. His mission has been accomplished, he has brought us safely through the fire. I think Uncle Alfred will go with him. (He by the way was one of the bell ringers last night and says he got swung right off his feet!) I expect they will give us the pigeons which will be something.

And so the hard thing for me to realise and face up to is that now I am on my own again. I must go back to training myself as a hero, but now life will have gone back to ordinary again. Nothing very much happens in St Saviour's. It is not a place for heroes.

But Mister Rudge was a hero even though the people in the Street used to laugh at him and call him names. Last night I think they were sorry, I think their hearts smote them. And Finn is a true hero as well, and he has lived in St Saviour's and so I must hold fast to my idea and not be discoraged.

I shall do my daily feat of daring as usual and I resolve to carry on with my RAF exercises as well. This is my New Year Resolution. I do not know if I will ever be a hero. But now I at least know what real heroes are like apart from Hercules, Perseus etc and know for sure that there is a place for them even in this day and age. They are not just people in books. They can change things.

This will be the last entry in the Chronicle of St Saviour's. But I hereby resolve that I will begin a new Chronicle, not really for posterity, for myself, and this will be a Chronicle of the making of a hero. This is what I hope. It will be up to me. Anything can happen, from now on.

Signed as a true and faithful record

Edward Flack